The League of the Scarlet Pimpernel

The League of the Scarlet Pimpernel

Baroness Emmuska Orczy

MINT EDITIONS

The League of the Scarlet Pimpernel was first published in 1919.

This edition published by Mint Editions 2021.

ISBN 9781513272184 | E-ISBN 9781513277189

Published by Mint Editions®

minteditionbooks.com

Publishing Director: Jennifer Newens
Design & Production: Rachel Lopez Metzger
Project Manager: Micaela Clark
Typesetting: Westchester Publishing Services

Contents

I

Sir Percy Explains

I

It was not, Heaven help us all! a very uncommon occurrence these days: a woman almost unsexed by misery, starvation, and the abnormal excitement engendered by daily spectacles of revenge and of cruelty. They were to be met with every day, round every street corner, these harridans, more terrible far than were the men.

This one was still comparatively young, thirty at most; would have been good-looking too, for the features were really delicate, the nose chiselled, the brow straight, the chin round and small. But the mouth! Heavens, what a mouth! Hard and cruel and thin-lipped; and those eyes! sunken and rimmed with purple; eyes that told tales of sorrow and, yes! of degradation. The crowd stood round her, sullen and apathetic; poor, miserable wretches like herself, staring at her antics with lack-lustre eyes and an ever-recurrent contemptuous shrug of the shoulders.

The woman was dancing, contorting her body in the small circle of light formed by a flickering lanthorn which was hung across the street from house to house, striking the muddy pavement with her shoeless feet, all to the sound of a be-ribboned tambourine which she struck now and again with her small, grimy hand. From time to time she paused, held out the tambourine at arm's length, and went the round of the spectators, asking for alms. But at her approach the crowd at once seemed to disintegrate, to melt into the humid evening air; it was but rarely that a greasy token fell into the outstretched tambourine. Then as the woman started again to dance the crowd gradually reassembled, and stood, hands in pockets, lips still sullen and contemptuous, but eyes watchful of the spectacle. There were such few spectacles these days, other than the monotonous processions of tumbrils with their load of aristocrats for the guillotine!

So the crowd watched, and the woman danced. The lanthorn overhead threw a weird light on red caps and tricolour cockades, on the sullen faces of the men and the shoulders of the women, on the dancer's weird antics and her flying, tattered skirts. She was obviously tired, as a poor, performing cur might be, or a bear prodded along to uncongenial buffoonery. Every time that she paused and solicited alms with her tambourine the crowd dispersed, and some of them laughed because she insisted.

"Voyons," she said with a weird attempt at gaiety, "a couple of sous for the entertainment, citizen! You have stood here half an hour. You can't have it all for nothing, what?"

The man—young, square-shouldered, thick-lipped, with the look of a bully about his well-clad person—retorted with a coarse insult, which the woman resented. There were high words; the crowd for the most part ranged itself on the side of the bully. The woman backed against the wall nearest to her, held feeble, emaciated hands up to her ears in a vain endeavour to shut out the hideous jeers and ribald jokes which were the natural weapons of this untamed crowd.

Soon blows began to rain; not a few fell upon the unfortunate woman. She screamed, and the more she screamed the louder did the crowd jeer, the uglier became its temper. Then suddenly it was all over. How it happened the woman could not tell. She had closed her eyes, feeling sick and dizzy; but she had heard a loud call, words spoken in English (a language which she understood), a pleasant laugh, and a brief but violent scuffle. After that the hurrying retreat of many feet, the click of sabots on the uneven pavement and patter of shoeless feet, and then silence.

She had fallen on her knees and was cowering against the wall, had lost consciousness probably for a minute or two. Then she heard that pleasant laugh again and the soft drawl of the English tongue.

"I love to see those beggars scuttling off, like so many rats to their burrows, don't you, Ffoulkes?"

"They didn't put up much fight, the cowards!" came from another voice, also in English. "A dozen of them against this wretched woman. What had best be done with her?"

"I'll see to her," rejoined the first speaker. "You and Tony had best find the others. Tell them I shall be round directly."

It all seemed like a dream. The woman dared not open her eyes lest reality—hideous and brutal—once more confronted her. Then all at once she felt that her poor, weak body, encircled by strong arms, was lifted off the ground, and that she was being carried down the street, away from the light projected by the lanthorn overhead, into the sheltering darkness of a yawning porte cochere. But she was not then fully conscious.

II

When she reopened her eyes she was in what appeared to be the lodge of a concierge. She was lying on a horsehair sofa. There was a sense of warmth and of security around her. No wonder that it still seemed like a dream. Before her stood a man, tall and straight, surely a being from another world—or so he appeared to the poor wretch who, since uncountable time, had set eyes on none but the most miserable dregs of struggling humanity, who had seen little else but rags, and faces either cruel or wretched. This man was clad in a huge caped coat, which made his powerful figure seem preternaturally large. His hair was fair and slightly curly above his low, square brow; the eyes beneath their heavy lids looked down on her with unmistakable kindness.

The poor woman struggled to her feet. With a quick and pathetically humble gesture she drew her ragged, muddy skirts over her ankles and her tattered kerchief across her breast.

"I had best go now, Monsieur. . . citizen," she murmured, while a hot flush rose to the roots of her unkempt hair. "I must not stop here. . . I—"

"You are not going, Madame," he broke in, speaking now in perfect French and with a great air of authority, as one who is accustomed to being implicitly obeyed, "until you have told me how, a lady of culture and of refinement, comes to be masquerading as a street-dancer. The game is a dangerous one, as you have experienced to-night."

"It is no game, Monsieur. . . citizen," she stammered; "nor yet a masquerade. I have been a street-dancer all my life, and—"

By way of an answer he took her hand, always with that air of authority which she never thought to resent.

"This is not a street-dancer's hand; Madame," he said quietly. "Nor is your speech that of the people."

She drew her hand away quickly, and the flush on her haggard face deepened.

"If you will honour me with your confidence, Madame," he insisted.

The kindly words, the courtesy of the man, went to the poor creature's heart. She fell back upon the sofa and with her face buried in her arms she sobbed out her heart for a minute or two. The man waited quite patiently. He had seen many women weep these days, and had dried many a tear through deeds of valour and of self-sacrifice, which were for ever recorded in the hearts of those whom he had succoured.

When this poor woman had succeeded in recovering some semblance of self-control, she turned her wan, tear-stained face to him and said simply:

"My name is Madeleine Lannoy, Monsieur. My husband was killed during the emeutes at Versailles, whilst defending the persons of the Queen and of the royal children against the fury of the mob. When I was a girl I had the misfortune to attract the attentions of a young doctor named Jean Paul Marat. You have heard of him, Monsieur?"

The other nodded.

"You know him, perhaps," she continued, "for what he is: the most cruel and revengeful of men. A few years ago he threw up his lucrative appointment as Court physician to Monseigneur le Comte d'Artois, and gave up the profession of medicine for that of journalist and politician. Politician! Heaven help him! He belongs to the most bloodthirsty section of revolutionary brigands. His creed is pillage, murder, and revenge; and he chooses to declare that it is I who, by rejecting his love, drove him to these foul extremities. May God forgive him that abominable lie! The evil we do, Monsieur, is within us; it does not come from circumstance. I, in the meanwhile, was a happy wife. My husband, M. de Lannoy, who was an officer in the army, idolised me. We had one child, a boy—"

She paused, with another catch in her throat. Then she resumed, with calmness that, in view of the tale she told, sounded strangely weird:

"In June last year my child was stolen from me—stolen by Marat in hideous revenge for the supposed wrong which I had done him. The details of that execrable outrage are of no importance. I was decoyed from home one day through the agency of a forged message purporting to come from a very dear friend whom I knew to be in grave trouble at the time. Oh! the whole thing was thoroughly well thought out, I can assure you!" she continued, with a harsh laugh which ended in a heartrending sob. "The forged message, the suborned servant, the threats of terrible reprisals if anyone in the village gave me the slightest warning or clue. When the whole miserable business was accomplished, I was just like a trapped animal inside a cage, held captive by immovable bars of obstinate silence and cruel indifference. No one would help me. No one ostensibly knew anything; no one had seen anything, heard anything. The child was gone! My servants, the people in the village—some of whom I could have sworn were true and sympathetic—only shrugged their shoulders. 'Que voulez-vous, Madame? Children of bourgeois as well as of aristos were often taken up by the State to be brought up as true patriots and no longer pampered like so many lap-dogs.'

"Three days later I received a letter from that inhuman monster, Jean Paul Marat. He told me that he had taken my child away from me, not from any idea of revenge for my disdain in the past, but from a spirit of pure patriotism. My boy, he said, should not be brought up with the same ideas of bourgeois effeteness and love of luxury which had disgraced the nation for centuries. No! he should be reared amongst men who had realised the true value of fraternity and equality and the ideal of complete liberty for the individual to lead his own life, unfettered by senseless prejudices of education and refinement. Which means, Monsieur," the poor woman went on with passionate misery, "that my child is to be reared up in the company of all that is most vile and most degraded in the disease-haunted slums of indigent Paris; that, with the connivance of that execrable fiend Marat, my only son will, mayhap, come back to me one day a potential thief, a criminal probably, a drink-sodden reprobate at best. Such things are done every day in this glorious Revolution of ours—done in the sacred name of France and of Liberty. And the moral murder of my child is to be my punishment for daring to turn a deaf ear to the indign passion of a brute!"

Once more she paused, and when the melancholy echo of her broken voice had died away in the narrow room, not another murmur broke the stillness of this far-away corner of the great city.

The man did not move. He stood looking down upon the poor woman before him, a world of pity expressed in his deep-set eyes. Through the absolute silence around there came the sound as of a gentle flutter, the current of cold air, mayhap, sighing through the ill-fitting shutters, or the soft, weird soughing made by unseen things. The man's heart was full of pity, and it seemed as if the Angel of Compassion had come at his bidding and enfolded the sorrowing woman with his wings.

A moment or two later she was able to finish her pathetic narrative.

"Do you marvel, Monsieur," she said, "that I am still sane—still alive? But I only live to find my child. I try and keep my reason in order to fight the devilish cunning of a brute on his own ground. Up to now all my inquiries have been in vain. At first I squandered money, tried judicial means, set an army of sleuth-hounds on the track. I tried bribery, corruption. I went to the wretch himself and abased myself in the dust before him. He only laughed at me and told me that his love for me had died long ago; he now was lavishing its treasures upon the faithful friend and companion—that awful woman, Simonne Evrard—who had stood by him in the darkest hours of his misfortunes. Then it was that I decided to adopt different tactics. Since my child was to be reared in the midst of murderers and thieves, I, too, would haunt their abodes. I became a street-singer, dancer, what you will. I wear rags now and solicit alms. I haunt the most disreputable cabarets in the lowest slums of Paris. I listen and I spy; I question every man, woman, and child who might afford some clue, give me some indication. There is hardly a house in these parts that I have not visited and whence I have not been kicked out as an importunate beggar or worse. Gradually I am narrowing the circle of my investigations. Presently I shall get a clue. I shall! I know I shall! God cannot allow this monstrous thing to go on!"

Again there was silence. The poor woman had completely broken down. Shame, humiliation, passionate grief, had made of her a mere miserable wreckage of humanity.

The man waited awhile until she was composed, then he said simply:

"You have suffered terribly, Madame; but chiefly, I think, because you have been alone in your grief. You have brooded over it until it has threatened your reason. Now, if you will allow me to act as your friend, I will pledge you my word that I will find your son for you. Will you trust me sufficiently to give up your present methods and place yourself entirely in my hands? There are more than a dozen gallant gentlemen, who are my friends, and who will help me in my search. But for this I must have a free hand, and only help from you when I require it. I can find you lodgings where you will be quite safe under the protection of my wife, who is as like an angel as any man or woman I have ever met on this earth. When your son is once more in your arms, you will, I hope, accompany us to England, where so many of your friends have already found a refuge. If this meets with your approval, Madame, you may command me, for with your permission I mean to be your most devoted servant."

Dante, in his wild imaginations of hell and of purgatory and fleeting glimpses of paradise, never put before us the picture of a soul that was lost and found heaven, after a cycle of despair. Nor could Madeleine Lannoy ever explain her feelings at that moment, even to herself. To begin with, she could not quite grasp the reality of this ray of hope, which came to her at the darkest hour of her misery. She stared at the man before her as she would on an ethereal vision; she fell on her knees and buried her face in her hands.

What happened afterwards she hardly knew; she was in a state of semi-consciousness. When she once more woke to reality, she was in comfortable lodgings; she moved and talked and ate and lived like a human being. She was no longer a pariah, an outcast, a poor, half-demented creature, insentient save for an infinite capacity for suffering. She suffered still, but she no longer despaired. There had been such marvellous power and confidence in that man's voice when he said: "I pledge you my word." Madeleine Lannoy lived now in hope and a sweet sense of perfect mental and bodily security. Around her there was an influence, too, a presence which she did not often see, but always felt to be there: a woman, tall and graceful and sympathetic, who was always ready to cheer, to comfort, and to help. Her name was Marguerite. Madame Lannoy never knew her by any other. The man had spoken of her as being as like an angel as could be met on this earth, and poor Madeleine Lannoy fully agreed with him.

III

Even that bloodthirsty tiger, Jean Paul Marat, has had his apologists. His friends have called him a martyr, a selfless and incorruptible exponent of social and political ideals. We may take it that Simonne Evrard loved him, for a more impassioned obituary speech was, mayhap, never spoken than the one which she delivered before the National Assembly in honour of that sinister demagogue, whose writings and activities will for ever sully some of the really fine pages of that revolutionary era.

But with those apologists we have naught to do. History has talked its fill of the inhuman monster. With the more intimate biographists alone has this true chronicle any concern. It is one of these who tells us that on or about the eighteenth day of Messidor, in the year I of the Republic (a date which corresponds with the sixth of July, 1793, of our own calendar), Jean Paul Marat took an additional man into his service, at the instance of Jeannette Marechal, his cook and maid-of-all-work. Marat was at this time a martyr to an unpleasant form of skin disease, brought on by the terrible privations which he had endured during the few years preceding his association with Simonne Evrard, the faithful friend and housekeeper, whose small fortune subsequently provided him with some degree of comfort.

The man whom Jeannette Marechal, the cook, introduced into the household of No. 30, Rue des Cordeliers, that worthy woman had literally picked one day out of the gutter where he was grabbing for scraps of food like some wretched starving cur. He appeared to be known to the police of the section, his identity book proclaiming him to be one Paul Mole, who had served his time in gaol for larceny. He professed himself willing to do any work required of him, for the merest pittance and some kind of roof over his head. Simonne Evrard allowed Jeannette to take him in, partly out of compassion and partly with a view to easing the woman's own burden, the only other domestic in the house—a man named Bas—being more interested in politics and the meetings of the Club des Jacobins than he was in his master's ailments. The man Mole, moreover, appeared to know something of medicine and of herbs and how to prepare the warm baths which alone eased the unfortunate Marat from pain. He was powerfully built, too, and though he muttered and grumbled a great deal, and indulged in prolonged fits of sulkiness, when he would not open his mouth to anyone, he was, on the whole, helpful and good-tempered.

There must also have been something about his whole wretched personality which made a strong appeal to the "Friend of the People," for it is quite evident that within a few days Paul Mole had won no small measure of his master's confidence.

Marat, sick, fretful, and worried, had taken an unreasoning dislike to his servant Bas. He was thankful to have a stranger about him, a man who was as miserable as he himself had been a very little while ago; who, like himself, had lived in cellars and in underground burrows, and lived on the scraps of food which even street-curs had disdained.

On the seventh day following Mole's entry into the household, and while the latter was preparing his employer's bath, Marat said abruptly to him:

"You'll go as far as the Chemin de Pantin to-day for me, citizen. You know your way?"

"I can find it, what?" muttered Mole, who appeared to be in one of his surly moods.

"You will have to go very circumspectly," Marat went on, in his cracked and feeble voice. "And see to it that no one spies upon your movements. I have many enemies, citizen. . . one especially. . . a woman. . . She is always prying and spying on me. . . So beware of any woman you see lurking about at your heels."

Mole gave a half-audible grunt in reply.

"You had best go after dark," the other rejoined after awhile. "Come back to me after nine o'clock. It is not far to the Chemin de Pantin—

just where it intersects the Route de Meaux. You can get there and back before midnight. The people will admit you. I will give you a ring—the only thing I possess. . . It has little or no value," he added with a harsh, grating laugh. "It will not be worth your while to steal it. You will have to see a brat and report to me on his condition—his appearance, what? . . . Talk to him a bit. . . See what he says and let me know. It is not difficult."

"No, citizen."

Mole helped the suffering wretch into his bath. Not a movement, not a quiver of the eyelid betrayed one single emotion which he may have felt—neither loathing nor sympathy, only placid indifference. He was just a half-starved menial, thankful to accomplish any task for the sake of satisfying a craving stomach. Marat stretched out his shrunken limbs in the herbal water with a sigh of well-being.

"And the ring, citizen?" Mole suggested presently.

The demagogue held up his left hand—it was emaciated and disfigured by disease. A cheap-looking metal ring, set with a false stone, glistened upon the fourth finger.

"Take it off," he said curtly.

The ring must have all along been too small for the bony hand of the once famous Court physician. Even now it appeared embedded in the flabby skin and refused to slide over the knuckle.

"The water will loosen it," remarked Mole quietly.

Marat dipped his hand back into the water, and the other stood beside him, silent and stolid, his broad shoulders bent, his face naught but a mask, void and expressionless beneath its coating of grime.

One or two seconds went by. The air was heavy with steam and a medley of evil-smelling fumes, which hung in the close atmosphere of the narrow room. The sick man appeared to be drowsy, his head rolled over to one side, his eyes closed. He had evidently forgotten all about the ring.

A woman's voice, shrill and peremptory, broke the silence which had become oppressive:

"Here, citizen Mole, I want you! There's not a bit of wood chopped up for my fire, and how am I to make the coffee without firing, I should like to know?"

"The ring, citizen," Mole urged gruffly.

Marat had been roused by the woman's sharp voice. He cursed her for a noisy harridan; then he said fretfully:

"It will do presently—when you are ready to start. I said nine o'clock. . . it is only four now. I am tired. Tell citizeness Evrard to bring me some hot coffee in an hour's time. . . You can go and fetch me the Moniteur now, and take back these proofs to citizen Dufour. You will find him at the 'Cordeliers,' or else at the printing works. . . Come back at nine o'clock. . . I am tired now. . . too tired to tell you where to find the house which is off the Chemin de Pantin. Presently will do. . ."

Even while he spoke he appeared to drop into a fitful sleep. His two hands were hidden under the sheet which covered the bath. Mole watched him in silence for a moment or two, then he turned on his heel and shuffled off through the ante-room into the kitchen beyond, where presently he sat down, squatting in an angle by the stove, and started with his usual stolidness to chop wood for the citizeness' fire.

When this task was done, and he had received a chunk of sour bread for his reward from Jeannette Marechal, the cook, he shuffled out of the place and into the street, to do his employer's errands.

IV

Paul Mole had been to the offices of the Moniteur and to the printing works of L'Ami du Peuple. He had seen the citizen Dufour at the Club and, presumably, had spent the rest of his time wandering idly about the streets of the quartier, for he did not return to the Rue des Cordeliers until nearly nine o'clock.

As soon as he came to the top of the street, he fell in with the crowd which had collected outside No. 30. With his habitual slouchy gait and the steady pressure of his powerful elbows, he pushed his way to the door, whilst gleaning whisperings and rumours on his way.

"The citizen Marat has been assassinated."

"By a woman."

"A mere girl."

"A wench from Caen. Her name is Corday."

"The people nearly tore her to pieces awhile ago."

"She is as much as guillotined already."

The latter remark went off with a loud guffaw and many a ribald joke.

Mole, despite his great height, succeeded in getting through unperceived. He was of no account, and he knew his way inside the house. It was full of people: journalists, gaffers, women and men—the usual crowd that come to gape. The citizen Marat was a great personage.

The Friend of the People. An Incorruptible, if ever there was one. Just look at the simplicity, almost the poverty, in which he lived! Only the aristos hated him, and the fat bourgeois who battened on the people. Citizen Marat had sent hundreds of them to the guillotine with a stroke of his pen or a denunciation from his fearless tongue.

Mole did not pause to listen to these comments. He pushed his way through the throng up the stairs, to his late employer's lodgings on the first floor.

The anteroom was crowded, so were the other rooms; but the greatest pressure was around the door immediately facing him, the one which gave on the bathroom. In the kitchen on his right, where awhile ago he had been chopping wood under a flood of abuse from Jeannette Marechal, he caught sight of this woman, cowering by the hearth, her filthy apron thrown over her head, and crying—yes! crying for the loathsome creature, who had expiated some of his abominable crimes at the hands of a poor, misguided girl, whom an infuriated mob was even now threatening to tear to pieces in its rage.

The parlour and even Simonne's room were also filled with people: men, most of whom Mole knew by sight; friends or enemies of the ranting demagogue who lay murdered in the very bath which his casual servant had prepared for him. Every one was discussing the details of the murder, the punishment of the youthful assassin. Simonne Evrard was being loudly blamed for having admitted the girl into citizen Marat's room. But the wench had looked so simple, so innocent, and she said she was the bearer of a message from Caen. She had called twice during the day, and in the evening the citizen himself said that he would see her. Simonne had been for sending her away. But the citizen was peremptory. And he was so helpless. . . in his bath. . . name of a name, the pitiable affair!

No one paid much attention to Mole. He listened for a while to Simonne's impassioned voice, giving her version of the affair; then he worked his way stolidly into the bathroom.

It was some time before he succeeded in reaching the side of that awful bath wherein lay the dead body of Jean Paul Marat. The small room was densely packed—not with friends, for there was not a man or woman living, except Simonne Evrard and her sisters, whom the bloodthirsty demagogue would have called "friend"; but his powerful personality had been a menace to many, and now they came in crowds to see that he was really dead, that a girl's feeble hand had actually done the deed which they themselves had only contemplated. They stood about whispering, their heads averted from the ghastly spectacle of this miserable creature, to whom even death had failed to lend his usual attribute of tranquil dignity.

The tiny room was inexpressibly hot and stuffy. Hardly a breath of outside air came in through the narrow window, which only gave on the bedroom beyond. An evil-smelling oil-lamp swung from the low ceiling and shed its feeble light on the upturned face of the murdered man.

Mole stood for a moment or two, silent and pensive, beside that hideous form. There was the bath, just as he had prepared it: the board spread over with a sheet and laid across the bath, above which only the head and shoulders emerged, livid and stained. One hand, the left, grasped the edge of the board with the last convulsive clutch of supreme agony.

On the fourth finger of that hand glistened the shoddy ring which Marat had said was not worth stealing. Yet, apparently, it roused the cupidity of the poor wretch who had served him faithfully for these last few days, and who now would once more be thrown, starving and friendless, upon the streets of Paris.

Mole threw a quick, furtive glance around him. The crowd which had come to gloat over the murdered Terrorist stood about whispering, with heads averted, engrossed in their own affairs. He slid his hand surreptitiously over that of the dead man. With dexterous manipulation he lifted the finger round which glistened the metal ring. Death appeared to have shrivelled the flesh still more upon the bones, to have contracted the knuckles and shrunk the tendons. The ring slid off quite easily. Mole had it in his hand, when suddenly a rough blow struck him on the shoulder.

"Trying to rob the dead?" a stern voice shouted in his ear. "Are you a disguised aristo, or what?"

At once the whispering ceased. A wave of excitement went round the room. Some people shouted, others pressed forward to gaze on the abandoned wretch who had been caught in the act of committing a gruesome deed.

"Robbing the dead!"

They were experts in evil, most of these men here. Their hands were indelibly stained with some of the foulest crimes ever recorded in history. But there was something ghoulish in this attempt to plunder that awful thing lying there, helpless, in the water. There was also a great relief to nerve-tension in shouting Horror and Anathema with self-righteous indignation; and additional excitement in the suggested "aristo in disguise."

Mole struggled vigorously. He was powerful and his fists were heavy. But he was soon surrounded, held fast by both arms, whilst half a dozen hands tore at his tattered clothes, searched him to his very skin, for the booty which he was thought to have taken from the dead.

"Leave me alone, curse you!" he shouted, louder than his aggressors. "My name is Paul Mole, I tell you. Ask the citizeness Evrard. I waited on citizen Marat. I prepared his bath. I was the only friend who did not turn away from him in his sickness and his poverty. Leave me alone, I say! Why," he added, with a hoarse laugh, "Jean Paul in his bath was as naked as on the day he was born!"

"'Tis true," said one of those who had been most active in rummaging through Mole's grimy rags. "There's nothing to be found on him."

But suspicion once aroused was not easily allayed. Mole's protestations became more and more vigorous and emphatic. His papers were all in order, he vowed. He had them on him: his own identity papers, clear for anyone to see. Someone had dragged them out of his pocket; they were dank and covered with splashes of mud—hardly legible. They were handed over to a man who stood in the immediate circle of light projected by the lamp. He seized them and examined them carefully. This man was short and slight, was dressed in well-made cloth clothes; his hair was held in at the nape of the next in a modish manner with a black taffeta bow. His hands were clean, slender, and claw-like, and he wore the tricolour scarf of office round his waist which proclaimed him to be a member of one of the numerous Committees which tyrannised over the people.

The papers appeared to be in order, and proclaimed the bearer to be Paul Mole, a native of Besancon, a carpenter by trade. The identity book had recently been signed by Jean Paul Marat, the man's latest employer, and been counter-signed by the Commissary of the section.

The man in the tricolour scarf turned with some acerbity on the crowd who was still pressing round the prisoner.

"Which of you here," he queried roughly, "levelled an unjust accusation against an honest citizen?"

But, as usual in such cases, no one replied directly to the charge. It was not safe these days to come into conflict with men like Mole. The Committees were all on their side, against the bourgeois as well as against the aristos. This was the reign of the proletariat, and the sans-culotte always emerged triumphant in a conflict against the well-to-do. Nor was it good to rouse the ire of citizen Chauvelin, one of the most powerful, as he was the most pitiless members of the Committee of Public Safety. Quiet, sarcastic rather than aggressive, something of the aristo, too, in his clean linen and well-cut clothes, he had not even yielded to the defunct Marat in cruelty and relentless persecution of aristocrats.

Evidently his sympathies now were all with Mole, the out-at-elbows, miserable servant of an equally miserable master. His pale-coloured, deep-set eyes challenged the crowd, which gave way before him, slunk back into the corners, away from his coldly threatening glance. Thus he found himself suddenly face to face with Mole, somewhat isolated from the rest, and close to the tin bath with its grim contents. Chauvelin had the papers in his hand.

"Take these, citizen," he said curtly to the other. "They are all in order."

He looked up at Mole as he said this, for the latter, though his shoulders were bent, was unusually tall, and Mole took the papers from him. Thus for the space of a few seconds the two men looked into one another's face, eyes to eyes—and suddenly Chauvelin felt an icy sweat coursing down his spine. The eyes into which he gazed had a strange, ironical twinkle in them, a kind of good-humoured arrogance, whilst through the firm, clear-cut lips, half hidden by a dirty and ill-kempt beard, there came the sound—oh! a mere echo—of a quaint and inane laugh.

The whole thing—it seemed like a vision—was over in a second. Chauvelin, sick and faint with the sudden rush of blood to his head, closed his eyes for one brief instant. The next, the crowd had closed round him; anxious inquiries reached his re-awakened senses.

But he uttered one quick, hoarse cry:

"Hebert! A moi! Are you there?"

"Present, citizen!" came in immediate response. And a tall figure in the tattered uniform affected by the revolutionary guard stepped briskly out of the crowd. Chauvelin's claw-like hand was shaking visibly.

"The man Mole," he called in a voice husky with excitement. "Seize him at once! And, name of a dog! do not allow a living soul in or out of the house!"

Hebert turned on his heel. The next moment his harsh voice was heard above the din and the general hubbub around:

"Quite safe, citizen!" he called to his chief. "We have the rogue right enough!"

There was much shouting and much cursing, a great deal of bustle and confusion, as the men of the Surete closed the doors of the defunct demagogue's lodgings. Some two score men, a dozen or so women, were locked in, inside the few rooms which reeked of dirt and of disease. They jostled and pushed, screamed and protested. For two or three minutes the din was quite deafening. Simonne Evrard pushed her way up to the forefront of the crowd.

"What is this I hear?" she queried peremptorily. "Who is accusing citizen Mole? And of what, I should like to know? I am responsible for everyone inside these apartments. . . and if citizen Marat were still alive—"

Chauvelin appeared unaware of all the confusion and of the woman's protestations. He pushed his way through the crowd to the corner of the anteroom where Mole stood, crouching and hunched up, his grimy hands idly fingering the papers which Chauvelin had returned to him a moment ago. Otherwise he did not move.

He stood, silent and sullen; and when Chauvelin, who had succeeded in mastering his emotion, gave the peremptory command: "Take this man to the depot at once. And do not allow him one instant out of your sight!" he made no attempt at escape.

He allowed Hebert and the men to seize him, to lead him away. He followed without a word, without a struggle. His massive figure was hunched up like that of an old man; his hands, which still clung to his identity papers, trembled slightly like those of a man who is very frightened and very helpless. The men of the Surete handled him very roughly, but he made no protest. The woman Evrard did all the protesting, vowing that the people would not long tolerate such tyranny. She even forced her way up to Hebert. With a gesture of fury she tried to strike him in the face, and continued, with a loud voice, her insults and objurgations, until, with a movement of his bayonet, he pushed her roughly out of the way.

After that Paul Mole, surrounded by the guard, was led without ceremony out of the house. Chauvelin gazed after him as if he had been brought face to face with a ghoul.

V

Chauvelin hurried to the depot. After those few seconds wherein he had felt dazed, incredulous, almost under a spell, he had quickly regained the mastery of his nerves, and regained, too, that intense joy which anticipated triumph is wont to give.

In the out-at-elbows, half-starved servant of the murdered Terrorist, citizen Chauvelin, of the Committee of Public Safety, had recognised his arch enemy, that meddlesome and adventurous Englishman who chose to hide his identity under the pseudonym of the Scarlet Pimpernel. He knew that he could reckon on Hebert; his orders not to allow the prisoner one moment out of sight would of a certainty be strictly obeyed.

Hebert, indeed, a few moments later, greeted his chief outside the doors of the depot with the welcome news that Paul Mole was safely under lock and key.

"You had no trouble with him?" Chauvelin queried, with ill-concealed eagerness.

"No, no! citizen, no trouble," was Hebert's quick reply. "He seems to be a well-known rogue in these parts," he continued with a complacent guffaw; "and some of his friends tried to hustle us at the corner of the Rue de Tourraine; no doubt with a view to getting the prisoner away. But we were too strong for them, and Paul Mole is now sulking in his cell and still protesting that his arrest is an outrage against the liberty of the people."

Chauvelin made no further remark. He was obviously too excited to speak. Pushing past Hebert and the men of the Surete who stood about the dark and narrow passages of the depot, he sought the Commissary of the Section in the latter's office.

It was now close upon ten o'clock. The citizen Commissary Cuisinier had finished his work for the day and was preparing to go home and to bed. He was a family man, had been a respectable bourgeois in his day, and though he was a rank opportunist and had sacrificed not only his political convictions but also his conscience to the exigencies of the time, he still nourished in his innermost heart a secret contempt for the revolutionary brigands who ruled over France at this hour.

To any other man than citizen Chauvelin, the citizen Commissary would, no doubt, have given a curt refusal to a request to see a prisoner at this late hour of the evening. But Chauvelin was not a man to be denied, and whilst muttering various objections in his ill-kempt beard, Cuisinier, nevertheless, gave orders that the citizen was to be conducted at once to the cells.

Paul Mole had in truth turned sulky. The turnkey vowed that the prisoner had hardly stirred since first he had been locked up in the common cell. He sat in a corner at the end of the bench, with his face turned to the wall, and paid no heed either to his fellow-prisoners or to the facetious remarks of the warder.

Chauvelin went up to him, made some curt remark. Mole kept an obstinate shoulder turned towards him—a grimy shoulder, which showed naked through a wide rent in his blouse. This portion of the cell was well-nigh in total darkness; the feeble shaft of light which came through the open door hardly penetrated to this remote angle of the squalid burrow. The same sense of mystery and unreality overcame Chauvelin again as he looked on the miserable creature in whom, an hour ago, he had recognised the super-exquisite Sir Percy Blakeney. Now he could only see a vague outline in the gloom: the stooping shoulders, the long limbs, that naked piece of shoulder which caught a feeble reflex from the distant light. Nor did any amount of none too gentle prodding on the part of the warder induce him to change his position.

"Leave him alone," said Chauvelin curly at last. "I have seen all that I wished to see."

The cell was insufferably hot and stuffy. Chauvelin, finical and queasy, turned away with a shudder of disgust. There was nothing to be got now out of a prolonged interview with his captured foe. He had seen him: that was sufficient. He had seen the super-exquisite Sir Percy Blakeney locked up in a common cell with some of the most scrubby and abject rogues which the slums of indigent Paris could yield, having apparently failed in some undertaking which had demanded for its fulfilment not only tattered clothes and grimy hands, but menial service with a beggarly and disease-ridden employer, whose very propinquity must have been positive torture to the fastidious dandy.

Of a truth this was sufficient for the gratification of any revenge. Chauvelin felt that he could now go contentedly to rest after an evening's work excellently done.

He gave order that Mole should be put in a separate cell, denied all intercourse with anyone outside or in the depot, and that he should be guarded on sight day and night. After that he went his way.

VI

The following morning citizen Chauvelin, of the Committee of Public Safety, gave due notice to citizen Fouquier-

Tinville, the Public Prosecutor, that the dangerous English spy, known to the world as the Scarlet Pimpernel, was now safely under lock and key, and that he must be transferred to the Abbaye prison forthwith and to the guillotine as quickly as might be. No one was to take any risks this time; there must be no question either of discrediting his famous League or of obtaining other more valuable information out of him. Such methods had proved disastrous in the past.

There were no safe Englishmen these days, except the dead ones, and it would not take citizen Fouquier-Tinville much thought or time to frame an indictment against the notorious Scarlet Pimpernel, which would do away with the necessity of a prolonged trial. The revolutionary government was at war with England now, and short work could be made of all poisonous spies.

By order, therefore, of the Committee of Public Safety, the prisoner, Paul Mole, was taken out of the cells of the depot and conveyed in a closed carriage to the Abbaye prison. Chauvelin had the pleasure of watching this gratifying spectacle from the windows of the Commissariat. When he saw the closed carriage drive away, with Hebert and two men inside and two others on the box, he turned to citizen Commissary Cuisinier with a sigh of intense satisfaction.

"There goes the most dangerous enemy our glorious revolution has had," he said, with an accent of triumph which he did not attempt to disguise.

Cuisinier shrugged his shoulders.

"Possibly," he retorted curtly. "He did not seem to me to be very dangerous and his papers were quite in order."

To this assertion Chauvelin made no reply. Indeed, how could he explain to this stolid official the subtle workings of an intriguing brain? Had he himself not had many a proof of how little the forging of identity papers or of passports troubled the members of that accursed League? Had he not seen the Scarlet Pimpernel, that exquisite Sir Percy Blakeney, under disguises that were so grimy and so loathsome that they would have repelled the most abject, suborned spy?

Indeed, all that was wanted now was the assurance that Hebert—who himself had a deadly and personal grudge against the Scarlet Pimpernel—would not allow him for one moment out of his sight.

Fortunately as to this, there was no fear. One hint to Hebert and the man was as keen, as determined, as Chauvelin himself.

"Set your mind at rest, citizen," he said with a rough oath. "I guessed how matters stood the moment you gave me the order. I knew you would not take all that trouble for a real Paul Mole. But have no fear! That accursed Englishman has not been one second out of my sight, from the moment I arrested him in the late citizen Marat's lodgings, and by Satan! he shall not be either, until I have seen his impudent head fall under the guillotine."

He himself, he added, had seen to the arrangements for the disposal of the prisoner in the Abbaye: an inner cell, partially partitioned off in one of the guard-rooms, with no egress of its own, and only a tiny grated air-hole high up in the wall, which gave on an outside corridor, and through which not even a cat could manage to slip. Oh! the prisoner was well guarded! The citizen Representative need, of a truth, have no fear! Three or four men—of the best and most trustworthy—had not left the guard-room since the morning. He himself (Hebert) had kept the accursed Englishman in sight all night, had personally conveyed him to the Abbaye, and had only left the guard-room a moment ago in order to speak with the citizen Representative. He was going back now at once, and would not move until the order came for the prisoner to be conveyed to the Court of Justice and thence to summary execution.

For the nonce, Hebert concluded with a complacent chuckle, the Englishman was still crouching dejectedly in a corner of his new cell, with little of him visible save that naked shoulder through his torn shirt, which, in the process of transference from one prison to another, had become a shade more grimy than before.

Chauvelin nodded, well satisfied. He commended Hebert for his zeal, rejoiced with him over the inevitable triumph. It would be well to avenge that awful humiliation at Calais last September. Nevertheless, he felt anxious and nervy; he could not comprehend the apathy assumed by the factitious Mole. That the apathy was assumed Chauvelin was keen enough to guess. What it portended he could not conjecture. But that the Englishman would make a desperate attempt at escape was, of course, a foregone conclusion. It rested with Hebert and a guard that could neither be bribed nor fooled into treachery, to see that such an attempt remained abortive.

What, however, had puzzled citizen Chauvelin all along was the motive which had induced Sir Percy Blakeney to play the role of menial to Jean Paul Marat. Behind it there lay, undoubtedly, one of those subtle intrigues for which that insolent Scarlet Pimpernel was famous; and with it was associated an attempt at theft upon the murdered body of the demagogue. . . an attempt which had failed, seeing that the supposititious Paul Mole had been searched and nothing suspicious been found upon his person.

Nevertheless, thoughts of that attempted theft disturbed Chauvelin's equanimity. The old legend of the crumpled roseleaf was applicable in his case. Something of his intense satisfaction would pale if this final enterprise of the audacious adventurer were to be brought to a triumphant close in the end.

VII

THAT SAME FORENOON, ON HIS return from the Abbaye and the depot, Chauvelin found that a visitor was waiting for him. A woman, who gave her name as Jeannette Marechal, desired to speak with the citizen Representative. Chauvelin knew the woman as his colleague Marat's maid-of-all-work, and he gave orders that she should be admitted at once.

Jeannette Marechal, tearful and not a little frightened, assured the citizen Representative that her errand was urgent. Her late employer had so few friends; she did not know to whom to turn until she bethought herself of citizen Chauvelin. It took him some little time to disentangle the tangible facts out of the woman's voluble narrative. At first the words: "Child. . . Chemin de Pantin. . . Leridan," were only a medley of sounds which conveyed no meaning to his ear. But when occasion demanded, citizen Chauvelin was capable of infinite patience. Gradually he understood what the woman was driving at.

"The child, citizen!" she reiterated excitedly. "What's to be done about him? I know that citizen Marat would have wished—"

"Never mind now what citizen Marat would have wished," Chauvelin broke in quietly. "Tell me first who this child is."

"I do not know, citizen," she replied.

"How do you mean, you do not know? Then I pray you, citizeness, what is all this pother about?"

"About the child, citizen," reiterated Jeannette obstinately.

"What child?"

"The child whom citizen Marat adopted last year and kept at that awful house on the Chemin de Pantin."

"I did not know citizen Marat had adopted a child," remarked Chauvelin thoughtfully.

"No one knew," she rejoined. "Not even citizeness Evrard. I was the only one who knew. I had to go and see the child once every month. It was a wretched, miserable brat," the woman went on, her shrivelled old breast vaguely stirred, mayhap, by some atrophied feeling of motherhood. "More than half-starved. . . and the look in its eyes, citizen! It was enough to make you cry! I could see by his poor little emaciated body and his nice little hands and feet that he ought never to have been put in that awful house, where—"

She paused, and that quick look of furtive terror, which was so often to be met with in the eyes of the timid these days, crept into her wrinkled face.

"Well, citizeness," Chauvelin rejoined quietly, "why don't you proceed? That awful house, you were saying. Where and what is that awful house of which you speak?"

"The place kept by citizen Leridan, just by Bassin de l'Ourcq," the woman murmured. "You know it, citizen."

Chauvelin nodded. He was beginning to understand.

"Well, now, tell me," he said, with that bland patience which had so oft served him in good stead in his unavowable profession. "Tell me. Last year citizen Marat adopted—we'll say adopted—a child, whom he placed in the Leridans' house on the Pantin road. Is that correct?"

"That is just how it is, citizen. And I—"

"One moment," he broke in somewhat more sternly, as the woman's garrulity was getting on his nerves. "As you say, I know the Leridans' house. I have had cause to send children there myself. Children of aristos or of fat bourgeois, whom it was our duty to turn into good citizens. They are not pampered there, I imagine," he went on drily; "and if citizen Marat sent his—er—adopted son there, it was not with a view to having him brought up as an aristo, what?"

"The child was not to be brought up at all," the woman said gruffly. "I have often heard citizen Marat say that he hoped the brat would prove a thief when he grew up, and would take to alcoholism like a duck takes to water."

"And you know nothing of the child's parents?"

"Nothing, citizen. I had to go to Pantin once a month and have a look at him and report to citizen Marat. But I always had the same tale to tell. The child was looking more and more like a young reprobate every time I saw him."

"Did citizen Marat pay the Leridans for keeping the child?"

"Oh, no, citizen! The Leridans make a trade of the children by sending them out to beg. But this one was not to be allowed out yet.

Citizen Marat's orders were very stern, and he was wont to terrify the Leridans with awful threats of the guillotine if they ever allowed the child out of their sight."

Chauvelin sat silent for a while. A ray of light had traversed the dark and tortuous ways of his subtle brain. While he mused the woman became impatient. She continued to talk on with the volubility peculiar to her kind. He paid no heed to her, until one phrase struck his ear.

"So now," Jeannette Marechal was saying, "I don't know what to do. The ring has disappeared, and the Leridans are suspicious."

"The ring?" queried Chauvelin curtly. "What ring?"

"As I was telling you, citizen," she replied querulously, "when I went to see the child, the citizen Marat always gave me this ring to show to the Leridans. Without I brought the ring they would not admit me inside their door. They were so terrified with all the citizen's threats of the guillotine."

"And now you say the ring has disappeared. Since when?"

"Well, citizen," replied Jeannette blandly, "since you took poor Paul Mole into custody."

"What do you mean?" Chauvelin riposted. "What had Paul Mole to do with the child and the ring?"

"Only this, citizen, that he was to have gone to Pantin last night instead of me. And thankful I was not to have to go. Citizen Marat gave the ring to Mole, I suppose. I know he intended to give it to him. He spoke to me about it just before that execrable woman came and murdered him. Anyway, the ring has gone and Mole too. So I imagine that Mole has the ring and—"

"That's enough!" Chauvelin broke in roughly. "You can go!"

"But, citizen—"

"You can go, I said," he reiterated sharply. "The matter of the child and the Leridans and the ring no longer concerns you. You understand?"

"Y—y—yes, citizen," murmured Jeannette, vaguely terrified.

And of a truth the change in citizen Chauvelin's demeanour was enough to scare any timid creature. Not that he raved or ranted or screamed. Those were not his ways. He still sat beside his desk as he had done before, and his slender hand, so like the talons of a vulture, was clenched upon the arm of his chair. But there was such a look of inward fury and of triumph in his pale, deep-set eyes, such lines of cruelty around his thin, closed lips, that Jeannette Marechal, even with the picture before her mind of Jean Paul Marat in his maddest moods, fled, with the unreasoning terror of her kind, before the sternly controlled, fierce passion of this man.

Chauvelin never noticed that she went. He sat for a long time, silent and immovable. Now he understood. Thank all the Powers of Hate and Revenge, no thought of disappointment was destined to embitter the overflowing cup of his triumph. He had not only brought his arch-enemy to his knees, but had foiled one of his audacious ventures. How clear the whole thing was! The false Paul Mole, the newly acquired menial in the household of Marat, had wormed himself into the confidence of his employer in order to wrest from him the secret of the aristo's child. Bravo! bravo! my gallant Scarlet Pimpernel! Chauvelin now could see it all. Tragedies such as that which had placed an aristo's child in the power of a cunning demon like Marat were not rare these days, and Chauvelin had been fitted by nature and by temperament to understand and appreciate an execrable monster of the type of Jean Paul Marat.

And Paul Mole, the grimy, degraded servant of the indigent demagogue, the loathsome mask which hid the fastidious personality of Sir Percy Blakeney, had made a final and desperate effort to possess himself of the ring which would deliver the child into his power. Now, having failed in his machinations, he was safe under lock and key—guarded on sight. The next twenty-four hours would see him unmasked, awaiting his trial and condemnation under the scathing indictment prepared by Fouquier-Tinville, the unerring Public Prosecutor. The day after that, the tumbril and the guillotine for that execrable English spy, and the boundless sense of satisfaction that his last intrigue had aborted in such a signal and miserable manner.

Of a truth Chauvelin at this hour had every cause to be thankful, and it was with a light heart that he set out to interview the Leridans.

VIII

The Leridans, anxious, obsequious, terrified, were only too ready to obey the citizen Representative in all things.

They explained with much complacency that, even though they were personally acquainted with Jeannette Marechal, when the citizeness presented herself this very morning without the ring they had refused her permission to see the brat.

Chauvelin, who in his own mind had already reconstructed the whole tragedy of the stolen child, was satisfied that Marat could not have chosen more efficient tools for the execution of his satanic revenge than these two hideous products of revolutionary Paris.

Grasping, cowardly, and avaricious, the Leridans would lend themselves to any abomination for a sufficiency of money; but no money on earth would induce them to risk their own necks in the process. Marat had obviously held them by threats of the guillotine. They knew the power of the "Friend of the People," and feared him accordingly. Chauvelin's scarf of office, his curt, authoritative manner, had an equally awe-inspiring effect upon the two miserable creatures. They became absolutely abject, cringing, maudlin in their protestations of good-will and loyalty. No one, they vowed, should as much as see the child—ring or no ring—save the citizen Representative himself. Chauvelin, however, had no wish to see the child. He was satisfied that its name was Lannoy—for the child had remembered it when first he had been brought to the Leridans. Since then he had apparently forgotten it, even though he often cried after his "Maman!"

Chauvelin listened to all these explanations with some impatience. The child was nothing to him, but the Scarlet Pimpernel had desired to rescue it from out of the clutches of the Leridans; had risked his all—and lost it—in order to effect that rescue! That in itself was a sufficient inducement for Chauvelin to interest himself in the execution of Marat's vengeance, whatever its original mainspring may have been.

At any rate, now he felt satisfied that the child was safe, and that the Leridans were impervious to threats or bribes which might land them on the guillotine.

All that they would own to was to being afraid.

"Afraid of what?" queried Chauvelin sharply.

That the brat may be kidnapped. . . stolen. Oh! he could not be decoyed. . . they were too watchful for that! But apparently there were mysterious agencies at work. . .

"Mysterious agencies!" Chauvelin laughed aloud at the suggestion. The "mysterious agency" was even now rotting in an obscure cell at the Abbaye. What other powers could be at work on behalf of the brat?

Well, the Leridans had had a warning!

What warning?

"A letter," the man said gruffly. "But as neither my wife nor I can read—"

"Why did you not speak of this before?" broke in Chauvelin roughly. "Let me see the letter."

The woman produced a soiled and dank scrap of paper from beneath her apron. Of a truth she could not read its contents, for they were writ in English in the form of a doggerel rhyme which caused Chauvelin to utter a savage oath.

"When did this come?" he asked. "And how?"

"This morning, citizen," the woman mumbled in reply. "I found it outside the door, with a stone on it to prevent the wind from blowing it away. What does it mean, citizen?" she went on, her voice shaking with terror, for of a truth the citizen Representative looked as if he had seen some weird and unearthly apparition.

He gave no reply for a moment or two, and the two catiffs had no conception of the tremendous effort at self-control which was hidden behind the pale, rigid mask of the redoubtable man.

"It probably means nothing that you need fear," Chauvelin said quietly at last. "But I will see the Commissary of the Section myself, and tell him to send a dozen men of the Surete along to watch your house and be at your beck and call if need be. Then you will feel quite safe, I hope."

"Oh, yes! quite safe, citizen!" the woman replied with a sigh of genuine relief. Then only did Chauvelin turn on his heel and go his way.

IX

But that crumpled and soiled scrap of paper given to him by the woman Leridan still lay in his clenched hand as he strode back rapidly citywards. It seemed to scorch his palm. Even before he had glanced at the contents he knew what they were. That atrocious English doggerel, the signature—a five-petalled flower traced in crimson! How well he knew them!

"We seek him here, we seek him there!"

The most humiliating moments in Chauvelin's career were associated with that silly rhyme, and now here it was, mocking him even when he knew that his bitter enemy lay fettered and helpless, caught in a trap, out of which there was no escape possible; even though he knew for a positive certainty that the mocking voice which had spoken those rhymes on that far-off day last September would soon be stilled for ever.

No doubt one of that army of abominable English spies had placed this warning outside the Leridans' door. No doubt they had done that with a view to throwing dust in the eyes of the Public Prosecutor and causing a confusion in his mind with regard to the identity of the prisoner at the Abbaye, all to the advantage of their chief.

The thought that such a confusion might exist, that Fouquier-Tinville might be deluded into doubting the real personality of Paul Mole, brought an icy sweat all down Chauvelin's spine. He hurried along the interminably long Chemin de Pantin, only paused at the Barriere du Combat in order to interview the Commissary of the Section on the matter of sending men to watch over the Leridans' house. Then, when he felt satisfied that this would be effectively and quickly done, an unconquerable feeling of restlessness prompted him to hurry round to the lodgings of the Public Prosecutor in the Rue Blanche—just to see him, to speak with him, to make quite sure.

Oh! he must be sure that no doubts, no pusillanimity on the part of any official would be allowed to stand in the way of the consummation of all his most cherished dreams. Papers or no papers, testimony or no testimony, the incarcerated Paul Mole was the Scarlet Pimpernel—of this Chauvelin was as certain as that he was alive. His every sense had testified to it when he stood in the narrow room of the Rue des Cordeliers, face to face—eyes gazing into eyes—with his sworn enemy.

Unluckily, however, he found the Public Prosecutor in a surly and obstinate mood, following on an interview which he had just had with citizen Commissary Cuisinier on the matter of the prisoner Paul Mole.

"His papers are all in order, I tell you," he said impatiently, in answer to Chauvelin's insistence. "It is as much as my head is worth to demand a summary execution."

"But I tell you that, those papers of his are forged," urged Chauvelin forcefully.

"They are not," retorted the other. "The Commissary swears to his own signature on the identity book. The concierge at the Abbaye swears that he knows Mole, so do all the men of the Surete who have seen him. The Commissary has known him as an indigent, good-for-nothing lubbard who has begged his way in the streets of Paris ever since he was released from gaol some months ago, after he had served a term for larceny. Even your own man Hebert admits to feeling doubtful on the point. You have had the nightmare, citizen," concluded Fouquier-Tinville with a harsh laugh.

"But, name of a dog!" broke in Chauvelin savagely. "You are not proposing to let the man go?"

"What else can I do?" the other rejoined fretfully. "We shall get into terrible trouble if we interfere with a man like Paul Mole. You know yourself how it is these days. We should have the whole of the rabble of Paris clamouring for our blood. If, after we have guillotined him, he is proved to be a good patriot, it will be my turn next. No! I thank you!"

"I tell you, man," retorted Chauvelin desperately, "that the man is not Paul Mole—that he is the English spy whom we all know as the Scarlet Pimpernel."

"Eh Bien!" riposted Fouquier-Tinville. "Bring me more tangible proof that our prisoner is not Paul Mole and I'll deal with him quickly enough, never fear. But if by to-morrow morning you do not satisfy me on the point. . . I must let him go his way."

A savage oath rose to Chauvelin's lips. He felt like a man who has been running, panting to reach a goal, who sees that goal within easy distance of him, and is then suddenly captured, caught in invisible meshes which hold him tightly, and against which he is powerless to struggle. For the moment he hated Fouquier-Tinville with a deadly hatred, would have tortured and threatened him until he wrung a consent, an admission, out of him.

Name of a name! when that damnable English spy was actually in his power, the man was a pusillanimous fool to allow the rich prize to slip from his grasp! Chauvelin felt as if he were choking; his slender fingers worked nervily around his cravat; beads of perspiration trickled unheeded down his pallid forehead.

Then suddenly he had an inspiration—nothing less! It almost seemed as if Satan, his friend, had whispered insinuating words into his ear. That scrap of paper! He had thrust it awhile ago into the breast pocket of his coat. It was still there, and the Public Prosecutor wanted a tangible proof. . . Then, why not. . . ?

Slowly, his thoughts still in the process of gradual coordination, Chauvelin drew that soiled scrap of paper out of his pocket. Fouquier-Tinville, surly and ill-humoured, had his back half-turned towards him, was moodily picking at his teeth. Chauvelin had all the leisure which he required. He smoothed out the creases in the paper and spread it out carefully upon the desk close to the other man's elbow. Fouquier-Tinville looked down on it, over his shoulder.

"What is that?" he queried.

"As you see, citizen," was Chauvelin's bland reply. "A message, such as you yourself have oft received, methinks, from our mutual enemy, the Scarlet Pimpernel."

But already the Public Prosecutor had seized upon the paper, and of a truth Chauvelin had no longer cause to complain of his colleague's indifference. That doggerel rhyme, no less than the signature, had the power to rouse Fouquier-Tinville's ire, as it had that of disturbing Chauvelin's well-studied calm.

"What is it?" reiterated the Public Prosecutor, white now to the lips.

"I have told you, citizen," rejoined Chauvelin imperturbably. "A message from that English spy. It is also the proof which you have demanded of me—the tangible proof that the prisoner, Paul Mole, is none other than the Scarlet Pimpernel."

"But," exclaimed the other hoarsely, "where did you get this?"

"It was found in the cell which Paul Mole occupied in the depot of the Rue de Tourraine, where he was first incarcerated. I picked it up there after he was removed. . . the ink was scarcely dry upon it."

The lie came quite glibly to Chauvelin's tongue. Was not every method good, every device allowable, which would lead to so glorious an end?

"Why did you not tell me of this before?" queried Fouquier-Tinville, with a sudden gleam of suspicion in his deep-set eyes.

"You had not asked me for a tangible proof before," replied Chauvelin blandly. "I myself was so firmly convinced of what I averred that I had well-nigh forgotten the existence of this damning scrap of paper."

Damning indeed! Fouquier-Tinville had seen such scraps of paper before. He had learnt the doggerel rhyme by heart, even though the English tongue was quite unfamiliar to him. He loathed the English—the entire nation—with all that deadly hatred which a divergence of political aims will arouse in times of acute crises. He hated the English government, Pitt and Burke and even Fox, the happy-go-lucky apologist of the young Revolution. But, above all, he hated that League of English spies—as he was pleased to call them—whose courage, resourcefulness, as well as reckless daring, had more than once baffled his own hideous schemes of murder, of pillage, and of rape.

Thank Beelzebub and his horde of evil spirits, citizen Chauvelin had been clear-sighted enough to detect that elusive Pimpernel under the disguise of Paul Mole.

"You have deserved well of your country," said Tinville with lusty fervour, and gave Chauvelin a vigorous slap on the shoulder. "But for you I should have allowed that abominable spy to slip through our fingers."

"I have succeeded in convincing you, citizen?" Chauvelin retorted dryly.

"Absolutely!" rejoined the other. "You may now leave the matter to me. And 'twill be friend Mole who will be surprised to-morrow," he added with a harsh guffaw, "when he finds himself face to face with me, before a Court of Justice."

He was all eagerness, of course. Such a triumph for him! The indictment of the notorious Scarlet Pimpernel on a charge of espionage would be the crowning glory of his career! Let other men look to their laurels! Those who brought that dangerous enemy of revolution to the guillotine would for ever be proclaimed as the saviours of France.

"A short indictment," he said, when Chauvelin, after a lengthy discussion on various points, finally rose to take his leave, "but a scathing one! I tell you, citizen Chauvelin, that to-morrow you will be the first to congratulate me on an unprecedented triumph."

He had been arguing in favour of a sensational trial and no less sensational execution. Chauvelin, with his memory harking back on many mysterious abductions at the very foot of the guillotine, would have liked to see his elusive enemy quietly put to death amongst a batch of traitors, who would help to mask his personality until after the guillotine had fallen, when the whole of Paris should ring with the triumph of this final punishment of the hated spy.

In the end, the two friends agreed upon a compromise, and parted well pleased with the turn of events which a kind Fate had ordered for their own special benefit.

X

THUS SATISFIED, CHAUVELIN RETURNED TO the Abbaye. Hebert was safe and trustworthy, but Hebert, too, had been assailed with the same doubts which had well-nigh wrecked Chauvelin's triumph, and with such doubts in his mind he might slacken his vigilance.

Name of a name! every man in charge of that damnable Scarlet Pimpernel should have three pairs of eyes wherewith to watch his movements. He should have the alert brain of a Robespierre, the physical strength of a Danton, the relentlessness of a Marat. He should be a giant in sheer brute force, a tiger in caution, an elephant in weight, and a mouse in stealthiness!

Name of a name! but 'twas only hate that could give such powers to any man!

Hebert, in the guard-room, owned to his doubts. His comrades, too, admitted that after twenty-four hours spent on the watch, their minds were in a whirl. The Citizen Commissary had been so sure—so was the chief concierge of the Abbaye even now; and the men of the Surete! . . . they themselves had seen the real Mole more than once. . . and this man in the cell. . . Well, would the citizen Representative have a final good look at him?

"You seem to forget Calais, citizen Hebert," Chauvelin said sharply, "and the deadly humiliation you suffered then at the hands of this man who is now your prisoner. Surely your eyes should have been, at least, as keen as mine own."

Anxious, irritable, his nerves well-nigh on the rack, he nevertheless crossed the guard-room with a firm step and entered the cell where the prisoner was still lying upon the palliasse, as he had been all along, and still presenting that naked piece of shoulder through the hole in his shirt.

"He has been like this the best part of the day," Hebert said with a shrug of the shoulders. "We put his bread and water right under his nose. He ate and he drank, and I suppose he slept. But except for a good deal of swearing, he has not spoken to any of us."

He had followed his chief into the cell, and now stood beside the palliasse, holding a small dark lantern in his hand. At a sign from Chauvelin he flashed the light upon the prisoner's averted head.

Mole cursed for awhile, and muttered something about "good patriots" and about "retribution." Then, worried by the light, he turned slowly round, and with fish-like, bleary eyes looked upon his visitor.

The words of stinging irony and triumphant sarcasm, all fully prepared, froze on Chauvelin's lips. He gazed upon the prisoner, and a weird sense of something unfathomable and mysterious came over him as he gazed. He himself could not have defined that feeling: the very next moment he was prepared to ridicule his own cowardice—yes, cowardice! because for a second or two he had felt positively afraid.

Afraid of what, forsooth? The man who crouched here in the cell was his arch-enemy, the Scarlet Pimpernel—the man whom he hated most bitterly in all the world, the man whose death he desired more than that of any other living creature. He had been apprehended by the very side of the murdered man whose confidence he had all but gained. He himself (Chauvelin) had at that fateful moment looked into the factitious Mole's eyes, had seen the mockery in them, the lazy insouciance which was the chief attribute of Sir Percy Blakeney. He had heard a faint echo of that inane laugh which grated upon his nerves. Hebert had then laid hands upon this very same man; agents of the Surete had barred every ingress and egress to the house, had conducted their prisoner straightway to the depot and thence to the Abbaye, had since that moment guarded him on sight, by day and by night. Hebert and the other men as well as the chief warder, all swore to that!

No, no! There could be no doubt! There was no doubt! The days of magic were over! A man could not assume a personality other than his own; he could not fly out of that personality like a bird out of its cage. There on the palliasse in the miserable cell were the same long limbs, the broad shoulders, the grimy face with the three days' growth of stubbly beard—the whole wretched personality of Paul Mole, in fact, which hid the exquisite one of Sir Percy Blakeney, Bart. And yet! . . .

A cold sweat ran down Chauvelin's spine as he gazed, mute and immovable, into those fish-like, bleary eyes, which were not—no! they were not those of the real Scarlet Pimpernel.

The whole situation became dreamlike, almost absurd. Chauvelin was not the man for such a mock-heroic, melodramatic situation. Commonsense, reason, his own cool powers of deliberation, would soon reassert themselves. But for the moment he was dazed. He had worked too hard, no doubt; had yielded too much to excitement, to triumph, and to hate. He turned to Hebert, who was standing stolidly by, gave him a few curt orders in a clear and well-pitched voice. Then he walked out of the cell, without bestowing another look on the prisoner.

Mole had once more turned over on his palliasse and, apparently, had gone to sleep. Hebert, with a strange and puzzled laugh, followed his chief out of the cell.

XI

At first Chauvelin had the wish to go back and see the Public Prosecutor—to speak with him—to tell him—what? Yes, what? That he, Chauvelin, had all of a sudden been assailed with the same doubts which already had worried Hebert and the others?—that he had told a deliberate lie when he stated that the incriminating doggerel rhyme had been found in Mole's cell? No, no! Such an admission would not only be foolish, it would be dangerous now, whilst he himself was scarce prepared to trust to his own senses. After all, Fouquier-Tinville was in the right frame of mind for the moment. Paul Mole, whoever he was, was safely under lock and key.

The only danger lay in the direction of the house on the Chemin de Pantin. At the thought Chauvelin felt giddy and faint. But he would allow himself no rest. Indeed, he could not have rested until something approaching certainty had once more taken possession of his soul. He could not—would not—believe that he had been deceived. He was still prepared to stake his very life on the identity of the prisoner at the Abbaye. Tricks of light, the flash of the lantern, the perfection of the disguise, had caused a momentary illusion—nothing more.

Nevertheless, that awful feeling of restlessness which had possessed him during the last twenty-four hours once more drove him to activity. And although commonsense and reason both pulled one way, an eerie sense of superstition whispered in his ear the ominous words, "If, after all!"

At any rate, he would see the Leridans, and once more make sure of them; and, late as was the hour, he set out for the lonely house on the Pantin Road.

Just inside the Barriere du Combat was the Poste de Section, where Commissary Burban was under orders to provide a dozen men of the Surete, who were to be on the watch round and about the house of the Leridans. Chauvelin called in on the Commissary, who assured him that the men were at their post.

Thus satisfied, he crossed the Barriere and started at a brisk walk down the long stretch of the Chemin de Pantin. The night was dark. The rolling clouds overhead hid the face of the moon and presaged the storm. On the right, the irregular heights of the Buttes Chaumont loomed out dense and dark against the heavy sky, whilst to the left, on ahead, a faintly glimmering, greyish streak of reflected light revealed the proximity of the canal.

Close to the spot where the main Route de Meux intersects the Chemin de Pantin, Chauvelin slackened his pace. The house of the Leridans now lay immediately on his left; from it a small, feeble ray of light, finding its way no doubt through an ill-closed shutter, pierced the surrounding gloom. Chauvelin, without hesitation, turned up a narrow track which led up to the house across a field of stubble. The next moment a peremptory challenge brought him to a halt.

"Who goes there?"

"Public Safety," replied Chauvelin. "Who are you?"

"Of the Surete," was the counter reply. "There are a dozen of us about here."

"When did you arrive?"

"Some two hours ago. We marched out directly after you left the orders at the Commissariat."

"You are prepared to remain on the watch all night?"

"Those are our orders, citizen," replied the man.

"You had best close up round the house, then. And, name of a dog!" he added, with a threatening ring in his voice. "Let there be no slackening of vigilance this night. No one to go in or out of that house, no one to approach it under any circumstances whatever. Is that understood?"

"Those were our orders from the first, citizen," said the man simply.

"And all has been well up to now?"

"We have seen no one, citizen."

The little party closed in around their chief and together they marched up to the house. Chauvelin, on tenterhooks, walked quicker than the others. He was the first to reach the door. Unable to find the bell-pull in the dark, he knocked vigorously.

The house appeared silent and wrapped in sleep. No light showed from within save that one tiny speck through the cracks of an ill-fitting shutter, in a room immediately overhead.

In response to Chauvelin's repeated summons, there came anon the sound of someone moving in one of the upstairs rooms, and presently the light overhead disappeared, whilst a door above was heard to open and to close and shuffling footsteps to come slowly down the creaking stairs.

A moment or two later the bolts and bars of the front door were unfastened, a key grated in the rusty lock, a chain rattled in its socket, and then the door was opened slowly and cautiously.

The woman Leridan appeared in the doorway. She held a guttering tallow candle high above her head. Its flickering light illumined Chauvelin's slender figure.

"Ah! the citizen Representative!" the woman exclaimed, as soon as she recognised him. "We did not expect you again to-day, and at this late hour, too. I'll tell my man—"

"Never mind your man," broke in Chauvelin impatiently, and pushed without ceremony past the woman inside the house. "The child? Is it safe?"

He could scarcely control his excitement. There was a buzzing, as of an angry sea, in his ears. The next second, until the woman spoke, seemed like a cycle of years.

"Quite safe, citizen," she said placidly. "Everything is quite safe. We were so thankful for those men of the Surete. We had been afraid before, as I told the citizen Representative, and my man and I could not rest for anxiety. It was only after they came that we dared go to bed."

A deep sigh of intense relief came from the depths of Chauvelin's heart. He had not realised himself until this moment how desperately anxious he had been. The woman's reassuring words appeared to lift a crushing weight from his mind. He turned to the man behind him.

"You did not tell me," he said, "that some of you had been here already."

"We have not been here before," the sergeant in charge of the little platoon said in reply. "I do not know what the woman means."

"Some of your men came about three hours ago," the woman retorted; "less than an hour after the citizen Representative was here. I remember that my man and I marvelled how quickly they did come, but they said that they had been on duty at the Barriere du Combat when the citizen arrived, and that he had dispatched them off at once. They said they had run all the way. But even so, we thought it was quick work—"

The words were smothered in her throat in a cry of pain, for, with an almost brutal gesture, Chauvelin had seized her by the shoulders.

"Where are those men?" he queried hoarsely. "Answer!"

"In there, and in there," the woman stammered, well-nigh faint with terror as she pointed to two doors, one on each side of the passage. "Three in each room. They are asleep now, I should say, as they seem so quiet. But they were an immense comfort to us, citizen. . . we were so thankful to have them in the house. . ."

But Chauvelin had snatched the candle from her hand. Holding it high above his head, he strode to the door on the right of the passage. It was ajar. He pushed it open with a vicious kick. The room beyond was in total darkness.

"Is anyone here?" he queried sharply.

Nothing but silence answered him. For a moment he remained there on the threshold, silent and immovable as a figure carved in stone. He had just a sufficiency of presence of mind and of will power not to drop the candle, to stand there motionless, with his back turned to the woman and to the men who had crowded in, in his wake. He would not let them see the despair, the rage and grave superstitious fear, which distorted every line of his pallid face.

He did not ask about the child. He would not trust himself to speak, for he had realised already how completely he had been baffled. Those abominable English spies had watched their opportunity, had worked on the credulity and the fears of the Leridans and, playing the game at which they and their audacious chief were such unconquerable experts, they had made their way into the house under a clever ruse.

The men of the Surete, not quite understanding the situation, were questioning the Leridans. The man, too, corroborated his wife's story. Their anxiety had been worked upon at the moment that it was most acute. After the citizen Representative left them, earlier in the evening, they had received another mysterious message which they had been unable to read, but which had greatly increased their alarm. Then, when the men of the Surete came. . . Ah! they had no cause to doubt that they were men of the Surete! . . . their clothes, their speech, their appearance. . . figure to yourself, even their uniforms! They spoke so nicely, so reassuringly. The Leridans were so thankful to see them! Then they made themselves happy in the two rooms below, and for additional safety the Lannoy child was brought down from its attic and put to sleep in the one room with the men of the Surete.

After that the Leridans went to bed. Name of a dog! how were they to blame? Those men and the child had disappeared, but they (the Leridans) would go to the guillotine swearing that they were not to blame.

Whether Chauvelin heard all these jeremiads, he could not afterwards have told you. But he did not need to be told how it had all been done. It had all been so simple, so ingenious, so like the methods usually adopted by that astute Scarlet Pimpernel! He saw it all so clearly before him. Nobody was to blame really, save he himself—he, who alone knew and understood the adversary with whom he had to deal.

But these people here should not have the gratuitous spectacle of a man enduring the torments of disappointment and of baffled revenge. Whatever Chauvelin was suffering now would for ever remain the secret of his own soul. Anon, when the Leridans' rasping voices died away in one of the more distant portions of the house and the men of the Surete were busy accepting refreshment and gratuity from the two terrified wretches, he had put down the candle with a steady hand and then walked with a firm step out of the house.

Soon the slender figure was swallowed up in the gloom as he strode back rapidly towards the city.

XII

Citizen Fouquier-Tinville had returned home from the Palais at a very late hour that same evening. His household in his simple lodgings in the Place Dauphine was already abed: his wife and the twins were asleep. He himself had sat down for a moment in the living-room, in dressing-gown and slippers, and with the late edition of the Moniteur in his hand, too tired to read.

It was half-past ten when there came a ring at the front door bell. Fouquier-Tinville, half expecting citizen Chauvelin to pay him a final visit, shuffled to the door and opened it.

A visitor, tall, well-dressed, exceedingly polite and urbane, requested a few minutes' conversation with citizen Fouquier-Tinville.

Before the Public Prosecutor had made up his mind whether to introduce such a late-comer into his rooms, the latter had pushed his way through the door into the ante-chamber, and with a movement as swift as it was unexpected, had thrown a scarf round Fouquier-Tinville's neck and wound it round his mouth, so that the unfortunate man's call for help was smothered in his throat.

So dexterously and so rapidly indeed had the miscreant acted, that his victim had hardly realised the assault before he found himself securely gagged and bound to a chair in his own ante-room, whilst that dare-devil stood before him, perfectly at his ease, his hands buried in the capacious pockets of his huge caped coat, and murmuring a few casual words of apology.

"I entreat you to forgive, citizen," he was saying in an even and pleasant voice, "this necessary violence on my part towards you. But my errand is urgent, and I could not allow your neighbours or your household to disturb the few minutes' conversation which I am obliged to have with you. My friend Paul Mole," he went on, after a slight pause, "is in grave danger of his life owing to a hallucination on the part of our mutual friend citizen Chauvelin; and I feel confident that you yourself are too deeply enamoured of your own neck to risk it wilfully by sending an innocent and honest patriot to the guillotine."

Once more he paused and looked down upon his unwilling interlocutor, who, with muscles straining against the cords that held him, and with eyes nearly starting out of their sockets in an access of fear and of rage, was indeed presenting a pitiful spectacle.

"I dare say that by now, citizen," the brigand continued imperturbably, "you will have guessed who I am. You and I have oft crossed invisible swords before; but this, methinks, is the first time that we have met face to face. I pray you, tell my dear friend M. Chauvelin that you have seen me. Also that there were two facts which he left entirely out of his calculations, perfect though these were. The one fact was that there were two Paul Moles—one real and one factitious. Tell him that, I pray you. It was the factitious Paul Mole who stole the ring and who stood for one moment gazing into clever citizen Chauvelin's eyes. But that same factitious Paul Mole had disappeared in the crowd even before your colleague had recovered his presence of mind. Tell him, I pray you, that the elusive Pimpernel whom he knows so well never assumes a fanciful disguise. He discovered the real Paul Mole first, studied him, learned his personality, until his own became a perfect replica of the miserable caitiff. It was the false Paul Mole who induced Jeannette Marechal to introduce him originally into the household of citizen Marat. It was he who gained the confidence of his employer; he, for a consideration, borrowed the identity papers of his real prototype. He again who for a few francs induced the real Paul Mole to follow him into the house of the murdered demagogue and to mingle there with the throng. He who thrust the identity papers back into the hands of their rightful owner whilst he himself was swallowed up by the crowd. But it was the real Paul Mole who was finally arrested and who is now lingering in the Abbaye prison, whence you, citizen Fouquier-Tinville, must free him on the instant, on pain of suffering yourself for the nightmares of your friend."

"The second fact," he went on with the same good-humoured pleasantry, "which our friend citizen Chauvelin had forgotten was that, though I happen to have aroused his unconquerable ire, I am but one man amongst a league of gallant English gentlemen. Their chief, I am proud to say; but without them, I should be powerless. Without one of them near me, by the side of the murdered Marat, I could not have rid myself of the ring in time, before other rough hands searched me to my skin. Without them, I could not have taken Madeleine Lannoy's child from out that terrible hell, to which a miscreant's lustful revenge had condemned the poor innocent. But while citizen Chauvelin, racked with triumph as well as with anxiety, was rushing from the Leridans' house to yours, and thence to the Abbaye prison, to gloat over his captive enemy, the League of the Scarlet Pimpernel carefully laid and carried out its plans at leisure. Disguised as men of the Surete, we took advantage of the Leridans' terror to obtain access into the house. Frightened to death by our warnings, as well as by citizen Chauvelin's threats, they not only admitted us into their house, but actually placed Madeleine Lannoy's child in our charge. Then they went contentedly to bed, and we, before the real men of the Surete arrived upon the scene, were already safely out of the way. My gallant English friends are some way out of Paris by now, escorting Madeleine Lannoy and her child into safety. They will return to Paris, citizen," continued the audacious adventurer, with a laugh full of joy and of unconquerable vitality, "and be my henchmen as before in many an adventure which will cause you and citizen Chauvelin to gnash your teeth with rage. But I myself will remain in Paris," he concluded lightly. "Yes, in Paris; under your very nose, and entirely at your service!"

The next second he was gone, and Fouquier-Tinville was left to marvel if the whole apparition had not been a hideous dream. Only there was no doubt that he was gagged and tied to a chair with cords: and here his wife found him, an hour later, when she woke from her first sleep, anxious because he had not yet come to bed.

II

A Question of Passports

Bibot was very sure of himself. There never was, never had been, there never would be again another such patriotic citizen of the Republic as was citizen Bibot of the Town Guard.

And because his patriotism was so well known among the members of the Committee of Public Safety, and his uncompromising hatred of the aristocrats so highly appreciated, citizen Bibot had been given the most important military post within the city of Paris.

He was in command of the Porte Montmartre, which goes to prove how highly he was esteemed, for, believe me, more treachery had been going on inside and out of the Porte Montmartre than in any other quarter of Paris. The last commandant there, citizen Ferney, was guillotined for having allowed a whole batch of aristocrats—traitors to the Republic, all of them—to slip through the Porte Montmartre and to find safety outside the walls of Paris. Ferney pleaded in his defence that these traitors had been spirited away from under his very nose by the devil's agency, for surely that meddlesome Englishman who spent his time in rescuing aristocrats—traitors, all of them—from the clutches of Madame la Guillotine must be either the devil himself, or at any rate one of his most powerful agents.

"Nom de Dieu! just think of his name! The Scarlet Pimpernel they call him! No one knows him by any other name! and he is preternaturally tall and strong and superhumanly cunning! And the power which he has of being transmuted into various personalities—rendering himself quite unrecognisable to the eyes of the most sharp-seeing patriot of France, must of a surety be a gift of Satan!"

But the Committee of Public Safety refused to listen to Ferney's explanations. The Scarlet Pimpernel was only an ordinary mortal—an exceedingly cunning and meddlesome personage it is true, and endowed with a superfluity of wealth which enabled him to break the thin crust of patriotism that overlay the natural cupidity of many Captains of the Town Guard—but still an ordinary man for all that! and no true lover of the Republic should allow either superstitious terror or greed to interfere with the discharge of his duties which at the Porte Montmartre consisted in detaining any and every person—aristocrat, foreigner, or otherwise traitor to the Republic—who could not give a satisfactory reason for desiring to leave Paris. Having detained such persons, the patriot's next duty was to hand them over to the Committee of Public Safety, who would then decide whether Madame la Guillotine would have the last word over them or not.

And the guillotine did nearly always have the last word to say, unless the Scarlet Pimpernel interfered.

The trouble was, that that same accursed Englishman interfered at times in a manner which was positively terrifying. His impudence, certes, passed all belief. Stories of his daring and of his impudence were abroad which literally made the lank and greasy hair of every patriot curl with wonder. 'Twas even whispered—not too loudly, forsooth—that certain members of the Committee of Public Safety had measured their skill and valour against that of the Englishman and emerged from the conflict beaten and humiliated, vowing vengeance which, of a truth, was still slow in coming.

Citizen Chauvelin, one of the most implacable and unyielding members of the Committee, was known to have suffered overwhelming shame at the hands of that daring gang, of whom the so-called Scarlet Pimpernel was the accredited chief. Some there were who said that citizen Chauvelin had for ever forfeited his prestige, and even endangered his head by measuring his well-known astuteness against that mysterious League of spies.

But then Bibot was different!

He feared neither the devil, nor any Englishman. Had the latter the strength of giants and the protection of every power of evil, Bibot was ready for him. Nay! he was aching for a tussle, and haunted the purlieus of the Committees to obtain some post which would enable him to come to grips with the Scarlet Pimpernel and his League.

Bibot's zeal and perseverance were duly rewarded, and anon he was appointed to the command of the guard at the Porte Montmartre.

A post of vast importance as aforesaid; so much so, in fact, that no less a person than citizen Jean Paul Marat himself came to speak with Bibot on that third day of Nivose in the year I of the Republic, with a view to impressing upon him the necessity of keeping his eyes open, and of suspecting every man, woman, and child indiscriminately until they had proved themselves to be true patriots.

"Let no one slip through your fingers, citizen Bibot," Marat admonished with grim earnestness. "That accursed Englishman is cunning and resourceful, and his impudence surpasses that of the devil himself."

"He'd better try some of his impudence on me!" commented Bibot with a sneer, "he'll soon find out that he no longer has a Ferney to deal with. Take it from me, citizen Marat, that if a batch of aristocrats escape out of Paris within the next few days, under the guidance of the d—d Englishman, they will have to find some other way than the Porte Montmartre."

"Well said, citizen!" commented Marat. "But be watchful to-night. . . to-night especially. The Scarlet Pimpernel is rampant in Paris just now."

"How so?"

"The ci-devant Duc and Duchesse de Montreux and the whole of their brood—sisters, brothers, two or three children, a priest, and several servants—a round dozen in all, have been condemned to death. The guillotine for them to-morrow at daybreak! Would it could have been to-night," added Marat, whilst a demoniacal leer contorted his face which already exuded lust for blood from every pore. "Would it could have been to-night. But the guillotine has been busy; over four hundred executions to-day. . . and the tumbrils are full—the seats bespoken in advance—and still they come. . . But to-morrow morning at daybreak Madame la Guillotine will have a word to say to the whole of the Montreux crowd!"

"But they are in the Conciergerie prison surely, citizen! out of the reach of that accursed Englishman?"

"They are on their way, an I mistake not, to the prison at this moment. I came straight on here after the condemnation, to which I listened with true joy. Ah, citizen Bibot! the blood of these hated aristocrats is good to behold when it drips from the blade of the guillotine. Have a care, citizen Bibot, do not let the Montreux crowd escape!"

"Have no fear, citizen Marat! But surely there is no danger! They have been tried and condemned! They are, as you say, even now on their way—well guarded, I presume—to the Conciergerie prison!—to-morrow at daybreak, the guillotine! What is there to fear?"

"Well! well!" said Marat, with a slight tone of hesitation, "it is best, citizen Bibot, to be over-careful these times."

Even whilst Marat spoke his face, usually so cunning and so vengeful, had suddenly lost its look of devilish cruelty which was almost superhuman in the excess of its infamy, and a greyish hue—suggestive of terror—had spread over the sunken cheeks. He clutched Bibot's arm, and leaning over the table he whispered in his ear:

"The Public Prosecutor had scarce finished his speech to-day, judgment was being pronounced, the spectators were expectant and still, only the Montreux woman and some of the females and children were blubbering and moaning, when suddenly, it seemed from nowhere, a small piece of paper fluttered from out the assembly and alighted on the desk in front of the Public Prosecutor. He took the paper up and glanced at its contents. I saw that his cheeks had paled, and that his hand trembled as he handed the paper over to me."

"And what did that paper contain, citizen Marat?" asked Bibot, also speaking in a whisper, for an access of superstitious terror was gripping him by the throat.

"Just the well-known accursed device, citizen, the small scarlet flower, drawn in red ink, and the few words: 'To-night the innocent men and women now condemned by this infamous tribunal will be beyond your reach!'"

"And no sign of a messenger?"

"None."

"And when did—"

"Hush!" said Marat peremptorily, "no more of that now. To your post, citizen, and remember—all are suspect! let none escape!"

The two men had been sitting outside a small tavern, opposite the Porte Montmartre, with a bottle of wine between them, their elbows resting on the grimy top of a rough wooden table. They had talked in whispers, for even the walls of the tumble-down cabaret might have had ears.

Opposite them the city wall—broken here by the great gate of Montmartre—loomed threateningly in the fast-gathering dusk of this winter's afternoon. Men in ragged red shirts, their unkempt heads crowned with Phrygian caps adorned with a tricolour cockade, lounged against the wall, or sat in groups on the top of piles of refuse that littered the street, with a rough deal plank between them and a greasy pack of cards in their grimy fingers. Guns and bayonets were propped against the wall. The gate itself had three means of egress; each of these was guarded by two men with fixed bayonets at their shoulders, but otherwise dressed like the others, in rags—with bare legs that looked blue and numb in the cold—the sans-culottes of revolutionary Paris.

Bibot rose from his seat, nodding to Marat, and joined his men.

From afar, but gradually drawing nearer, came the sound of a ribald song, with chorus accompaniment sung by throats obviously surfeited with liquor.

For a moment—as the sound approached—Bibot turned back once more to the Friend of the People.

"Am I to understand, citizen," he said, "that my orders are not to let anyone pass through these gates to-night?"

"No, no, citizen," replied Marat, "we dare not do that. There are a number of good patriots in the city still. We cannot interfere with their liberty or—"

And the look of fear of the demagogue—himself afraid of the human whirlpool which he has let loose—stole into Marat's cruel, piercing eyes.

"No, no," he reiterated more emphatically, "we cannot disregard the passports issued by the Committee of Public Safety. But examine each passport carefully, citizen Bibot! If you have any reasonable ground for suspicion, detain the holder, and if you have not—"

The sound of singing was quite near now. With another wink and a final leer, Marat drew back under the shadow of the cabaret, and Bibot swaggered up to the main entrance of the gate.

"Qui va la?" he thundered in stentorian tones as a group of some half-dozen people lurched towards him out of the gloom, still shouting hoarsely their ribald drinking song.

The foremost man in the group paused opposite citizen Bibot, and with arms akimbo, and legs planted well apart tried to assume a rigidity of attitude which apparently was somewhat foreign to him at this moment.

"Good patriots, citizen," he said in a thick voice which he vainly tried to render steady.

"What do you want?" queried Bibot.

"To be allowed to go on our way unmolested."

"What is your way?"

"Through the Porte Montmartre to the village of Barency."

"What is your business there?"

This query delivered in Bibot's most pompous manner seemed vastly to amuse the rowdy crowd. He who was the spokesman turned to his friends and shouted hilariously:

"Hark at him, citizens! He asks me what is our business. Oh, citizen Bibot, since when have you become blind? A dolt you've always been, else you had not asked the question."

But Bibot, undeterred by the man's drunken insolence, retorted gruffly:

"Your business, I want to know."

"Bibot! my little Bibot!" cooed the bibulous orator now in dulcet tones, "dost not know us, my good Bibot? Yet we all know thee, citizen—Captain Bibot of the Town Guard, eh, citizens! Three cheers for the citizen captain!"

When the noisy shouts and cheers from half a dozen hoarse throats had died down, Bibot, without more ado, turned to his own men at the gate.

"Drive these drunken louts away!" he commanded; "no one is allowed to loiter here."

Loud protest on the part of the hilarious crowd followed, then a slight scuffle with the bayonets of the Town Guard. Finally the spokesman, somewhat sobered, once more appealed to Bibot.

"Citizen Bibot! you must be blind not to know me and my mates! And let me tell you that you are doing yourself a deal of harm by interfering with the citizens of the Republic in the proper discharge of their duties, and by disregarding their rights of egress through this gate, a right confirmed by passports signed by two members of the Committee of Public Safety."

He had spoken now fairly clearly and very pompously. Bibot, somewhat impressed and remembering Marat's admonitions, said very civilly:

"Tell me your business then, citizen, and show me your passports. If everything is in order you may go your way."

"But you know me, citizen Bibot?" queried the other.

"Yes, I know you—unofficially, citizen Durand."

"You know that I and the citizens here are the carriers for citizen Legrand, the market gardener of Barency?"

"Yes, I know that," said Bibot guardedly, "unofficially."

"Then, unofficially, let me tell you, citizen, that unless we get to Barency this evening, Paris will have to do without cabbages and potatoes to-morrow. So now you know that you are acting at your own risk and peril, citizen, by detaining us."

"Your passports, all of you," commanded Bibot.

He had just caught sight of Marat still sitting outside the tavern opposite, and was glad enough, in this instance, to shelve his responsibility on the shoulders of the popular "Friend of the People." There was general searching in ragged pockets for grimy papers with official seals thereon, and whilst Bibot ordered one of his men to take the six passports across the road to citizen Marat for his inspection, he himself, by the last rays of the setting winter sun, made close examination of the six men who desired to pass through the Porte Montmartre.

As the spokesman had averred, he—Bibot—knew every one of these men. They were the carriers to citizen Legrand, the Barency market gardener. Bibot knew every face. They passed with a load of fruit and vegetables in and out of Paris every day. There was really and absolutely no cause for suspicion, and when citizen Marat returned the six passports, pronouncing them to be genuine, and recognising his own signature at the bottom of each, Bibot was at last satisfied, and the six bibulous carriers were allowed to pass through the gate, which they did, arm in arm, singing a wild curmagnole, and vociferously cheering as they emerged out into the open.

But Bibot passed an unsteady hand over his brow. It was cold, yet he was in a perspiration. That sort of thing tells on a man's nerves. He rejoined Marat, at the table outside the drinking booth, and ordered a fresh bottle of wine.

The sun had set now, and with the gathering dusk a damp mist descended on Montmartre. From the wall opposite, where the men sat playing cards, came occasional volleys of blasphemous oaths. Bibot was feeling much more like himself. He had half forgotten the incident of the six carriers, which had occurred nearly half an hour ago.

Two or three other people had, in the meanwhile, tried to pass through the gates, but Bibot had been suspicious and had detained them all.

Marat having commended him for his zeal took final leave of him. Just as the demagogue's slouchy, grimy figure was disappearing down a side street there was the loud clatter of hoofs from that same direction, and the next moment a detachment of the mounted Town Guard, headed by an officer in uniform, galloped down the ill-paved street.

Even before the troopers had drawn rein the officer had hailed Bibot.

"Citizen," he shouted, and his voice was breathless, for he had evidently ridden hard and fast, "this message to you from the citizen Chief Commissary of the Section. Six men are wanted by the Committee of Public Safety. They are disguised as carriers in the employ of a market gardener, and have passports for Barency! . . . The passports are stolen: the men are traitors—escaped aristocrats—and their spokesman is that d—d Englishman, the Scarlet Pimpernel."

Bibot tried to speak; he tugged at the collar of his ragged shirt; an awful curse escaped him.

"Ten thousand devils!" he roared.

"On no account allow these people to go through," continued the officer. "Keep their passports. Detain them! . . . Understand?"

Bibot was still gasping for breath even whilst the officer, ordering a quick "Turn!" reeled his horse round, ready to gallop away as far as he had come.

"I am for the St. Denis Gate—Grosjean is on guard there!" he shouted. "Same orders all round the city. No one to leave the gates! . . . Understand?"

His troopers fell in. The next moment he would be gone, and those cursed aristocrats well in safety's way.

"Citizen Captain!"

The hoarse shout at last contrived to escape Bibot's parched throat. As if involuntarily, the officer drew rein once more.

"What is it? Quick!—I've no time. That confounded Englishman may be at the St. Denis Gate even now!"

"Citizen Captain," gasped Bibot, his breath coming and going like that of a man fighting for his life. "Here! . . . at this gate! . . . not half an hour ago. . . six men. . . carriers. . . market gardeners. . . I seemed to know their faces. . ."

"Yes! yes! market gardener's carriers," exclaimed the officer gleefully, "aristocrats all of them. . . and that d—d Scarlet Pimpernel. You've got them? You've detained them? . . . Where are they? . . . Speak, man, in the name of hell! . . ."

"Gone!" gasped Bibot. His legs would no longer bear him. He fell backwards on to a heap of street debris and refuse, from which lowly vantage ground he contrived to give away the whole miserable tale.

"Gone! half an hour ago. Their passports were in order! . . . I seemed to know their faces! Citizen Marat was here. . . He, too—"

In a moment the officer had once more swung his horse round, so that the animal reared, with wild forefeet pawing the air, with champing of bit, and white foam scattered around.

"A thousand million curses!" he exclaimed. "Citizen Bibot, your head will pay for this treachery. Which way did they go?"

A dozen hands were ready to point in the direction where the merry party of carriers had disappeared half an hour ago; a dozen tongues gave rapid, confused explanations.

"Into it, my men!" shouted the officer; "they were on foot! They can't have gone far. Remember the Republic has offered ten thousand francs for the capture of the Scarlet Pimpernel."

Already the heavy gates had been swung open, and the officer's voice once more rang out clear through a perfect thunder-clap of fast galloping hoofs:

"Ventre a terre! Remember!—ten thousand francs to him who first sights the Scarlet Pimpernel!"

The thunder-clap died away in the distance, the dust of four score hoofs was merged in the fog and in the darkness; the voice of the captain was raised again through the mist-laden air. One shout. . . a shout of triumph. . . then silence once again.

Bibot had fainted on the heap of debris.

His comrades brought him wine to drink. He gradually revived. Hope came back to his heart; his nerves soon steadied themselves as the heavy beverage filtrated through into his blood.

"Bah!" he exclaimed as he pulled himself together, "the troopers were well-mounted. . . the officer was enthusiastic; those carriers could not have walked very far. And, in any case, I am free from blame. Citoyen Marat himself was here and let them pass!"

A shudder of superstitious terror ran through him as he recollected the whole scene: for surely he knew all the faces of the six men who had gone through the gate. The devil indeed must have given the mysterious Englishman power to transmute himself and his gang wholly into the bodies of other people.

More than an hour went by. Bibot was quite himself again, bullying, commanding, detaining everybody now.

At that time there appeared to be a slight altercation going on, on the farther side of the gate. Bibot thought it his duty to go and see what the noise was about. Someone wanting to get into Paris instead of out of it at this hour of the night was a strange occurrence.

Bibot heard his name spoken by a raucous voice. Accompanied by two of his men he crossed the wide gates in order to see what was happening. One of the men held a lanthorn, which he was swinging high above his head. Bibot saw standing there before him, arguing with the guard by the gate, the bibulous spokesman of the band of carriers.

He was explaining to the sentry that he had a message to deliver to the citizen commanding at the Porte Montmartre.

"It is a note," he said, "which an officer of the mounted guard gave me. He and twenty troopers were galloping down the great North Road not far from Barency. When they overtook the six of us they drew rein, and the officer gave me this note for citizen Bibot and fifty francs if I would deliver it tonight."

"Give me the note!" said Bibot calmly.

But his hand shook as he took the paper; his face was livid with fear and rage.

The paper had no writing on it, only the outline of a small scarlet flower done in red—the device of the cursed Englishman, the Scarlet Pimpernel.

"Which way did the officer and the twenty troopers go," he stammered, "after they gave you this note?"

"On the way to Calais," replied the other, "but they had magnificent horses, and didn't spare them either. They are a league and more away by now!"

All the blood in Bibot's body seemed to rush up to his head, a wild buzzing was in his ears. . .

And that was how the Duc and Duchesse de Montreux, with their servants and family, escaped from Paris on that third day of Nivose in the year I of the Republic.

III

Two Good Patriots

Being the deposition of citizeness Fanny Roussell, who was brought up, together with her husband, before the Tribunal of the Revolution on a charge of treason—both being subsequently acquitted.

My name is Fanny Roussell, and I am a respectable married woman, and as good a patriot as any of you sitting there.

Aye, and I'll say it with my dying breath, though you may send me to the guillotine. . . as you probably will, for you are all thieves and murderers, every one of you, and you have already made up your minds that I and my man are guilty of having sheltered that accursed Englishman whom they call the Scarlet Pimpernel. . . and of having helped him to escape.

But I'll tell you how it all happened, because, though you call me a traitor to the people of France, yet am I a true patriot and will prove it to you by telling you exactly how everything occurred, so that you may be on your guard against the cleverness of that man, who, I do believe, is a friend and confederate of the devil. . . else how could he have escaped that time?

Well! it was three days ago, and as bitterly cold as anything that my man and I can remember. We had no travellers staying in the house, for we are a good three leagues out of Calais, and too far for the folk who have business in or about the harbour. Only at midday the coffee-room would get full sometimes with people on their way to or from the port.

But in the evenings the place was quite deserted, and so lonely that at times we fancied that we could hear the wolves howling in the forest of St. Pierre.

It was close on eight o'clock, and my man was putting up the shutters, when suddenly we heard the tramp of feet on the road outside, and then the quick word, "Halt!"

The next moment there was a peremptory knock at the door. My man opened it, and there stood four men in the uniform of the 9th Regiment of the Line. . . the same that is quartered at Calais. The uniform, of course, I knew well, though I did not know the men by sight.

"In the name of the People and by the order of the Committee of Public Safety!" said one of the men, who stood in the forefront, and who, I noticed, had a corporal's stripe on his left sleeve.

He held out a paper, which was covered with seals and with writing, but as neither my man nor I can read, it was no use our looking at it.

Hercule—that is my husband's name, citizens—asked the corporal what the Committee of Public Safety wanted with us poor hoteliers of a wayside inn.

"Only food and shelter for to-night for me and my men," replied the corporal, quite civilly.

"You can rest here," said Hercule, and he pointed to the benches in the coffee-room, "and if there is any soup left in the stockpot, you are welcome to it."

Hercule, you see, is a good patriot, and he had been a soldier in his day. . . No! no. . . do not interrupt me, any of you. . . you would only be saying that I ought to have known. . . but listen to the end.

"The soup we'll gladly eat," said the corporal very pleasantly. "As for shelter. . . well! I am afraid that this nice warm coffee-room will not exactly serve our purpose. We want a place where we can lie hidden, and at the same time keep a watch on the road. I noticed an outhouse as we came. By your leave we will sleep in there."

"As you please," said my man curtly.

He frowned as he said this, and it suddenly seemed as if some vague suspicion had crept into Hercule's mind.

The corporal, however, appeared unaware of this, for he went on quite cheerfully:

"Ah! that is excellent! Entre nous, citizen, my men and I have a desperate customer to deal with. I'll not mention his name, for I see you have guessed it already. A small red flower, what? . . . Well, we know that he must be making straight for the port of Calais, for he has been traced through St. Omer and Ardres. But he cannot possibly enter Calais city to-night, for we are on the watch for him. He must seek shelter somewhere for himself and any other aristocrat he may have with him, and, bar this house, there is no other place between Ardres and Calais where he can get it. The night is bitterly cold, with a snow blizzard raging round. I and my men have been detailed to watch this road, other patrols are guarding those that lead toward Boulogne and to Gravelines; but I have an idea, citizen, that our fox is making for Calais, and that to me will fall the honour of handing that tiresome scarlet flower to the Public Prosecutor en route for Madame la Guillotine."

Now I could not really tell you, citizens, what suspicions had by this time entered Hercule's head or mine; certainly what suspicions we did have were still very vague.

I prepared the soup for the men and they ate it heartily, after which my husband led the way to the outhouse where we sometimes stabled a traveller's horse when the need arose.

It is nice and dry, and always filled with warm, fresh straw. The entrance into it immediately faces the road; the corporal declared that nothing would suit him and his men better.

They retired to rest apparently, but we noticed that two men remained on the watch just inside the entrance, whilst the two others curled up in the straw.

Hercule put out the lights in the coffee-room, and then he and I went upstairs—not to bed, mind you—but to have a quiet talk together over the events of the past half-hour.

The result of our talk was that ten minutes later my man quietly stole downstairs and out of the house. He did not, however, go out by the front door, but through a back way which, leading through a cabbage-patch and then across a field, cuts into the main road some two hundred metres higher up.

Hercule and I had decided that he would walk the three leagues into Calais, despite the cold, which was intense, and the blizzard, which was nearly blinding, and that he would call at the post of gendarmerie at the city gates, and there see the officer in command and tell him the exact state of the case. It would then be for that officer to decide what was to be done; our responsibility as loyal citizens would be completely covered.

Hercule, you must know, had just emerged from our cabbage-patch on to the field when he was suddenly challenged:

"Qui va la?"

He gave his name. His certificate of citizenship was in his pocket; he had nothing to fear. Through the darkness and the veil of snow he had discerned a small group of men wearing the uniform of the 9th Regiment of the Line.

"Four men," said the foremost of these, speaking quickly and commandingly, "wearing the same uniform that I and my men are wearing. . . have you seen them?"

"Yes," said Hercule hurriedly.

"Where are they?"

"In the outhouse close by."

The other suppressed a cry of triumph.

"At them, my men!" he said in a whisper, "and you, citizen, thank your stars that we have not come too late."

"These men. . ." whispered Hercule. "I had my suspicions."

"Aristocrats, citizen," rejoined the commander of the little party, "and one of them is that cursed Englishman—the Scarlet Pimpernel."

Already the soldiers, closely followed by Hercule, had made their way through our cabbage-patch back to the house.

The next moment they had made a bold dash for the barn. There was a great deal of shouting, a great deal of swearing and some firing, whilst Hercule and I, not a little frightened, remained in the coffee-room, anxiously awaiting events.

Presently the group of soldiers returned, not the ones who had first come, but the others. I noticed their leader, who seemed to be exceptionally tall.

He looked very cheerful, and laughed loudly as he entered the coffee-room. From the moment that I looked at his face I knew, somehow, that Hercule and I had been fooled, and that now, indeed, we stood eye to eye with that mysterious personage who is called the Scarlet Pimpernel.

I screamed, and Hercule made a dash for the door; but what could two humble and peaceful citizens do against this band of desperate men, who held their lives in their own hands? They were four and we were two, and I do believe that their leader has supernatural strength and power.

He treated us quite kindly, even though he ordered his followers to bind us down to our bed upstairs, and to tie a cloth round our mouths so that our cries could not be distinctly heard.

Neither my man nor I closed an eye all night, of course, but we heard the miscreants moving about in the coffee-room below. But they did no mischief, nor did they steal any of the food or wines.

At daybreak we heard them going out by the front door, and their footsteps disappearing toward Calais. We found their discarded uniforms lying in the coffee-room. They must have entered Calais by daylight, when the gates were opened—just like other peaceable citizens. No doubt they had forged passports, just as they had stolen uniforms.

Our maid-of-all-work released us from our terrible position in the course of the morning, and we released the soldiers of the 9th Regiment of the Line, whom we found bound and gagged, some of them wounded, in the outhouse.

That same afternoon we were arrested, and here we are, ready to die if we must, but I swear that I have told you the truth, and I ask you, in the name of justice, if we have done anything wrong, and if we did not act like loyal and true citizens, even though we were pitted against an emissary of the devil?

IV

The Old Scarecrow

I

Nobody in the quartier could quite recollect when it was that the new Public Letter-Writer first set up in business at the angle formed by the Quai des Augustins and the Rue Dauphine, immediately facing the Pont Neuf; but there he certainly was on the 28th day of February, 1793, when Agnes, with eyes swollen with tears, a market basket on her arm, and a look of dreary despair on her young face, turned that selfsame angle on her way to the Pont Neuf, and nearly fell over the rickety construction which sheltered him and his stock-in-trade.

"Oh, mon Dieu! citizen Lepine, I had no idea you were here," she exclaimed as soon as she had recovered her balance.

"Nor I, citizeness, that I should have the pleasure of seeing you this morning," he retorted.

"But you were always at the other corner of the Pont Neuf," she argued.

"So I was," he replied, "so I was. But I thought I would like a change. The Faubourg St. Michel appealed to me; most of my clients came to me from this side of the river—all those on the other side seem to know how to read and write."

"I was just going over to see you," she remarked.

"You, citizeness," he exclaimed in unfeigned surprise, "what should procure a poor public writer the honour of—"

"Hush, in God's name!" broke in the young girl quickly as she cast a rapid, furtive glance up and down the quai and the narrow streets which converged at this angle.

She was dressed in the humblest and poorest of clothes, her skimpy shawl round her shoulders could scarce protect her against the cold of this cruel winter's morning; her hair was entirely hidden beneath a frilled and starched cap, and her feet were encased in coarse worsted stockings and sabots, but her hands were delicate and fine, and her face had that nobility of feature and look of patient resignation in the midst of overwhelming sorrow which proclaimed a lofty refinement both of soul and of mind.

The old Letter-Writer was surveying the pathetic young figure before him through his huge horn-rimmed spectacles, and she smiled on him through her fast-gathering tears. He used to have his pitch at the angle of the Pont Neuf, and whenever Agnes had walked past it, she had nodded to him and bidden him "Good morrow!" He had at times done little commissions for her and gone on errands when she needed a messenger; to-day, in the midst of her despair, she had suddenly thought of him and that rumour credited him with certain knowledge which she would give her all to possess.

She had sallied forth this morning with the express purpose of speaking with him; but now suddenly she felt afraid, and stood looking at him for a moment or two, hesitating, wondering if she dared tell him—one never knew those days into what terrible pitfall an ill-considered word might lead one.

A scarecrow he was, that old Public Letter-Writer, more like a great, gaunt bird than a human being, with those spectacles of his, and his long, very sparse and very lanky fringe of a beard which fell from his cheeks and chin and down his chest for all the world like a crumpled grey bib. He was wrapped from head to foot in a caped coat which had once been green in colour, but was now of many hues not usually seen in rainbows. He wore his coat all buttoned down the front, like a dressing-gown, and below the hem there peeped out a pair of very large feet encased in boots which had never been a pair. He sat upon a rickety, straw-bottomed chair under an improvised awning which was made up of four poles and a bit of sacking. He had a table in front of him—a table partially and very insecurely propped up by a bundle of old papers and books, since no two of its four legs were completely whole—and on the table there was a neckless bottle half-filled with ink, a few sheets of paper and a couple of quill pens.

The young girl's hesitation had indeed not lasted more than a few seconds.

Furtively, like a young creature terrified of lurking enemies, she once more glanced to right and left of her and down the two streets and the river bank, for Paris was full of spies these days—human bloodhounds ready for a few sous to sell their fellow-creatures' lives. It was middle morning now, and a few passers-by were hurrying along wrapped to the nose in mufflers, for the weather was bitterly cold.

Agnes waited until there was no one in sight, then she leaned forward over the table and whispered under her breath:

"They say, citizen, that you alone in Paris know the whereabouts of the English milor'—of him who is called the Scarlet Pimpernel. . ."

"Hush-sh-sh!" said the old man quickly, for just at that moment two men had gone by, in ragged coats and torn breeches, who had leered at Agnes and her neat cap and skirt as they passed. Now they had turned the angle of the street and the old man, too, sank his voice to a whisper.

"I know nothing of any Englishman," he muttered.

"Yes, you do," she rejoined insistently. "When poor Antoine Carre was somewhere in hiding and threatened with arrest, and his mother dared not write to him lest her letter be intercepted, she spoke to you about the English milor', and the English milor' found Antoine Carre and took him and his mother safely out of France. Mme. Carre is my godmother. . . I saw her the very night when she went to meet the English milor' at his commands. I know all that happened then. . . I know that you were the intermediary."

"And if I was," he muttered sullenly as he fiddled with his pen and paper, "maybe I've had cause to regret it. For a week after that Carre episode I dared not show my face in the streets of Paris; for nigh on a fortnight I dared not ply my trade. . . I have only just ventured again to set up in business. I am not going to risk my old neck again in a hurry. . ."

"It is a matter of life and death," urged Agnes, as once more the tears rushed to her pleading eyes and the look of misery settled again upon her face.

"Your life, citizeness?" queried the old man, "or that of citizen-deputy Fabrice?"

"Hush!" she broke in again, as a look of real terror now overspread her face. Then she added under her breath: "You know?"

"I know that Mademoiselle Agnes de Lucines is fiancee to the citizen-deputy Arnould Fabrice," rejoined the old man quietly, "and that it is Mademoiselle Agnes de Lucines who is speaking with me now."

"You have known that all along?"

"Ever since mademoiselle first tripped past me at the angle of the Pont Neuf dressed in winsey kirtle and wearing sabots on her feet. . ."

"But how?" she murmured, puzzled, not a little frightened, for his knowledge might prove dangerous to her. She was of gentle birth, and as such an object of suspicion to the Government of the Republic and of the Terror; her mother was a hopeless cripple, unable to move: this together with her love for Arnould Fabrice had kept Agnes de Lucines in France these days, even though she was in hourly peril of arrest.

"Tell me what has happened," the old man said, unheeding her last anxious query. "Perhaps I can help. . ."

"Oh! you cannot—the English milor' can and will if only we could know where he is. I thought of him the moment I received that awful man's letter—and then I thought of you. . ."

"Tell me about the letter—quickly," he interrupted her with some impatience. "I'll be writing something—but talk away, I shall hear every word. But for God's sake be as brief as you can."

He drew some paper nearer to him and dipped his pen in the ink. He appeared to be writing under her dictation. Thin, flaky snow had begun to fall and settled in a smooth white carpet upon the frozen ground, and the footsteps of the passers-by sounded muffled as they hurried along. Only the lapping of the water of the sluggish river close by broke the absolute stillness of the air.

Agnes de Lucines' pale face looked ethereal in this framework of white which covered her shoulders and the shawl crossed over her bosom: only her eyes, dark, appealing, filled with a glow of immeasurable despair, appeared tensely human and alive.

"I had a letter this morning," she whispered, speaking very rapidly, "from citizen Heriot—that awful man—you know him?"

"Yes, yes!"

"He used to be valet in the service of deputy Fabrice. Now he, too, is a member of the National Assembly. . . he is arrogant and cruel and vile. He hates Arnould Fabrice and he professes himself passionately in love with me."

"Yes, yes!" murmured the old man, "but the letter?"

"It came this morning. In it he says that he has in his possession a number of old letters, documents and manuscripts which are quite enough to send deputy Fabrice to the guillotine. He threatens to place all those papers before the Committee of Public Safety unless. . . unless I. . ."

She paused, and a deep blush, partly of shame, partly of wrath, suffused her pale cheeks.

"Unless you accept his grimy hand in marriage," concluded the man dryly.

Her eyes gave him answer. With pathetic insistence she tried now to glean a ray of hope from the old scarecrow's inscrutable face. But he was bending over his writing: his fingers were blue with cold, his great shoulders were stooping to his task.

"Citizen," she pleaded.

"Hush!" he muttered, "no more now. The very snowflakes are made up of whispers that may reach those bloodhounds yet. The English milor' shall know of this. He will send you a message if he thinks fit."

"Citizen—"

"Not another word, in God's name! Pay me five sous for this letter and pray Heaven that you have not been watched."

She shivered and drew her shawl closer round her shoulders, then she counted out five sous with elaborate care and laid them out upon the table. The old man took up the coins. He blew into his fingers, which looked paralysed with the cold. The snow lay over everything now; the rough awning had not protected him or his wares.

Agnes turned to go. The last she saw of him, as she went up the Rue Dauphine, was one broad shoulder still bending over the table, and clad in the shabby, caped coat all covered with snow like an old Santa Claus.

II

It was half-an-hour before noon, and citizen-deputy Heriot was preparing to go out to the small tavern round the corner where he habitually took his dejeuner. Citizen Rondeau, who for the consideration of ten sous a day looked after Heriot's paltry creature-comforts, was busy tidying up the squalid apartment which the latter occupied on the top floor of a lodging-house in the Rue Cocatrice. This apartment consisted of three rooms leading out of one another; firstly there was a dark and narrow antichambre wherein slept the aforesaid citizen-servant; then came a sitting-room sparsely furnished with a few chairs, a centre table and an iron stove, and finally there was the bedroom wherein the most conspicuous object was a large oak chest clamped with wide iron hinges and a massive writing-desk; the bed and a very primitive washstand were in an alcove at the farther end of the room and partially hidden by a tapestry curtain.

At exactly half-past seven that morning there came a peremptory knock at the door of the antichambre, and as Rondeau was busy in the bedroom, Heriot went himself to see who his unexpected visitor might be. On the landing outside stood an extraordinary-looking individual—more like a tall and animated scarecrow than a man—who in a tremulous voice asked if he might speak with the citizen Heriot.

"That is my name," said the deputy gruffly, "what do you want?"

He would have liked to slam the door in the old scarecrow's face, but the latter, with the boldness which sometimes besets the timid, had already stepped into the anti-chambre and was now quietly sauntering through to the next room into the one beyond. Heriot, being a representative of the people and a social democrat of the most advanced type, was supposed to be accessible to every one who desired speech with him. Though muttering sundry curses, he thought it best not to go against his usual practice, and after a moment's hesitation he followed his unwelcome visitor.

The latter was in the sitting-room by this time; he had drawn a chair close to the table and sat down with the air of one who has a perfect right to be where he is; as soon as Heriot entered he said placidly:

"I would desire to speak alone with the citizen-deputy."

And Heriot, after another slight hesitation, ordered Rondeau to close the bedroom door.

"Keep your ears open in case I call," he added significantly.

"You are cautious, citizen," merely remarked the visitor with a smile.

To this Heriot vouchsafed no reply. He, too, drew a chair forward and sat opposite his visitor, then he asked abruptly: "Your name and quality?"

"My name is Lepine at your service," said the old man, "and by profession I write letters at the rate of five sous or so, according to length, for those who are not able to do it for themselves."

"Your business with me?" queried Heriot curtly.

"To offer you two thousand francs for the letters which you stole from deputy Fabrice when you were his valet," replied Lepine with perfect calm.

In a moment Heriot was on his feet, jumping up as if he had been stung; his pale, short-sighted eyes narrowed till they were mere slits, and through them he darted a quick, suspicious glance at the extraordinary out-at-elbows figure before him. Then he threw back his head and laughed till the tears streamed down his cheeks and his sides began to ache.

"This is a farce, I presume, citizen," he said when he had recovered something of his composure.

"No farce, citizen," replied Lepine calmly. "The money is at your disposal whenever you care to bring the letters to my pitch at the angle of the Rue Dauphine and the Quai des Augustins, where I carry on my business."

"Whose money is it? Agnes de Lucines' or did that fool Fabrice send you?"

"No one sent me, citizen. The money is mine—a few savings I possess—I honour citizen Fabrice—I would wish to do him service by purchasing certain letters from you."

Then as Heriot, moody and sullen, remained silent and began pacing up and down the long, bare floor of the room, Lepine added persuasively, "Well! what do you say? Two thousand francs for a packet of letters—not a bad bargain these hard times."

"Get out of this room," was Heriot's fierce and sudden reply.

"You refuse?"

"Get out of this room!"

"As you please," said Lepine as he, too, rose from his chair. "But before I go, citizen Heriot," he added, speaking very quietly, "let me tell you one thing. Mademoiselle Agnes de Lucines would far sooner cut off her right hand than let yours touch it even for one instant. Neither she nor deputy Fabrice would ever purchase their lives at such a price."

"And who are you—you mangy old scarecrow?" retorted Heriot, who was getting beside himself with rage, "that you should assert these things? What are those people to you, or you to them, that you should interfere in their affairs?"

"Your question is beside the point, citizen," said Lepine blandly; "I am here to propose a bargain. Had you not better agree to it?"

"Never!" reiterated Heriot emphatically.

"Two thousand francs," reiterated the old man imperturbably.

"Not if you offered me two hundred thousand," retorted the other fiercely. "Go and tell that, to those who sent you. Tell them that I—Heriot—would look upon a fortune as mere dross against the delight of seeing that man Fabrice, whom I hate beyond everything in earth or hell, mount up the steps to the guillotine. Tell them that I know that Agnes de Lucines loathes me, that I know that she loves him. I know that I cannot win her save by threatening him. But you are wrong, citizen Lepine," he continued, speaking more and more calmly as his passions of hatred and of love seemed more and more to hold him in their grip; "you are wrong if you think that she will not strike a bargain with me in order to save the life of Fabrice, whom she loves. Agnes de Lucines will be my wife within the month, or Arnould Fabrice's head will fall under the guillotine, and you, my interfering friend, may go to the devil, if you please."

"That would be but a tame proceeding, citizen, after my visit to you," said the old man, with unruffled sang-froid. "But let me, in my turn, assure you of this, citizen Heriot," he added, "that Mlle. de Lucines will never be your wife, that Arnould Fabrice will not end his valuable life under the guillotine—and that you will never be allowed to use against him the cowardly and stolen weapon which you possess."

Heriot laughed—a low, cynical laugh and shrugged his thin shoulders:

"And who will prevent me, I pray you?" he asked sarcastically.

The old man made no immediate reply, but he came just a step or two closer to the citizen-deputy and, suddenly drawing himself up to his full height, he looked for one brief moment down upon the mean and sordid figure of the ex-valet. To Heriot it seemed as if the whole man had become transfigured; the shabby old scarecrow looked all of a sudden like a brilliant and powerful personality; from his eyes there flashed down a look of supreme contempt and of supreme pride, and Heriot—unable to understand this metamorphosis which was more apparent to his inner consciousness than to his outward sight, felt his knees shake under him and all the blood rush back to his heart in an agony of superstitious terror.

From somewhere there came to his ear the sound of two words: "I will!" in reply to his own defiant query. Surely those words uttered by a man conscious of power and of strength could never have been spoken by the dilapidated old scarecrow who earned a precarious living by writing letters for ignorant folk.

But before he could recover some semblance of presence of mind citizen Lepine had gone, and only a loud and merry laugh seemed to echo through the squalid room.

Heriot shook off the remnant of his own senseless terror; he tore open the door of the bedroom and shouted to Rondeau, who truly was thinking that the citizen-deputy had gone mad:

"After him!—after him! Quick! curse you!" he cried.

"After whom?" gasped the man.

"The man who was here just now—an aristo."

"I saw no one—but the Public Letter-Writer, old Lepine—I know him well—"

"Curse you for a fool!" shouted Heriot savagely, "the man who was here was that cursed Englishman—the one whom they call the Scarlet Pimpernel. Run after him—stop him, I say!"

"Too late, citizen," said the other placidly; "whoever was here before is certainly half-way down the street by now."

III

"No use, Ffoulkes," said Sir Percy Blakeney to his friend half-an-hour later, "the man's passions of hatred and desire are greater than his greed."

The two men were sitting together in one of Sir Percy Blakeney's many lodgings—the one in the Rue des Petits Peres—and Sir Percy had just put Sir Andrew Ffoulkes au fait with the whole sad story of Arnould Fabrice's danger and Agnes de Lucines' despair.

"You could do nothing with the brute, then?" queried Sir Andrew.

"Nothing," replied Blakeney. "He refused all bribes, and violence would not have helped me, for what I wanted was not to knock him down, but to get hold of the letters."

"Well, after all, he might have sold you the letters and then denounced Fabrice just the same."

"No, without actual proofs he could not do that. Arnould Fabrice is not a man against whom a mere denunciation would suffice. He has the grudging respect of every faction in the National Assembly. Nothing but irrefutable proof would prevail against him—and bring him to the guillotine."

"Why not get Fabrice and Mlle. de Lucines safely over to England?"

"Fabrice would not come. He is not of the stuff that emigres are made of. He is not an aristocrat; he is a republican by conviction, and a demmed honest one at that. He would scorn to run away, and Agnes de Lucines would not go without him."

"Then what can we do?"

"Filch those letters from that brute Heriot," said Blakeney calmly.

"House-breaking, you mean!" commented Sir Andrew Ffoulkes dryly.

"Petty theft, shall we say?" retorted Sir Percy. "I can bribe the lout who has charge of Heriot's rooms to introduce us into his master's sanctum this evening when the National Assembly is sitting and the citizen-deputy safely out of the way."

And the two men—one of whom was the most intimate friend of the Prince of Wales and the acknowledged darling of London society—thereupon fell to discussing plans for surreptitiously entering a man's room and committing larceny, which in normal times would entail, if discovered, a long term of imprisonment, but which, in these days, in Paris, and perpetrated against a member of the National Assembly, would certainly be punished by death.

IV

Citizen Rondeau, whose business it was to look after the creature comforts of deputy Heriot, was standing in the antichambre facing the two visitors whom he had just introduced into his master's apartments, and idly turning a couple of gold coins over and over between his grimy fingers.

"And mind, you are to see nothing and hear nothing of what goes on in the next room," said the taller of the two strangers; "and when we go there'll be another couple of louis for you. Is that understood?"

"Yes! it's understood," grunted Rondeau sullenly; "but I am running great risks. The citizen-deputy sometimes returns at ten o'clock, but sometimes at nine. . . I never know."

"It is now seven," rejoined the other; "we'll be gone long before nine."

"Well," said Rondeau surlily, "I go out now for my supper. I'll return in half an hour, but at half-past eight you must clear out."

Then he added with a sneer:

"Citizens Legros and Desgas usually come back with deputy Heriot of nights, and citizens Jeanniot and Bompard come in from next door for a game of cards. You wouldn't stand much chance if you were caught here."

"Not with you to back up so formidable a quintette of stalwarts," assented the tall visitor gaily. "But we won't trouble about that just now. We have a couple of hours before us in which to do all that we want. So au revoir, friend Rondeau. . . two more louis for your complaisance, remember, when we have accomplished our purpose."

Rondeau muttered something more, but the two strangers paid no further heed to him; they had already walked to the next room, leaving Rondeau in the antichambre.

Sir Percy Blakeney did not pause in the sitting-room where an oil lamp suspended from the ceiling threw a feeble circle of light above the centre table. He went straight through to the bedroom. Here, too, a small lamp was burning which only lit up a small portion of the room—the writing-desk and the oak chest—leaving the corners and the alcove, with its partially drawn curtains, in complete shadow.

Blakeney pointed to the oak chest and to the desk.

"You tackle the chest, Ffoulkes, and I will go for the desk," he said quietly, as soon as he had taken a rapid survey of the room. "You have your tools?"

Ffoulkes nodded, and anon in this squalid room, ill-lit, ill-ventilated, barely furnished, was presented one of the most curious spectacles of these strange and troublous times: two English gentlemen, the acknowledged dandies of London drawing-rooms, busy picking locks and filing hinges like any common house-thieves.

Neither of them spoke, and a strange hush fell over the room—a hush only broken by the click of metal against metal, and the deep breathing of the two men bending to their task. Sir Andrew Ffoulkes was working with a file on the padlocks of the oak chest, and Sir Percy Blakeney, with a bunch of skeleton keys, was opening the drawers of the writing-desk. These, when finally opened, revealed nothing of any importance; but when anon Sir Andrew was able to lift the lid of the oak chest, he disclosed an innumerable quantity of papers and documents tied up in neat bundles, docketed and piled up in rows and tiers to the very top of the chest.

"Quick to work, Ffoulkes," said Blakeney, as in response to his friend's call he drew a chair forward and, seating himself beside the chest, started on the task of looking through the hundreds of bundles which lay before him. "It will take us all our time to look through these."

Together now the two men set to work—methodically and quietly—piling up on the floor beside them the bundles of papers which they had already examined, and delving into the oak chest for others. No sound was heard save the crackling of crisp paper and an occasional exclamation from either of them when they came upon some proof or other of Heriot's propensity for blackmail.

"Agnes de Lucines is not the only one whom this brute is terrorising," murmured Blakeney once between his teeth; "I marvel that the man ever feels safe, alone in these lodgings, with no one but that weak-kneed Rondeau to protect him. He must have scores of enemies in this city who would gladly put a dagger in his heart or a bullet through his back."

They had been at work for close on half an hour when an exclamation of triumph, quickly smothered, escaped Sir Percy's lips.

"By Gad, Ffoulkes!" he said, "I believe I have got what we want!"

With quick, capable hands he turned over a bundle which he had just extracted from the chest. Rapidly he glanced through them. "I have them, Ffoulkes," he reiterated more emphatically as he put the bundle into his pocket; "now everything back in its place and—"

Suddenly he paused, his slender hand up to his lips, his head turned toward the door, an expression of tense expectancy in every line of his face.

"Quick, Ffoulkes," he whispered, "everything back into the chest, and the lid down."

"What ears you have," murmured Ffoulkes as he obeyed rapidly and without question. "I heard nothing."

Blakeney went to the door and bent his head to listen.

"Three men coming up the stairs," he said; "they are on the landing now."

"Have we time to rush them?"

"No chance! They are at the door. Two more men have joined them, and I can distinguish Rondeau's voice, too."

"The quintette," murmured Sir Andrew. "We are caught like two rats in a trap."

Even as he spoke the opening of the outside door could be distinctly heard, then the confused murmur of many voices. Already Blakeney and Ffoulkes had with perfect presence of mind put the finishing touches to the tidying of the room—put the chairs straight, shut down the lid of the oak chest, closed all the drawers of the desk.

"Nothing but good luck can save us now," whispered Blakeney as he lowered the wick of the lamp. "Quick now," he added, "behind that tapestry in the alcove and trust to our stars."

Securely hidden for the moment behind the curtains in the dark recess of the alcove the two men waited. The door leading into the sitting-room was ajar, and they could hear Heriot and his friends making merry irruption into the place. From out the confusion of general conversation they soon gathered that the debates in the Chamber had been so dull and uninteresting that, at a given signal, the little party had decided to adjourn to Heriot's rooms for their habitual game of cards. They could also hear Heriot calling to Rondeau to bring bottles and glasses, and vaguely they marvelled what Rondeau's attitude might be like at this moment. Was he brazening out the situation, or was he sick with terror?

Suddenly Heriot's voice came out more distinctly.

"Make yourselves at home, friends," he was saying; "here are cards, dominoes, and wine. I must leave you to yourselves for ten minutes whilst I write an important letter."

"All right, but don't be long," came in merry response.

"Not longer than I can help," rejoined Heriot. "I want my revenge against Bompard, remember. He did fleece me last night."

"Hurry on, then," said one of the men. "I'll play Desgas that return game of dominoes until then."

"Ten minutes and I'll be back," concluded Heriot.

He pushed open the bedroom door. The light within was very dim. The two men hidden behind the tapestry could hear him moving about the room muttering curses to himself. Presently the light of the lamp was shifted from one end of the room to the other. Through the opening between the two curtains Blakeney could just see Heriot's back as he placed the lamp at a convenient angle upon his desk, divested himself of his overcoat and muffler, then sat down and drew pen and paper closer to him. He was leaning forward, his elbow resting upon the table, his fingers fidgeting with his long, lank hair. He had closed the door when he entered, and from the other room now the voices of his friends sounded confused and muffled. Now and then an exclamation: "Double!" "Je. . . tiens!" "Cinq-deux!" an oath, a laugh, the click of glasses and bottles came out more clearly; but the rest of the time these sounds were more like a droning accompaniment to the scraping of Heriot's pen upon the paper when he finally began to write his letter.

Two minutes went by and then two more. The scratching of Heriot's pen became more rapid as he appeared to be more completely immersed in his work. Behind the curtain the two men had been waiting: Blakeney ready to act, Ffoulkes equally ready to interpret the slightest signal from his chief.

The next minute Blakeney had stolen out of the alcove, and his two hands—so slender and elegant looking, and yet with a grip of steel—had fastened themselves upon Heriot's mouth, smothering within the space of a second the cry that had been half-uttered. Ffoulkes was ready to complete the work of rendering the man helpless: one handkerchief made an efficient gag, another tied the ankles securely. Heriot's own coat-sleeves supplied the handcuffs, and the blankets off the bed tied around his legs rendered him powerless to move. Then the two men lifted this inert mass on to the bed and Ffoulkes whispered anxiously: "Now, what next?"

Heriot's overcoat, hat, and muffler lay upon a chair. Sir Percy, placing a warning finger upon his lips, quickly divested himself of his own coat, slipped that of Heriot on, twisted the muffler round his neck, hunched up his shoulders, and murmuring: "Now for a bit of luck!" once more lowered the light of the lamp and then went to the door.

"Rondeau!" he called. "Hey, Rondeau!" And Sir Percy himself was surprised at the marvellous way in which he had caught the very inflection of Heriot's voice.

"Hey, Rondeau!" came from one of the players at the table, "the citizen-deputy is calling you!"

They were all sitting round the table: two men intent upon their game of dominoes, the other two watching with equal intentness. Rondeau came shuffling out of the antichambre. His face, by the dim light of the oil lamp, looked jaundiced with fear.

"Rondeau, you fool, where are you?" called Blakeney once again.

The next moment Rondeau had entered the room. No need for a signal or an order this time. Ffoulkes knew by instinct what his chief's bold scheme would mean to them both if it succeeded. He retired into the darkest corner of the room as Rondeau shuffled across to the writing-desk. It was all done in a moment. In less time than it had taken to bind and gag Heriot, his henchman was laid out on the floor, his coat had been taken off him, and he was tied into a mummy-like bundle with Sir Andrew Ffoulkes' elegant coat fastened securely round his arms and chest. It had all been done in silence. The men in the next room were noisy and intent on their game; the slight scuffle, the quickly smothered cries had remained unheeded.

"Now, what next?" queried Sir Andrew Ffoulkes once more.

"The impudence of the d—l, my good Ffoulkes," replied Blakeney in a whisper, "and may our stars not play us false. Now let me make you look as like Rondeau as possible—there! Slip on his coat—now your hair over your forehead—your coat-collar up—your knees bent—that's better!" he added as he surveyed the transformation which a few deft strokes had made in Sir Andrew Ffoulkes' appearance. "Now all you have to do is to shuffle across the room—here's your prototype's handkerchief—of dubious cleanliness, it is true, but it will serve—blow your nose as you cross the room, it will hide your face. They'll not heed you—keep in the shadows and God guard you—I'll follow in a moment or two. . . but don't wait for me."

He opened the door, and before Sir Andrew could protest his chief had pushed him out into the room where the four men were still intent on their game. Through the open door Sir Percy now watched his friend who, keeping well within the shadows, shuffled quietly across the room. The next moment Sir Andrew was through and in the antichambre. Blakeney's acutely sensitive ears caught the sound of the opening of the outer door. He waited for a while, then he drew out of his pocket the bundle of letters which he had risked so much to obtain. There they were neatly docketed and marked: "The affairs of Arnould Fabrice."

Well! if he got away to-night Agnes de Lucines would be happy and free from the importunities of that brute Heriot; after that he must persuade her and Fabrice to go to England and to freedom.

For the moment his own safety was terribly in jeopardy; one false move—one look from those players round the table. . . Bah! even then—!

With an inward laugh he pushed open the door once more and stepped into the room. For the moment no one noticed him; the game was at its most palpitating stage; four shaggy heads met beneath the lamp and four pairs of eyes were gazing with rapt attention upon the intricate maze of the dominoes.

Blakeney walked quietly across the room; he was just midway and on a level with the centre table when a voice was suddenly raised from that tense group beneath the lamp: "Is it thou, friend Heriot?"

Then one of the men looked up and stared, and another did likewise and exclaimed: "It is not Heriot!"

In a moment all was confusion, but confusion was the very essence of those hair-breadth escapes and desperate adventures which were as the breath of his nostrils to the Scarlet Pimpernel. Before those four men had had time to jump to their feet, or to realise that something was wrong with their friend Heriot, he had run across the room, his hand was on the knob of the door—the door that led to the antichambre and to freedom.

Bompard, Desgas, Jeanniot, Legros were at his heels, but he tore open the door, bounded across the threshold, and slammed it to with such a vigorous bang that those on the other side were brought to a momentary halt. That moment meant life and liberty to Blakeney; already he had crossed the antichambre. Quite coolly and quietly now he took out the key from the inner side of the main door and slipped it to the outside. The next second—even as the four men rushed helter-skelter into the antichambre he was out on the landing and had turned the key in the door.

His prisoners were safely locked in—in Heriot's apartments—and Sir Percy Blakeney, calmly and without haste, was descending the stairs of the house in the Rue Cocatrice.

The next morning Agnes de Lucines received, through an anonymous messenger, the packet of letters which would so gravely have compromised Arnould Fabrice. Though the weather was more inclement than ever, she ran out into the streets, determined to seek out the old Public Letter-Writer and thank him for his mediation with the English milor, who surely had done this noble action.

But the old scarecrow had disappeared.

V

A Fine Bit of Work

I

"Sh! . . . sh! . . . It's the Englishman. I'd know his footstep anywhere—"

"God bless him!" murmured petite maman fervently.

Pere Lenegre went to the door; he stepped cautiously and with that stealthy foot-tread which speaks in eloquent silence of daily, hourly danger, of anguish and anxiety for lives that are dear.

The door was low and narrow—up on the fifth floor of one of the huge tenement houses in the Rue Jolivet in the Montmartre quarter of Paris. A narrow stone passage led to it—pitch-dark at all times, but dirty, and evil-smelling when the concierge—a free citizen of the new democracy—took a week's holiday from his work in order to spend whole afternoons either at the wineshop round the corner, or on the Place du Carrousel to watch the guillotine getting rid of some twenty aristocrats an hour for the glorification of the will of the people.

But inside the small apartment everything was scrupulously neat and clean. Petite maman was such an excellent manager, and Rosette was busy all the day tidying and cleaning the poor little home, which Pere Lenegre contrived to keep up for wife and daughter by working fourteen hours a day in the government saddlery.

When Pere Lenegre opened the narrow door, the entire framework of it was filled by the broad, magnificent figure of a man in heavy caped coat and high leather boots, with dainty frills of lace at throat and wrist, and elegant chapeau-bras held in the hand.

Pere Lenegre at sight of him, put a quick finger to his own quivering lips.

"Anything wrong, vieux papa?" asked the newcomer lightly.

The other closed the door cautiously before he made reply. But petite maman could not restrain her anxiety.

"My little Pierre, milor?" she asked as she clasped her wrinkled hands together, and turned on the stranger her tear-dimmed restless eyes.

"Pierre is safe and well, little mother," he replied cheerily. "We got him out of Paris early this morning in a coal cart, carefully hidden among the sacks. When he emerged he was black but safe. I drove the cart myself as far as Courbevoie, and there handed over your Pierre and those whom we got out of Paris with him to those of my friends who were going straight to England. There's nothing more to be afraid of, petite maman," he added as he took the old woman's wrinkled hands in both his own; "your son is now under the care of men who would die rather than see him captured. So make your mind at ease, Pierre will be in England, safe and well, within a week."

Petite maman couldn't say anything just then because tears were choking her, but in her turn she clasped those two strong and slender hands—the hands of the brave Englishman who had just risked his life in order to save Pierre from the guillotine—and she kissed them as fervently as she kissed the feet of the Madonna when she knelt before her shrine in prayer.

Pierre had been a footman in the household of unhappy Marie Antoinette. His crime had been that he remained loyal to her in words as well as in thought. A hot-headed but nobly outspoken harangue on behalf of the unfortunate queen, delivered in a public place, had at once marked him out to the spies of the Terrorists as suspect of intrigue against the safety of the Republic. He was denounced to the Committee of Public Safety, and his arrest and condemnation to the guillotine would have inevitably followed had not the gallant band of Englishmen, known as the League of the Scarlet Pimpernel, succeeded in effecting his escape.

What wonder that petite maman could not speak for tears when she clasped the hands of the noble leader of that splendid little band of heroes? What wonder that Pere Lenegre, when he heard that his son was safe murmured a fervent: "God bless you, milor, and your friends!" and that Rosette surreptitiously raised the fine caped coat to her lips, for Pierre was her twin-brother, and she loved him very dearly.

But already Sir Percy Blakeney had, with one of his characteristic cheery words, dissipated the atmosphere of tearful emotion which oppressed these kindly folk.

"Now, Papa Lenegre," he said lightly, "tell me why you wore such a solemn air when you let me in just now."

"Because, milor," replied the old man quietly, "that d——d concierge, Jean Baptiste, is a black-hearted traitor."

Sir Percy laughed, his merry, infectious laugh.

"You mean that while he has been pocketing bribes from me, he has denounced me to the Committee."

Pere Lenegre nodded: "I only heard it this morning," he said, "from one or two threatening words the treacherous brute let fall. He knows that you lodge in the Place des Trois Maries, and that you come here frequently. I would have given my life to warn you then and there," continued the old man with touching earnestness, "but I didn't know where to find you. All I knew was that you were looking after Pierre."

Even while the man spoke there darted from beneath the Englishman's heavy lids a quick look like a flash of sudden and brilliant light out of the lazy depths of his merry blue eyes; it was one of those glances of pure delight and exultation which light up the eyes of the true soldier when there is serious fighting to be done.

"La, man," he said gaily, "there was no cause to worry. Pierre is safe, remember that! As for me," he added with that wonderful insouciance which caused him to risk his life a hundred times a day with a shrug of his broad shoulders and a smile upon his lips; "as for me, I'll look after myself, never fear."

He paused awhile, then added gravely: "So long as you are safe, my good Lenegre, and petite maman, and Rosette."

Whereupon the old man was silent, petite maman murmured a short prayer, and Rosette began to cry. The hero of a thousand gallant rescues had received his answer.

"You, too, are on the black list, Pere Lenegre?" he asked quietly.

The old man nodded.

"How do you know?" queried the Englishman.

"Through Jean Baptiste, milor."

"Still that demmed concierge," muttered Sir Percy.

"He frightened petite maman with it all this morning, saying that he knew my name was down on the Sectional Committee's list as a 'suspect.' That's when he let fall a word or two about you, milor. He said it is known that Pierre has escaped from justice, and that you helped him to it.

"I am sure that we shall get a domiciliary visit presently," continued Pere Lenegre, after a slight pause. "The gendarmes have not yet been, but I fancy that already this morning early I saw one or two of the Committee's spies hanging about the house, and when I went to the workshop I was followed all the time."

The Englishman looked grave: "And tell me," he said, "have you got anything in this place that may prove compromising to any of you?"

"No, milor. But, as Jean Baptiste said, the Sectional Committee know about Pierre. It is because of my son that I am suspect."

The old man spoke quite quietly, very simply, like a philosopher who has long ago learned to put behind him the fear of death. Nor did petite maman cry or lament. Her thoughts were for the brave milor who had saved her boy; but her fears for her old man left her dry-eyed and dumb with grief.

There was silence in the little room for one moment while the angel of sorrow and anguish hovered round these faithful and brave souls, then the Englishman's cheery voice, so full of spirit and merriment, rang out once more—he had risen to his full, towering height, and now placed a kindly hand on the old man's shoulder:

"It seems to me, my good Lenegre," he said, "that you and I haven't many moments to spare if we mean to cheat those devils by saving your neck. Now, petite maman," he added, turning to the old woman, "are you going to be brave?"

"I will do anything, milor," she replied quietly, "to help my old man."

"Well, then," said Sir Percy Blakeney in that optimistic, light-hearted yet supremely authoritative tone of which he held the secret, "you and Rosette remain here and wait for the gendarmes. When they come, say nothing; behave with absolute meekness, and let them search your place from end to end. If they ask you about your husband say that you believe him to be at his workshop. Is that clear?"

"Quite clear, milor," replied petite maman.

"And you, Pere Lenegre," continued the Englishman, speaking now with slow and careful deliberation, "listen very attentively to the instructions I am going to give you, for on your implicit obedience to them depends not only your own life but that of these two dear women. Go at once, now, to the Rue Ste. Anne, round the corner, the second house on your right, which is numbered thirty-seven. The porte cochere stands open, go boldly through, past the concierge's box, and up the stairs to apartment number twelve, second floor. Here is the key of the apartment," he added, producing one from his coat pocket and handing it over to the old man. "The rooms are nominally occupied by a certain Maitre Turandot, maker of violins, and not even the concierge of the place knows that the hunchbacked and snuffy violin-maker and the meddlesome Scarlet Pimpernel, whom the Committee of Public Safety would so love to lay by the heels, are one and the same person. The apartment, then, is mine; one of the many which I occupy in Paris at different times," he went on. "Let yourself in quietly with this key, walk straight across the first room to a wardrobe, which you will see in front of you. Open it. It is hung full of shabby clothes; put these aside, and you will notice that the panels at the back do not fit very closely, as if the wardrobe was old or had been badly put together. Insert your fingers in the tiny aperture between the two middle panels. These slide back easily: there is a recess immediately behind them. Get in there; pull the doors of the wardrobe together first, then slide the back panels into their place. You will be perfectly safe there, as the house is not under suspicion at present, and even if the revolutionary guard, under some meddle-some sergeant or other, chooses to pay it a surprise visit, your hiding-place will be perfectly secure. Now is all that quite understood?"

"Absolutely, milor," replied Lenegre, even as he made ready to obey Sir Percy's orders, "but what about you? You cannot get out of this house, milor," he urged; "it is watched, I tell you."

"La!" broke in Blakeney, in his light-hearted way, "and do you think I didn't know that? I had to come and tell you about Pierre, and now I must give those worthy gendarmes the slip somehow. I have my rooms downstairs on the ground floor, as you know, and I must make certain arrangements so that we can all get out of Paris comfortably this evening. The demmed place is no longer safe either for you, my good Lenegre, or for petite maman and Rosette. But wherever I may be, meanwhile, don't worry about me. As soon as the gendarmes have been and gone, I'll go over to the Rue Ste. Anne and let you know what arrangements I've been able to make. So do as I tell you now, and in Heaven's name let me look after myself."

Whereupon, with scant ceremony, he hustled the old man out of the room.

Pere Lenegre had contrived to kiss petite maman and Rosette before he went. It was touching to see the perfect confidence with which these simple-hearted folk obeyed the commands of milor. Had he not saved Pierre in his wonderful, brave, resourceful way? Of a truth he would know how to save Pere Lenegre also. But, nevertheless, anguish gripped the women's hearts; anguish doubly keen since the saviour of Pierre was also in danger now.

When Pere Lenegre's shuffling footsteps had died away along the flagged corridor, the stranger once more turned to the two women.

"And now, petite maman," he said cheerily, as he kissed the old woman on both her furrowed cheeks, "keep up a good heart, and say your prayers with Rosette. Your old man and I will both have need of them."

He did not wait to say good-bye, and anon it was his firm footstep that echoed down the corridor. He went off singing a song, at the top of his voice, for the whole house to hear, and for that traitor, Jean Baptiste, to come rushing out of his room marvelling at the impudence of the man, and cursing the Committee of Public Safety who were so slow in sending the soldiers of the Republic to lay this impertinent Englishman by the heels.

II

A QUARTER OF AN HOUR later half dozen men of the Republican Guard, with corporal and sergeant in command, were in the small apartment on the fifth floor of the tenement house in the Rue Jolivet. They had demanded an entry in the name of the Republic, had roughly hustled petite maman and Rosette, questioned them to Lenegre's whereabouts, and not satisfied with the reply which they received, had turned the tidy little home topsy-turvy, ransacked every cupboard, dislocated every bed, table or sofa which might presumably have afforded a hiding place for a man.

Satisfied now that the "suspect" whom they were searching for was not on the premises, the sergeant stationed four of his men with the corporal outside the door, and two within, and himself sitting down in the centre of the room ordered the two women to stand before him and to answer his questions clearly on pain of being dragged away forthwith to the St. Lazare house of detention.

Petite maman smoothed out her apron, crossed her arms before her, and looked the sergeant quite straight in the face. Rosette's eyes were full of tears, but she showed no signs of fear either, although her shoulder—where one of the gendarmes had seized it so roughly—was terribly painful.

"Your husband, citizeness," asked the sergeant peremptorily, "where is he?"

"I am not sure, citizen," replied petite maman. "At this hour he is generally at the government works in the Quai des Messageries."

"He is not there now," asserted the sergeant. "We have knowledge that he did not go back to his work since dinner-time."

Petite maman was silent.

"Answer," ordered the sergeant.

"I cannot tell you more, citizen sergeant," she said firmly. "I do not know."

"You do yourself no good, woman, by this obstinacy," he continued roughly. "My belief is that your husband is inside this house, hidden away somewhere. If necessary I can get orders to have every apartment searched until he is found: but in that case it will go much harder with you and with your daughter, and much harder too with your husband than if he gave us no trouble and followed us quietly."

But with sublime confidence in the man who had saved Pierre and who had given her explicit orders as to what she should do, petite maman, backed by Rosette, reiterated quietly:

"I cannot tell you more, citizen sergeant, I do not know."

"And what about the Englishman?" queried the sergeant more roughly, "the man they call the Scarlet Pimpernel, what do you know of him?"

"Nothing, citizen," replied petite maman, "what should we poor folk know of an English milor?"

"You know at any rate this much, citizeness, that the English milor helped your son Pierre to escape from justice."

"If that is so," said petite maman quietly, "it cannot be wrong for a mother to pray to God to bless her son's preserver."

"It behooves every good citizen," retorted the sergeant firmly, "to denounce all traitors to the Republic."

"But since I know nothing about the Englishman, citizen sergeant—?"

And petite maman shrugged her thin shoulders as if the matter had ceased to interest her.

"Think again, citizeness," admonished the sergeant, "it is your husband's neck as well as your daughter's and your own that you are risking by so much obstinacy."

He waited a moment or two as if willing to give the old woman time to speak: then, when he saw that she kept her thin, quivering lips resolutely glued together he called his corporal to him.

"Go to the citizen Commissary of the Section," he commanded, "and ask for a general order to search every apartment in No. 24 Rue Jolivet. Leave two of our men posted on the first and third landings of this house and leave two outside this door. Be as quick as you can. You can be back here with the order in half an hour, or perhaps the committee will send me an extra squad; tell the citizen Commissary that this is a big house, with many corridors. You can go."

The corporal saluted and went.

Petite maman and Rosette the while were still standing quietly in the middle of the room, their arms folded underneath their aprons, their wide-open, anxious eyes fixed into space. Rosette's tears were falling slowly, one by one down her cheeks, but petite maman was dry-eyed. She was thinking, and thinking as she had never had occasion to think before.

She was thinking of the brave and gallant Englishman who had saved Pierre's life only yesterday. The sergeant, who sat there before her, had asked for orders from the citizen Commissary to search this big house from attic to cellar. That is what made petite maman think and think.

The brave Englishman was in this house at the present moment: the house would be searched from attic to cellar and he would be found, taken, and brought to the guillotine.

The man who yesterday had risked his life to save her boy was in imminent and deadly danger, and she—petite maman—could do nothing to save him.

Every moment now she thought to hear milor's firm tread resounding on stairs or corridor, every moment she thought to hear snatches of an English song, sung by a fresh and powerful voice, never after to-day to be heard in gaiety again.

The old clock upon the shelf ticked away these seconds and minutes while petite maman thought and thought, while men set traps to catch a fellow-being in a deathly snare, and human carnivorous beasts lay lurking for their prey.

III

Another quarter of an hour went by. Petite maman and Rosette had hardly moved. The shadows of evening were creeping into the narrow room, blurring the outlines of the pieces of furniture and wrapping all the corners in gloom.

The sergeant had ordered Rosette to bring in a lamp. This she had done, placing it upon the table so that the feeble light glinted upon the belt and buckles of the sergeant and upon the tricolour cockade which was pinned to his hat. Petite maman had thought and thought until she could think no more.

Anon there was much commotion on the stairs; heavy footsteps were heard ascending from below, then crossing the corridors on the various landings. The silence which reigned otherwise in the house, and which had fallen as usual on the squalid little street, void of traffic at this hour, caused those footsteps to echo with ominous power.

Petite maman felt her heart beating so vigorously that she could hardly breathe. She pressed her wrinkled hands tightly against her bosom.

There were the quick words of command, alas! so familiar in France just now, the cruel, peremptory words that invariably preceded an arrest, preliminaries to the dragging of some wretched—often wholly harmless—creature before a tribunal that knew neither pardon nor mercy.

The sergeant, who had become drowsy in the close atmosphere of the tiny room, roused himself at the sound and jumped to his feet. The door was thrown open by the men stationed outside even before the authoritative words, "Open! in the name of the Republic!" had echoed along the narrow corridor.

The sergeant stood at attention and quickly lifted his hand to his forehead in salute. A fresh squad of some half-dozen men of the Republican Guard stood in the doorway; they were under the command of an officer of high rank, a rough, uncouth, almost bestial-looking creature, with lank hair worn the fashionable length under his greasy chapeau-bras, and unkempt beard round an ill-washed and bloated face. But he wore the tricolour sash and badge which proclaimed him one of the military members of the Sectional Committee of Public Safety, and the sergeant, who had been so overbearing with the women just now, had assumed a very humble and even obsequious manner.

"You sent for a general order to the sectional Committee," said the new-comer, turning abruptly to the sergeant after he had cast a quick, searching glance round the room, hardly condescending to look on petite maman and Rosette, whose very souls were now gazing out of their anguish-filled eyes.

"I did, citizen commandant," replied the sergeant.

"I am not a commandant," said the other curtly. "My name is Rouget, member of the Convention and of the Committee of Public Safety. The sectional Committee to whom you sent for a general order of search thought that you had blundered somehow, so they sent me to put things right."

"I am not aware that I committed any blunder, citizen," stammered the sergeant dolefully. "I could not take the responsibility of making a domiciliary search all through the house. So I begged for fuller orders."

"And wasted the Committee's time and mine by such nonsense," retorted Rouget harshly. "Every citizen of the Republic worthy of the name should know how to act on his own initiative when the safety of the nation demands it."

"I did not know—I did not dare—" murmured the sergeant, obviously cowed by this reproof, which had been delivered in the rough, overbearing tones peculiar to these men who, one and all, had risen from the gutter to places of importance and responsibility in the newly-modelled State.

"Silence!" commanded the other peremptorily. "Don't waste any more of my time with your lame excuses. You have failed in zeal and initiative. That's enough. What else have you done? Have you got the man Lenegre?"

"No, citizen. He is not in hiding here, and his wife and daughter will not give us any information about him."

"That is their look-out," retorted Rouget with a harsh laugh. "If they give up Lenegre of their own free will the law will deal leniently with them, and even perhaps with him. But if we have to search the house for him, then it means the guillotine for the lot of them."

He had spoken these callous words without even looking on the two unfortunate women; nor did he ask them any further questions just then, but continued speaking to the sergeant:

"And what about the Englishman? The sectional Committee sent down some spies this morning to be on the look-out for him on or about this house. Have you got him?"

"Not yet, citizen. But—"

"Ah ca, citizen sergeant," broke in the other brusquely, "meseems that your zeal has been even more at fault than I had supposed. Have you done anything at all, then, in the matter of Lenegre or the Englishman?"

"I have told you, citizen," retorted the sergeant sullenly, "that I believe Lenegre to be still in this house. At any rate, he had not gone out of it an hour ago—that's all I know. And I wanted to search the whole of this house, as I am sure we should have found him in one of the other apartments. These people are all friends together, and will always help each other to evade justice. But the Englishman was no concern of mine. The spies of the Committee were ordered to watch for him, and when they reported to me I was to proceed with the arrest. I was not set to do any of the spying work. I am a soldier, and obey my orders when I get them."

"Very well, then, you'd better obey them now, citizen sergeant," was Rouget's dry comment on the other man's surly explanation, "for you seem to have properly blundered from first to last, and will be hard put to it to redeem your character. The Republic, remember, has no use for fools."

The sergeant, after this covert threat, thought it best, apparently, to keep his tongue, whilst Rouget continued, in the same aggressive, peremptory tone:

"Get on with your domiciliary visits at once. Take your own men with you, and leave me the others. Begin on this floor, and leave your sentry at the front door outside. Now let me see your zeal atoning for your past slackness. Right turn! Quick march!"

Then it was that petite maman spoke out. She had thought and thought, and now she knew what she ought to do; she knew that that cruel, inhuman wretch would presently begin his tramp up and down corridors and stairs, demanding admittance at every door, entering every apartment. She knew that the man who had saved her Pierre's life was in hiding somewhere in the house—that he would be found and dragged to the guillotine, for she knew that the whole governing body of this abominable Revolution was determined not to allow that hated Englishman to escape again.

She was old and feeble, small and thin—that's why everyone called her petite maman—but once she knew what she ought to do, then her spirit overpowered the weakness of her wizened body.

Now she knew, and even while that arrogant member of an execrated murdering Committee was giving final instructions to the sergeant, petite maman said, in a calm, piping voice:

"No need, citizen sergeant, to go and disturb all my friends and neighbours. I'll tell you where my husband is."

In a moment Rouget had swung round on his heel, a hideous gleam of satisfaction spread over his grimy face, and he said, with an ugly sneer:

"So! you have thought better of it, have you? Well, out with it! You'd better be quick about it if you want to do yourselves any good."

"I have my daughter to think of," said petite maman in a feeble, querulous way, "and I won't have all my neighbours in this house made unhappy because of me. They have all been kind neighbours. Will you promise not to molest them and to clear the house of soldiers if I tell you where Lenegre is?"

"The Republic makes no promises," replied Rouget gruffly. "Her citizens must do their duty without hope of a reward. If they fail in it, they are punished. But privately I will tell you, woman, that if you save us the troublesome and probably unprofitable task of searching this rabbit-warren through and through, it shall go very leniently with you and with your daughter, and perhaps—I won't promise, remember—perhaps with your husband also."

"Very good, citizen," said petite maman calmly. "I am ready."

"Ready for what?" he demanded.

"To take you to where my husband is in hiding."

"Oho! He is not in the house, then?"

"No."

"Where is he, then?"

"In the Rue Ste. Anne. I will take you there."

Rouget cast a quick, suspicious glance on the old woman, and exchanged one of understanding with the sergeant.

"Very well," he said after a slight pause. "But your daughter must come along too. Sergeant," he added, "I'll take three of your men with me; I have half a dozen, but it's better to be on the safe side. Post your fellows round the outer door, and on my way to the Rue Ste. Anne I will leave word at the gendarmerie that a small reinforcement be sent on to you at once. These can be here in five minutes; until then you are quite safe."

Then he added under his breath, so that the women should not hear: "The Englishman may still be in the house. In which case, hearing us depart, he may think us all gone and try to give us the slip. You'll know what to do?" he queried significantly.

"Of course, citizen," replied the sergeant.

"Now, then, citizeness—hurry up."

Once more there was tramping of heavy feet on stone stairs and corridors. A squad of soldiers of the Republican Guard, with two women in their midst, and followed by a member of the Committee of Public Safety, a sergeant, corporal and two or three more men, excited much anxious curiosity as they descended the steep flights of steps from the fifth floor.

Pale, frightened faces peeped shyly through the doorways at sound of the noisy tramp from above, but quickly disappeared again at sight of the grimy scarlet facings and tricolour cockades.

The sergeant and three soldiers remained stationed at the foot of the stairs inside the house. Then citizen Rouget roughly gave the order to proceed. It seemed strange that it should require close on a dozen men to guard two women and to apprehend one old man, but as the member of the Committee of Public Safety whispered to the sergeant before he finally went out of the house: "The whole thing may be a trap, and one can't be too careful. The Englishman is said to be very powerful; I'll get the gendarmerie to send you another half-dozen men, and mind you guard the house until my return."

IV

Five minutes later the soldiers, directed by petite maman, had reached No. 37 Rue Ste. Anne. The big outside door stood wide open, and the whole party turned immediately into the house.

The concierge, terrified and obsequious, rushed—trembling—out of his box.

"What was the pleasure of the citizen soldiers?" he asked.

"Tell him, citizeness," commanded Rouget curtly.

"We are going to apartment No. 12 on the second floor," said petite maman to the concierge.

"Have you a key of the apartment?" queried Rouget.

"No, citizen," stammered the concierge, "but—"

"Well, what is it?" queried the other peremptorily.

"Papa Turandot is a poor, harmless maker of volins," said the concierge. "I know him well, though he is not often at home. He lives with a daughter somewhere Passy way, and only uses this place as a workshop. I am sure he is no traitor."

"We'll soon see about that," remarked Rouget dryly.

Petite maman held her shawl tightly crossed over her bosom: her hands felt clammy and cold as ice. She was looking straight out before her, quite dry-eyed and calm, and never once glanced on Rosette, who was not allowed to come anywhere near her mother.

As there was no duplicate key to apartment No. 12, citizen Rouget ordered his men to break in the door. It did not take very long: the house was old and ramshackle and the doors rickety. The next moment the party stood in the room which a while ago the Englishman had so accurately described to pere Lenegre in petite maman's hearing.

There was the wardrobe. Petite maman, closely surrounded by the soldiers, went boldly up to it; she opened it just as milor had directed, and pushed aside the row of shabby clothes that hung there. Then she pointed to the panels that did not fit quite tightly together at the back. Petite maman passed her tongue over her dry lips before she spoke.

"There's a recess behind those panels," she said at last. "They slide back quite easily. My old man is there."

"And God bless you for a brave, loyal soul," came in merry, ringing accent from the other end of the room. "And God save the Scarlet Pimpernel!"

These last words, spoken in English, completed the blank amazement which literally paralysed the only three genuine Republican soldiers there—those, namely, whom Rouget had borrowed from the sergeant. As for the others, they knew what to do. In less than a minute they had overpowered and gagged the three bewildered soldiers.

Rosette had screamed, terror-stricken, from sheer astonishment, but petite maman stood quite still, her pale, tear-dimmed eyes fixed upon the man whose gay "God bless you!" had so suddenly turned her despair into hope.

How was it that in the hideous, unkempt and grimy Rouget she had not at once recognised the handsome and gallant milor who had saved her Pierre's life? Well, of a truth he had been unrecognisable, but now that he tore the ugly wig and beard from his face, stretched out his fine figure to its full height, and presently turned his lazy, merry eyes on her, she could have screamed for very joy.

The next moment he had her by the shoulders and had imprinted two sounding kisses upon her cheeks.

"Now, petite maman," he said gaily, "let us liberate the old man."

Pere Lenegre, from his hiding-place, had heard all that had been going on in the room for the last few moments. True, he had known exactly what to expect, for no sooner had he taken possession of the recess behind the wardrobe than milor also entered the apartment and then and there told him of his plans not only for pere's own safety, but for that of petite maman and Rosette who would be in grave danger if the old man followed in the wake of Pierre.

Milor told him in his usual light-hearted way that he had given the Committee's spies the slip.

"I do that very easily, you know," he explained. "I just slip into my rooms in the Rue Jolivet, change myself into a snuffy and hunchback violin-maker, and walk out of the house under the noses of the spies. In the nearest wine-shop my English friends, in various disguises, are all ready to my hand: half a dozen of them are never far from where I am in case they may be wanted."

These half-dozen brave Englishmen soon arrived one by one: one looked like a coal-heaver, another like a seedy musician, a third like a coach-driver. But they all walked boldly into the house and were soon all congregated in apartment No. 12. Here fresh disguises were assumed, and soon a squad of Republican Guards looked as like the real thing as possible.

Pere Lenegre admitted himself that though he actually saw milor transforming himself into citizen Rouget, he could hardly believe his eyes, so complete was the change.

"I am deeply grieved to have frightened and upset you so, petite maman," now concluded milor kindly, "but I saw no other way of getting you and Rosette out of the house and leaving that stupid sergeant and some of his men behind. I did not want to arouse in him even the faintest breath of suspicion, and of course if he had asked me for the written orders which he was actually waiting for, or if his corporal had returned sooner than I anticipated, there might have been trouble. But even then," he added with his usual careless insouciance, "I should have thought of some way of baffling those brutes."

"And now," he concluded more authoritatively, "it is a case of getting out of Paris before the gates close. Pere Lenegre, take your wife and daughter with you and walk boldly out of this house. The sergeant and his men have not vacated their post in the Rue Jolivet, and no one else can molest you. Go straight to the Porte de Neuilly, and on the other side wait quietly in the little cafe at the corner of the Avenue until I come. Your old passes for the barriers still hold good; you were only placed on the 'suspect' list this morning, and there has not been a hue and cry yet about you. In any case some of us will be close by to help you if needs be."

"But you, milor," stammered pere Lenegre, "and your friends—?"

"La, man," retorted Blakeney lightly, "have I not told you before never to worry about me and my friends? We have more ways than one of giving the slip to this demmed government of yours. All you've got to think of is your wife and your daughter. I am afraid that petite maman cannot take more with her than she has on, but we'll do all we can for her comfort until we have you all in perfect safety—in England—with Pierre."

Neither pere Lenegre, nor petite maman, nor Rosette could speak just then, for tears were choking them, but anon when milor stood nearer, petite maman knelt down, and, imprisoning his slender hand in her brown, wrinkled ones, she kissed it reverently.

He laughed and chided her for this.

"'Tis I should kneel to you in gratitude, petite maman," he said earnestly, "you were ready to sacrifice your old man for me."

"You have saved Pierre, milor," said the mother simply.

A minute later pere Lenegre and the two women were ready to go. Already milor and his gallant English friends were busy once more transforming themselves into grimy workmen or seedy middle-class professionals.

As soon as the door of apartment No. 12 finally closed behind the three good folk, my lord Tony asked of his chief:

"What about these three wretched soldiers, Blakeney?"

"Oh! they'll be all right for twenty-four hours. They can't starve till then, and by that time the concierge will have realised that there's something wrong with the door of No. 12 and will come in to investigate the matter. Are they securely bound, though?"

"And gagged! Rather!" exclaimed one of the others. "Odds life, Blakeney!" he added enthusiastically, "that was a fine bit of work!"

VI

How Jean Pierre Met the Scarlet Pimpernel

As told by Himself

I

Ah, monsieur! the pity of it, the pity! Surely there are sins which le bon Dieu Himself will condone. And if not—well, I had to risk His displeasure anyhow. Could I see them both starve, monsieur? I ask you! and M. le Vicomte had become so thin, so thin, his tiny, delicate bones were almost through his skin. And Mme. la Marquise! an angel, monsieur! Why, in the happy olden days, before all these traitors and assassins ruled in France, M. and Mme. la Marquise lived only for the child, and then to see him dying—yes, dying, there was no shutting one's eyes to that awful fact—M. le Vicomte de Mortain was dying of starvation and of disease.

There we were all herded together in a couple of attics—one of which little more than a cupboard—at the top of a dilapidated half-ruined house in the Rue des Pipots—Mme. la Marquise, M. le Vicomte and I—just think of that, monsieur! M. le Marquis had his chateau, as no doubt you know, on the outskirts of Lyons. A loyal high-born gentleman; was it likely, I ask you, that he would submit passively to the rule of those execrable revolutionaries who had murdered their King, outraged their Queen and Royal family, and, God help them! had already perpetrated every crime and every abomination for which of a truth there could be no pardon either on earth or in Heaven? He joined that plucky but, alas! small and ill-equipped army of royalists who, unable to save their King, were at least determined to avenge him.

Well, you know well enough what happened. The counter-revolution failed; the revolutionary army brought Lyons down to her knees after a siege of two months. She was then marked down as a rebel city, and after the abominable decree of October 9th had deprived her of her very name, and Couthon had exacted bloody reprisals from the entire population for its loyalty to the King, the infamous Laporte was sent down in order finally to stamp out the lingering remnants of the rebellion. By that time, monsieur, half the city had been burned down, and one-tenth and more of the inhabitants—men, women, and children—had been massacred in cold blood, whilst most of the others had fled in terror from the appalling scene of ruin and desolation. Laporte completed the execrable work so ably begun by Couthon. He was a very celebrated and skilful doctor at the Faculty of Medicine, now turned into a human hyena in the name of Liberty and Fraternity.

M. le Marquis contrived to escape with the scattered remnant of the Royalist army into Switzerland. But Mme la Marquise throughout all these strenuous times had stuck to her post at the chateau like the valiant creature that she was. When Couthon entered Lyons at the head of the revolutionary army, the whole of her household fled, and I was left alone to look after her and M. le Vicomte.

Then one day when I had gone into Lyons for provisions, I suddenly chanced to hear outside an eating-house that which nearly froze the marrow in my old bones. A captain belonging to the Revolutionary Guard was transmitting to his sergeant certain orders, which he had apparently just received.

The orders were to make a perquisition at ten o'clock this same evening in the chateau of Mortaine as the Marquis was supposed to be in hiding there, and in any event to arrest every man, woman, and child who was found within its walls.

"Citizen Laporte," the captain concluded, "knows for a certainty that the ci-devant Marquise and her brat are still there, even if the Marquis has fled like the traitor that he is. Those cursed English spies who call themselves the League of the Scarlet Pimpernel have been very active in Lyons of late, and citizen Laporte is afraid that they might cheat the guillotine of the carcase of those aristos, as they have already succeeded in doing in the case of a large number of traitors."

I did not, of course, wait to hear any more of that abominable talk. I sped home as fast as my old legs would carry me. That self-same evening, as soon as it was dark, Mme. la Marquise, carrying M. le Vicomte in her arms and I carrying a pack with a few necessaries on my back, left the ancestral home of the Mortaines never to return to it again: for within an hour of our flight a detachment of the revolutionary army made a descent upon the chateau; they ransacked it from attic to cellar, and finding nothing there to satisfy their lust of hate, they burned the stately mansion down to the ground.

We were obliged to take refuge in Lyons, at any rate for a time. Great as was the danger inside the city, it was infinitely greater on the high roads, unless we could arrange for some vehicle to take us a considerable part of the way to the frontier, and above all for some sort of passports—forged or otherwise—to enable us to pass the various toll-gates on the road, where vigilance was very strict. So we wandered through the ruined and deserted streets of the city in search of shelter, but found every charred and derelict house full of miserable tramps and destitutes like ourselves. Half dead with fatigue, Mme. la Marquise was at last obliged to take refuge in one of these houses which was situated in the Rue des Pipots. Every room was full to overflowing with a miserable wreckage of humanity thrown hither by the tide of anarchy and of bloodshed. But at the top of the house we found an attic. It was empty save for a couple of chairs, a table and a broken-down bedstead on which were a ragged mattress and pillow.

Here, monsieur, we spent over three weeks, at the end of which time M. le Vicomte fell ill, and then there followed days, monsieur, through which I would not like my worst enemy to pass.

Mme. la Marquise had only been able to carry away in her flight what ready money she happened to have in the house at the time. Securities, property, money belonging to aristocrats had been ruthlessly confiscated by the revolutionary government in Lyons. Our scanty resources rapidly became exhausted, and what was left had to be kept for milk and delicacies for M. le Vicomte. I tramped through the streets in search of a doctor, but most of them had been arrested on some paltry charge or other of rebellion, whilst others had fled from the city. There was only that infamous Laporte—a vastly clever doctor, I knew—but as soon take a lamb to a hungry lion as the Vicomte de Mortaine to that bloodthirsty cut-throat.

Then one day our last franc went and we had nothing left. Mme. la Marquise had not touched food for two days. I had stood at the corner of the street, begging all the day until I was driven off by the gendarmes. I had only obtained three sous from the passers-by. I bought some milk and took it home for M. le Vicomte. The following morning when I entered the larger attic I found that Mme. la Marquise had fainted from inanition.

I spent the whole of the day begging in the streets and dodging the guard, and even so I only collected four sous. I could have got more perhaps, only that at about midday the smell of food from an eating-house turned me sick and faint, and when I regained consciousness I found myself huddled up under a doorway and evening gathering in fast around me. If Mme. la Marquise could go two days without food I ought to go four. I struggled to my feet; fortunately I had retained possession of my four sous, else of a truth I would not have had the courage to go back to the miserable attic which was the only home I knew.

I was wending my way along as fast as I could—for I knew that Mme. la Marquise would be getting terribly anxious—when, just as I turned into the Rue Blanche, I spied two gentlemen—obviously strangers, for they were dressed with a luxury and care with which we had long ceased to be familiar in Lyons—walking rapidly towards me. A moment or two later they came to a halt, not far from where I was standing, and I heard the taller one of the two say to the other in English—a language with which I am vaguely conversant: "All right again this time, what, Tony?"

Both laughed merrily like a couple of schoolboys playing truant, and then they disappeared under the doorway of a dilapidated house, whilst I was left wondering how two such elegant gentlemen dared be abroad in Lyons these days, seeing that every man, woman and child who was dressed in anything but threadbare clothes was sure to be insulted in the streets for an aristocrat, and as often as not summarily arrested as a traitor.

However, I had other things to think about, and had already dismissed the little incident from my mind, when at the bottom of the Rue Blanche I came upon a knot of gaffers, men and women, who were talking and gesticulating very excitedly outside the door of a cook-shop. At first I did not take much notice of what was said: my eyes were glued to the front of the shop, on which were displayed sundry delicacies of the kind which makes a wretched, starved beggar's mouth water as he goes by; a roast capon especially attracted my attention, together with a bottle of red wine; these looked just the sort of luscious food which Mme. la Marquise would relish.

Well, sir, the law of God says: "Thou shalt not covet!" and no doubt that I committed a grievous sin when my hungry eyes fastened upon that roast capon and that bottle of Burgundy. We also know the stories of Judas Iscariot and of Jacob's children who sold their own brother Joseph into slavery—such a crime, monsieur, I took upon my conscience then; for just as the vision of Mme. la Marquise eating that roast capon and drinking that Burgundy rose before my eyes, my ears caught some fragments of the excited conversation which was going on all around me.

"He went this way!" someone said.

"No; that!" protested another.

"There's no sign of him now, anyway."

The owner of the shop was standing on his own doorstep, his legs wide apart, one arm on his wide hip, the other still brandishing the knife wherewith he had been carving for his customers.

"He can't have gone far," he said, as he smacked his thick lips.

"The impudent rascal, flaunting such fine clothes—like the aristo that he is."

"Bah! these cursed English! They are aristos all of them! And this one with his followers is no better than a spy!"

"Paid by that damned English Government to murder all our patriots and to rob the guillotine of her just dues."

"They say he had a hand in the escape of the ci-devant Duc de Sermeuse and all his brats from the very tumbril which was taking them to execution."

A cry of loathing and execration followed this statement. There was vigorous shaking of clenched fists and then a groan of baffled rage.

"We almost had him this time. If it had not been for these confounded, ill-lighted streets—"

"I would give something," concluded the shopkeeper, "if we could lay him by the heels."

"What would you give, citizen Dompierre?" queried a woman in the crowd, with a ribald laugh, "one of your roast capons?"

"Aye, little mother," he replied jovially, "and a bottle of my best Burgundy to boot, to drink confusion to that meddlesome Englishman and his crowd and a speedy promenade up the steps of the guillotine."

Monsieur, I assure you that at that moment my heart absolutely stood still. The tempter stood at my elbow and whispered, and I deliberately smothered the call of my conscience. I did what Joseph's brethren did, what brought Judas Iscariot to hopeless remorse. There was no doubt that the hue and cry was after the two elegantly dressed gentlemen whom I had seen enter the dilapidated house in the Rue Blanche. For a second or two I closed my eyes and deliberately conjured up the vision of Mme. la Marquise fainting for lack of food, and of M. le Vicomte dying for want of sustenance; then I worked my way to the door of the shop and accosted the burly proprietor with as much boldness as I could muster.

"The two Englishmen passed by me at the top of the Rue Blanche," I said to him. "They went into a house. . . I can show you which it is—"

In a moment I was surrounded by a screeching, gesticulating crowd. I told my story as best I could; there was no turning back now from the path of cowardice and of crime. I saw that brute Dompierre pick up the largest roast capon from the front of his shop, together with a bottle of that wine which I had coveted; then he thrust both these treasures into my trembling hands and said:

"En avant!"

And we all started to run up the street, shouting: "Death to the English spies!" I was the hero of the expedition. Dompierre and another man carried me, for I was too weak to go as fast as they wished. I was hugging the capon and the bottle of wine to my heart; I had need to do that, so as to still the insistent call of my conscience, for I felt a coward—a mean, treacherous, abominable coward!

When we reached the house and I pointed it out to Dompierre, the crowd behind us gave a cry of triumph. In the topmost storey a window was thrown open, two heads appeared silhouetted against the light within, and the cry of triumph below was answered by a merry, prolonged laugh from above.

I was too dazed to realise very clearly what happened after that. Dompierre, I know, kicked open the door of the house, and the crowd rushed in, in his wake. I managed to keep my feet and to work my way gradually out of the crowd. I must have gone on mechanically, almost unconsciously, for the next thing that I remember with any distinctness was that I found myself once more speeding down the Rue Blanche, with all the yelling and shouting some little way behind me.

With blind instinct, too, I had clung to the capon and the wine, the price of my infamy. I was terribly weak and felt sick and faint, but I struggled on for a while, until my knees refused me service and I came down on my two hands, whilst the capon rolled away into the gutter, and the bottle of Burgundy fell with a crash against the pavement, scattering its precious contents in every direction.

There I lay, wretched, despairing, hardly able to move, when suddenly I heard rapid and firm footsteps immediately behind me, and the next moment two firm hands had me under the arms, and I heard a voice saying:

"Steady, old friend. Can you get up? There! Is that better?"

The same firm hands raised me to my feet. At first I was too dazed to see anything, but after a moment or two I was able to look around me, and, by the light of a street lanthorn immediately overhead, I recognised the tall, elegantly dressed Englishman and his friend, whom I had just betrayed to the fury of Dompierre and a savage mob.

I thought that I was dreaming, and I suppose that my eyes betrayed the horror which I felt, for the stranger looked at me scrutinisingly for a moment or two, then he gave the quaintest laugh I had ever heard in all my life, and said something to his friend in English, which this time I failed to understand.

Then he turned to me:

"By my faith," he said in perfect French—so that I began to doubt if he was an English spy after all—"I verily believe that you are the clever rogue, eh? who obtained a roast capon and a bottle of wine from that fool Dompierre. He and his boon companions are venting their wrath on you, old compeer; they are calling you liar and traitor and cheat, in the intervals of wrecking what is left of the house, out of which my friend and I have long since escaped by climbing up the neighbouring gutter-pipes and scrambling over the adjoining roofs."

Monsieur, will you believe me when I say that he was actually saying all this in order to comfort me? I could have sworn to that because of the wonderful kindliness which shone out of his eyes, even through the good-humoured mockery wherewith he obviously regarded me. Do you know what I did then, monsieur? I just fell on my knees and loudly thanked God that he was safe; at which both he and his friend once again began to laugh, for all the world like two schoolboys who had escaped a whipping, rather than two men who were still threatened with death.

"Then it WAS you!" said the taller stranger, who was still laughing so heartily that he had to wipe his eyes with his exquisite lace handkerchief.

"May God forgive me," I replied.

The next moment his arm was again round me. I clung to him as to a rock, for of a truth I had never felt a grasp so steady and withal so gentle and kindly, as was his around my shoulders. I tried to murmur words of thanks, but again that wretched feeling of sickness and faintness overcame me, and for a second or two it seemed to me as if I were slipping into another world. The stranger's voice came to my ear, as it were through cotton-wool.

"The man is starving," he said. "Shall we take him over to your lodgings, Tony? They are safer than mine. He may be able to walk in a minute or two, if not I can carry him."

My senses at this partly returned to me, and I was able to protest feebly:

"No, no! I must go back—I must—kind sirs," I murmured. "Mme. la Marquise will be getting so anxious."

No sooner were these foolish words out of my mouth than I could have bitten my tongue out for having uttered them; and yet, somehow, it seemed as if it was the stranger's magnetic personality, his magic voice and kindly act towards me, who had so basely sold him to his enemies, which had drawn them out of me. He gave a low, prolonged whistle.

"Mme. la Marquise?" he queried, dropping his voice to a whisper.

Now to have uttered Mme. la Marquise de Mortaine's name here in Lyons, where every aristocrat was termed a traitor and sent without trial to the guillotine, was in itself an act of criminal folly, and yet—you may believe me, monsieur, or not—there was something within me just at that moment that literally compelled me to open my heart out to this stranger, whom I had so basely betrayed, and who requited my abominable crime with such gentleness and mercy. Before I fully realised what I was doing, monsieur, I had blurted out the whole history of Mme. la Marquise's flight and of M. le Vicomte's sickness to him. He drew me under the cover of an open doorway, and he and his friend listened to me without speaking a word until I had told them my pitiable tale to the end.

When I had finished he said quietly:

"Take me to see Mme. la Marquise, old friend. Who knows? perhaps I may be able to help."

Then he turned to his friend.

"Will you wait for me at my lodgings, Tony," he said, "and let Ffoulkes and Hastings know that I may wish to speak with them on my return?"

He spoke like one who had been accustomed all his life to give command, and I marvelled how his friend immediately obeyed him. Then when the latter had disappeared down the dark street, the stranger once more turned to me.

"Lean on my arm, good old friend," he said, "and we must try and walk as quickly as we can. The sooner we allay the anxieties of Mme. la Marquise the better."

I was still hugging the roast capon with one arm, with the other I clung to him as together we walked in the direction of the Rue des Pipots. On the way we halted at a respectable eating-house, where my protector gave me some money wherewith to buy a bottle of good wine and sundry provisions and delicacies which we carried home with us.

II

Never shall I forget the look of horror which came in Mme. la Marquise's eyes when she saw me entering our miserable attic in the company of a stranger. The last of the little bit of tallow candle flickered in its socket. Madame threw her emaciated arms over her child, just like some poor hunted animal defending its young. I could almost hear the cry of terror which died down in her throat ere it reached her lips. But then, monsieur, to see the light of hope gradually illuminating her pale, wan face as the stranger took her hand and spoke to her—oh! so gently and so kindly—was a sight which filled my poor, half-broken heart with joy.

"The little invalid must be seen by a doctor at once," he said, "after that only can we think of your ultimate safety."

Mme. la Marquise, who herself was terribly weak and ill, burst out crying. "Would I not have taken him to a doctor ere now?" she murmured through her tears. "But there is no doctor in Lyons. Those who have not been arrested as traitors have fled from this stricken city. And my little Jose is dying for want of medical care."

"Your pardon, madame," he rejoined gently, "one of the ablest doctors in France is at present in Lyons—"

"That infamous Laporte," she broke in, horrified. "He would snatch my sick child from my arms and throw him to the guillotine."

"He would save your boy from disease," said the stranger earnestly, "his own professional pride or professional honour, whatever he might choose to call it, would compel him to do that. But the moment the doctor's work was done, that of the executioner would commence."

"You see, milor," moaned Madame in pitiable agony, "that there is no hope for us."

"Indeed there is," he replied. "We must get M. le Vicomte well first—after that we shall see."

"But you are not proposing to bring that infamous Laporte to my child's bedside!" she cried in horror.

"Would you have your child die here before your eyes," retorted the stranger, "as he undoubtedly will this night?"

This sounded horribly cruel, and the tone in which it was said was commanding. There was no denying its truth. M. le Vicomte was dying.

I could see that. For a moment or two madame remained quite still, with her great eyes, circled with pain and sorrow, fixed upon the stranger. He returned her gaze steadily and kindly, and gradually that frozen look of horror in her pale face gave place to one of deep puzzlement, and through her bloodless lips there came the words, faintly murmured: "Who are you?"

He gave no direct reply, but from his little finger he detached a ring and held it out for her to see. I saw it too, for I was standing close by Mme. la Marquise, and the flickering light of the tallow candle fell full upon the ring. It was of gold, and upon it there was an exquisitely modelled, five-petalled little flower in vivid red enamel.

Madame la Marquise looked at the ring, then once again up into his face. He nodded assent, and my heart seemed even then to stop its beating as I gazed upon his face. Had we not—all of us—heard of the gallant Scarlet Pimpernel? And did I not know—far better than Mme. la Marquise herself—the full extent of his gallantry and his self-sacrifice? The hue and cry was after him. Human bloodhounds were even now on his track, and he spoke calmly of walking out again in the streets of Lyons and of affronting that infamous Laporte, who would find glory in sending him to death. I think he guessed what was passing in my mind, for he put a finger up to his lip and pointed significantly to M. le Vicomte.

But it was beautiful to see how completely Mme. la Marquise now trusted him. At his bidding she even ate a little of the food and drank some wine—and I was forced to do likewise. And even when anon he declared his intention of fetching Laporte immediately, she did not flinch. She kissed M. le Vicomte with passionate fervour, and then gave the stranger her solemn promise that the moment he returned she would take refuge in the next room and never move out of it until after Laporte had departed.

When he went I followed him to the top of the stairs. I was speechless with gratitude and also with fears for him. But he took my hand and said, with that same quaint, somewhat inane laugh which was so characteristic of him:

"Be of good cheer, old fellow! Those confounded murderers will not get me this time."

III

Less than half an hour later, monsieur, citizen Laporte, one of the most skilful doctors in France and one of the most bloodthirsty tyrants this execrable Revolution has known, was sitting at the bedside of M. le Vicomte de Mortaine, using all the skill, all the knowledge he possessed in order to combat the dread disease of which the child was dying, ere he came to save him—as he cynically remarked in my hearing—for the guillotine.

I heard afterwards how it all came about.

Laporte, it seems, was in the habit of seeing patients in his own house every evening after he had settled all his business for the day. What a strange contradiction in the human heart, eh, monsieur? The tiger turned lamb for the space of one hour in every twenty-four—the butcher turned healer. How well the English milor had gauged the strange personality of that redoubtable man! Professional pride—interest in intricate cases—call it what you will—was the only redeeming feature in Laporte's abominable character. Everything else in him, every thought, every action was ignoble, cruel and vengeful.

Milor that night mingled with the crowd who waited on the human hyena to be cured of their hurts. It was a motley crowd that filled the dreaded pro-consul's ante-chamber—men, women and children—all of them too much preoccupied with their own troubles to bestow more than a cursory glance on the stranger who, wrapped in a dark mantle, quietly awaited his turn. One or two muttered curses were flung at the aristo, one or two spat in his direction to express hatred and contempt, then the door which gave on the inner chamber would be flung open—a number called—one patient would walk out, another walk in—and in the ever-recurring incident the stranger for the nonce was forgotten.

His turn came—his number being called—it was the last on the list, and the ante-chamber was now quite empty save for him. He walked into the presence of the pro-consul. Claude Lemoine, who was on guard in the room at the time, told me that just for the space of two seconds the two men looked at one another. Then the stranger threw back his head and said quietly:

"There's a child dying of pleurisy, or worse, in an attic in the Rue des Pipots. There's not a doctor left in Lyons to attend on him, and the child will die for want of medical skill. Will you come to him, citizen doctor?"

It seems that for a moment or two Laporte hesitated.

"You look to me uncommonly like an aristo, and therefore a traitor," he said, "and I've half a mind—"

"To call your guard and order my immediate arrest," broke in milor with a whimsical smile, "but in that case a citizen of France will die for want of a doctor's care. Let me take you to the child's bedside, citizen doctor, you can always have me arrested afterwards."

But Laporte still hesitated.

"How do I know that you are not one of those English spies?" he began.

"Take it that I am," rejoined milor imperturbably, "and come and see the patient."

Never had a situation been carried off with so bold a hand. Claude Lemoine declared that Laporte's mouth literally opened for the call which would have summoned the sergeant of the guard into the room and ordered the summary arrest of this impudent stranger. During the veriest fraction of a second life and death hung in the balance for the gallant English milor. In the heart of Laporte every evil passion fought the one noble fibre within him. But the instinct of the skilful healer won the battle, and the next moment he had hastily collected what medicaments and appliances he might require, and the two men were soon speeding along the streets in the direction of the Rue des Pipots.

DURING THE WHOLE OF THAT night, milor and Laporte sat together by the bedside of M. le Vicomte. Laporte only went out once in order to fetch what further medicaments he required. Mme. la Marquise took the opportunity of running out of her hiding-place in order to catch a glimpse of her child. I saw her take milor's hand and press it against her heart in silent gratitude. On her knees she begged him to go away and leave her and the boy to their fate. Was it likely that he would go? But she was so insistent that at last he said:

"Madame, let me assure you that even if I were prepared to play the coward's part which you would assign to me, it is not in my power to do so at this moment. Citizen Laporte came to this house under the escort of six picked men of his guard. He has left these men stationed on the landing outside this door."

Madame la Marquise gave a cry of terror, and once more that pathetic look of horror came into her face. Milor took her hand and then pointed to the sick child.

"Madame," he said, "M. le Vicomte is already slightly better. Thanks to medical skill and a child's vigorous hold on life, he will live. The rest is in the hands of God."

Already the heavy footsteps of Laporte were heard upon the creaking stairs. Mme. la Marquise was forced to return to her hiding-place.

Soon after dawn he went. M. le Vicomte was then visibly easier. Laporte had all along paid no heed to me, but I noticed that once or twice during his long vigil by the sick-bed his dark eyes beneath their overhanging brows shot a quick suspicious look at the door behind which cowered Mme. la Marquise. I had absolutely no doubt in my mind then that he knew quite well who his patient was.

He gave certain directions to milor—there were certain fresh medicaments to be got during the day. While he spoke there was a sinister glint in his eyes—half cynical, wholly menacing—as he looked up into the calm, impassive face of milor.

"It is essential for the welfare of the patient that these medicaments be got for him during the day," he said dryly, "and the guard have orders to allow you to pass in and out. But you need have no fear," he added significantly, "I will leave an escort outside the house to accompany you on your way."

He gave a mocking, cruel laugh, the meaning of which was unmistakable. His well-drilled human bloodhounds would be on the track of the English spy, whenever the latter dared to venture out into the streets.

Mme. la Marquise and I were prisoners for the day. We spent it in watching alternately beside M. le Vicomte. But milor came and went as freely as if he had not been carrying his precious life in his hands every time that he ventured outside the house.

In the evening Laporte returned to see his patient, and again the following morning, and the next evening. M. le Vicomte was making rapid progress towards recovery.

The third day in the morning Laporte pronounced his patient to be out of danger, but said that he would nevertheless come again to see him at the usual hour in the evening. Directly he had gone, milor went out in order to bring in certain delicacies of which the invalid was now allowed to partake. I persuaded Madame to lie down and have a couple of hours' good sleep in the inner attic, while I stayed to watch over the child.

To my horror, hardly had I taken up my stand at the foot of the bed when Laporte returned; he muttered something as he entered about having left some important appliance behind, but I was quite convinced that he had been on the watch until milor was out of sight, and then slipped back in order to find me and Madame here alone.

He gave a glance at the child and another at the door of the inner attic, then he said in a loud voice:

"Yes, another twenty-four hours and my duties as doctor will cease and those of patriot will re-commence. But Mme. la Marquise de Mortaine need no longer be in any anxiety about her son's health, nor will Mme. la Guillotine be cheated of a pack of rebels."

He laughed, and was on the point of turning on his heel when the door which gave on the smaller attic was opened and Mme. la Marquise appeared upon the threshold.

Monsieur, I had never seen her look more beautiful than she did now in her overwhelming grief. Her face was as pale as death, her eyes, large and dilated, were fixed upon the human monster who had found it in his heart to speak such cruel words. Clad in a miserable, threadbare gown, her rich brown hair brought to the top of her head like a crown, she looked more regal than any queen.

But proud as she was, monsieur, she yet knelt at the feet of that wretch. Yes, knelt, and embraced his knees and pleaded in such pitiable accents as would have melted the heart of a stone. She pleaded, monsieur—ah, not for herself. She pleaded for her child and for me, her faithful servant, and she pleaded for the gallant gentleman who had risked his life for the sake of the child, who was nothing to him.

"Take me!" she said. "I come of a race that have always known how to die! But what harm has that innocent child done in this world? What harm has poor old Jean-Pierre done, and, oh. . . is the world so full of brave and noble men that the bravest of them all be so unjustly sent to death?"

Ah, monsieur, any man, save one of those abject products of that hideous Revolution, would have listened to such heartrending accents. But this man only laughed and turned on his heel without a word.

Shall I ever forget the day that went by? Mme. la Marquise was well-nigh prostrate with terror, and it was heartrending to watch the noble efforts which she made to amuse M. le Vicomte. The only gleams of sunshine which came to us out of our darkness were the brief appearances of milor. Outside we could hear the measured tramp of the guard that had been set there to keep us close prisoners. They were relieved every six hours, and, in fact, we were as much under arrest as if we were already incarcerated in one of the prisons of Lyons.

At about four o'clock in the afternoon milor came back to us after a brief absence. He stayed for a little while playing with M. le Vicomte. Just before leaving he took Madame's hand in his and said very earnestly, and sinking his voice to the merest whisper:

"To-night! Fear nothing! Be ready for anything! Remember that the League of the Scarlet Pimpernel have never failed to succour, and that I hereby pledge you mine honour that you and those you care for will be out of Lyons this night."

He was gone, leaving us to marvel at his strange words. Mme. la Marquise after that was just like a person in a dream. She hardly spoke to me, and the only sound that passed her lips was a quaint little lullaby which she sang to M. le Vicomte ere he dropped off to sleep.

The hours went by leaden-footed. At every sound on the stairs Madame started like a frightened bird. That infamous Laporte usually paid his visits at about eight o'clock in the evening, and after it became quite dark, Madame sat at the tiny window, and I felt that she was counting the minutes which still lay between her and the dreaded presence of that awful man.

At a quarter before eight o'clock we heard the usual heavy footfall on the stairs. Madame started up as if she had been struck. She ran to the bed—almost like one demented, and wrapping the one poor blanket round M. le Vicomte, she seized him in her arms. Outside we could hear Laporte's raucous voice speaking to the guard. His usual query: "Is all well?" was answered by the brief: "All well, citizen." Then he asked if the English spy were within, and the sentinel replied: "No, citizen, he went out at about five o'clock and has not come back since."

"Not come back since five o'clock?" said Laporte with a loud curse. "Pardi! I trust that that fool Caudy has not allowed him to escape."

"I saw Caudy about an hour ago, citizen," said the man.

"Did he say anything about the Englishman then?"

It seemed to us, who were listening to this conversation with bated breath, that the man hesitated a moment ere he replied; then he spoke with obvious nervousness.

"As a matter of fact, citizen," he said, "Caudy thought then that the Englishman was inside the house, whilst I was equally sure that I had seen him go downstairs an hour before."

"A thousand devils!" cried Laporte with a savage oath, "if I find that you, citizen sergeant, or Caudy have blundered there will be trouble for you."

To the accompaniment of a great deal more swearing he suddenly kicked open the door of our attic with his boot, and then came to a standstill on the threshold with his hands in the pockets of his breeches and his legs planted wide apart, face to face with Mme. la Marquise, who confronted him now, herself like a veritable tigress who is defending her young.

He gave a loud, mocking laugh.

"Ah, the aristos!" he cried, "waiting for that cursed Englishman, what? to drag you and your brat out of the claws of the human tiger. . . Not so, my fine ci-devant Marquise. The brat is no longer sick—he is well enough, anyhow, to breathe the air of the prisons of Lyons for a few days pending a final rest in the arms of Mme. la Guillotine. Citizen sergeant," he called over his shoulder, "escort these aristos to my carriage downstairs. When the Englishman returns, tell him he will find his friends under the tender care of Doctor Laporte. En avant, little mother," he added, as he gripped Mme. la Marquise tightly by the arm, "and you, old scarecrow," he concluded, speaking to me over his shoulder, "follow the citizen sergeant, or—"

Mme. la Marquise made no resistance. As I told you, she had been, since dusk, like a person in a dream; so what could I do but follow her noble example? Indeed, I was too dazed to do otherwise.

We all went stumbling down the dark, rickety staircase, Laporte leading the way with Mme. la Marquise, who had M. le Vicomte tightly clasped in her arms. I followed with the sergeant, whose hand was on my shoulder; I believe that two soldiers walked behind, but of that I cannot be sure.

At the bottom of the stairs through the open door of the house I caught sight of the vague outline of a large barouche, the lanthorns of which threw a feeble light upon the cruppers of two horses and of a couple of men sitting on the box.

Mme. la Marquise stepped quietly into the carriage. Laporte followed her, and I was bundled in in his wake by the rough hands of the soldiery. Just before the order was given to start, Laporte put his head out of the window and shouted to the sergeant:

"When you see Caudy tell him to report himself to me at once. I will be back here in half an hour; keep strict guard as before until then, citizen sergeant."

The next moment the coachman cracked his whip, Laporte called loudly, "En avant!" and the heavy barouche went rattling along the ill-paved streets.

Inside the carriage all was silence. I could hear Mme. la Marquise softly whispering to M. le Vicomte, and I marvelled how wondrously calm—nay, cheerful, she could be. Then suddenly I heard a sound which of a truth did make my heart stop its beating. It was a quaint and prolonged laugh which I once thought I would never hear again on this earth. It came from the corner of the barouche next to where Mme. la Marquise was so tenderly and gaily crooning to her child. And a kindly voice said merrily:

"In half an hour we shall be outside Lyons. To-morrow we'll be across the Swiss frontier. We've cheated that old tiger after all. What say you, Mme. la Marquise?"

It was milor's voice, and he was as merry as a school-boy.

"I told you, old Jean-Pierre," he added, as he placed that firm hand which I loved so well upon my knee, "I told you that those confounded murderers would not get me this time."

And to think that I did not know him, as he stood less than a quarter of an hour ago upon the threshold of our attic in the hideous guise of that abominable Laporte. He had spent two days in collecting old clothes that resembled those of that infamous wretch, and in taking possession of one of the derelict rooms in the house in the Rue des Pipots. Then while we were expecting every moment that Laporte would order our arrest, milor assumed the personality of the monster, hoodwinked the sergeant on the dark staircase, and by that wonderfully audacious coup saved Mme. la Marquise, M. le Vicomte and my humble self from the guillotine.

Money, of which he had plenty, secured us immunity on the way, and we were in safety over the Swiss frontier, leaving Laporte to eat out his tigerish heart with baffled rage.

VII

Out of the Jaws of Death

Being a fragment from the diary of Valentine Lemercier, in the possession of her great-granddaughter.

We were such a happy family before this terrible Revolution broke out; we lived rather simply, but very comfortably, in our dear old home just on the borders of the forest of Compiegne. Jean and Andre were the twins; just fifteen years old they were when King Louis was deposed from the throne of France which God had given him, and sent to prison like a common criminal, with our beautiful Queen Marie Antoinette and the Royal children, and Madame Elizabeth, who was so beloved by the poor!

Ah! that seems very, very long ago now. No doubt you know better than I do all that happened in our beautiful land of France and in lovely Paris about that time: goods and property confiscated, innocent men, women, and children condemned to death for acts of treason which they had never committed.

It was in August last year that they came to "Mon Repos" and arrested papa, and maman, and us four young ones and dragged us to Paris, where we were imprisoned in a narrow and horribly dank vault in the Abbaye, where all day and night through the humid stone walls we heard cries and sobs and moans from poor people, who no doubt were suffering the same sorrows and the same indignities as we were.

I had just passed my nineteenth birthday, and Marguerite was only thirteen. Maman was a perfect angel during that terrible time; she kept up our courage and our faith in God in a way that no one else could have done. Every night and morning we knelt round her knee and papa sat close beside her, and we prayed to God for deliverance from our own afflictions, and for the poor people who were crying and moaning all the day.

But of what went on outside our prison walls we had not an idea, though sometimes poor papa would brave the warder's brutalities and ask him questions of what was happening in Paris every day.

"They are hanging all the aristos to the street-lamps of the city," the man would reply with a cruel laugh, "and it will be your turn next."

We had been in prison for about a fortnight, when one day—oh! shall I ever forget it?—we heard in the distance a noise like the rumbling of thunder; nearer and nearer it came, and soon the sound became less confused, cries and shrieks could be heard above that rumbling din; but so weird and menacing did those cries seem that instinctively—though none of us knew what they meant—we all felt a nameless terror grip our hearts.

Oh! I am not going to attempt the awful task of describing to you all the horrors of that never-to-be-forgotten day. People, who to-day cannot speak without a shudder of the September massacres, have not the remotest conception of what really happened on that awful second day of that month.

We are all at peace and happy now, but whenever my thoughts fly back to that morning, whenever the ears of memory recall those hideous yells of fury and of hate, coupled with the equally horrible cries for pity, which pierced through the walls behind which the six of us were crouching, trembling, and praying, whenever I think of it all my heart still beats violently with that same nameless dread which held it in its deathly grip then.

Hundreds of men, women, and children were massacred in the prisons of that day—it was a St. Bartholomew even more hideous than the last.

Maman was trying in vain to keep our thoughts fixed upon God—papa sat on the stone bench, his elbows resting on his knees, his head buried in his hands; but maman was kneeling on the floor, with her dear arms encircling us all and her trembling lips moving in continuous prayer.

We felt that we were facing death—and what a death, O my God!

Suddenly the small grated window—high up in the dank wall—became obscured. I was the first to look up, but the cry of terror which rose from my heart was choked ere it reached my throat.

Jean and Andre looked up, too, and they shrieked, and so did Marguerite, and papa jumped up and ran to us and stood suddenly between us and the window like a tiger defending its young.

But we were all of us quite silent now. The children did not even cry; they stared, wide-eyed, paralysed with fear.

Only maman continued to pray, and we could hear papa's rapid and stertorous breathing as he watched what was going on at that window above.

Heavy blows were falling against the masonry round the grating, and we could hear the nerve-racking sound of a file working on the iron bars; and farther away, below the window, those awful yells of human beings transformed by hate and fury into savage beasts.

How long this horrible suspense lasted I cannot now tell you; the next thing I remember clearly is a number of men in horrible ragged clothing pouring into our vault-like prison from the window above; the next moment they rushed at us simultaneously—or so it seemed to me, for I was just then recommending my soul to God, so certain was I that in that same second I would cease to live.

It was all like a dream, for instead of the horrible shriek of satisfied hate which we were all expecting to hear, a whispering voice, commanding and low, struck our ears and dragged us, as it were, from out the abyss of despair into the sudden light of hope.

"If you will trust us," the voice whispered, "and not be afraid, you will be safely out of Paris within an hour."

Papa was the first to realise what was happening; he had never lost his presence of mind even during the darkest moment of this terrible time, and he said quite calmly and steadily now:

"What must we do?"

"Persuade the little ones not to be afraid, not to cry, to be as still and silent as may be," continued the voice, which I felt must be that of one of God's own angels, so exquisitely kind did it sound to my ear.

"They will be quiet and still without persuasion," said papa; "eh, children?"

And Jean, Andre, and Marguerite murmured: "Yes!" whilst maman and I drew them closer to us and said everything we could think of to make them still more brave.

And the whispering, commanding voice went on after awhile:

"Now will you allow yourselves to be muffled and bound, and, after that, will you swear that whatever happens, whatever you may see or hear, you will neither move nor speak? Not only your own lives, but those of many brave men will depend upon your fulfilment of this oath."

Papa made no reply save to raise his hand and eyes up to where God surely was watching over us all. Maman said in her gentle, even voice:

"For myself and my children, I swear to do all that you tell us."

A great feeling of confidence had entered into her heart, just as it had done into mine. We looked at one another and knew that we were both thinking of the same thing: we were thinking of the brave Englishman and his gallant little band of heroes, about whom we had heard many wonderful tales—how they had rescued a number of innocent people who were unjustly threatened with the guillotine; and we all knew that the tall figure, disguised in horrible rags, who spoke to us with such a gentle yet commanding voice, was the man whom rumour credited with supernatural powers, and who was known by the mysterious name of "The Scarlet Pimpernel."

Hardly had we sworn to do his bidding than his friends most unceremoniously threw great pieces of sacking over our heads, and then proceeded to tie ropes round our bodies. At least, I know that that is what one of them was doing to me, and from one or two whispered words of command which reached my ear I concluded that papa and maman and the children were being dealt with in the same summary way.

I felt hot and stifled under that rough bit of sacking, but I would not have moved or even sighed for worlds. Strangely enough, as soon as my eyes and ears were shut off from the sounds and sights immediately round me, I once more became conscious of the horrible and awful din which was going on, not only on the other side of our prison walls, but inside the whole of the Abbaye building and in the street beyond.

Once more I heard those terrible howls of rage and of satisfied hatred, uttered by the assassins who were being paid by the government of our beautiful country to butcher helpless prisoners in their hundreds.

Suddenly I felt myself hoisted up off my feet and slung up on to a pair of shoulders that must have been very powerful indeed, for I am no light weight, and once more I heard the voice, the very sound of which was delight, quite close to my ear this time, giving a brief and comprehensive command:

"All ready!—remember your part—en avant!"

Then it added in English. "Here, Tony, you start kicking against the door whilst we begin to shout!"

I loved those few words of English, and hoped that maman had heard them too, for it would confirm her—as it did me—in the happy knowledge that God and a brave man had taken our rescue in hand.

But from that moment we might have all been in the very antechamber of hell. I could hear the violent kicks against the heavy door of our prison, and our brave rescuers seemed suddenly to be transformed into a cageful of wild beasts. Their shouts and yells were as horrible as any that came to us from the outside, and I must say that the gentle, firm voice which I had learnt to love was as execrable as any I could hear.

Apparently the door would not yield, as the blows against it became more and more violent, and presently from somewhere above my head—the window presumably—there came a rough call, and a raucous laugh:

"Why? what in the name of—is happening here?"

And the voice near me answered back equally roughly: "A quarry of six—but we are caught in this confounded trap—get the door open for us, citizen—we want to get rid of this booty and go in search for more."

A horrible laugh was the reply from above, and the next instant I heard a terrific crash; the door had at last been burst open, either from within or without, I could not tell which, and suddenly all the din, the cries, the groans, the hideous laughter and bibulous songs which had sounded muffled up to now burst upon us with all their hideousness.

That was, I think, the most awful moment of that truly fearful hour. I could not have moved then, even had I wished or been able to do so; but I knew that between us all and a horrible, yelling, murdering mob there was now nothing—except the hand of God and the heroism of a band of English gentlemen.

Together they gave a cry—as loud, as terrifying as any that were uttered by the butchering crowd in the building, and with a wild rush they seemed to plunge with us right into the thick of the awful melee.

At least, that is what it all felt like to me, and afterwards I heard from our gallant rescuer himself that that is exactly what he and his friends did. There were eight of them altogether, and we four young ones had each been hoisted on a pair of devoted shoulders, whilst maman and papa were each carried by two men.

I was lying across the finest pair of shoulders in the world, and close to me was beating the bravest heart on God's earth.

Thus burdened, these eight noble English gentlemen charged right through an army of butchering, howling brutes, they themselves howling with the fiercest of them.

All around me I heard weird and terrific cries: "What ho! citizens—what have you there?"

"Six aristos!" shouted my hero boldly as he rushed on, forging his way through the crowd.

"What are you doing with them?" yelled a raucous voice.

"Food for the starving fish in the river," was the ready response. "Stand aside, citizen," he added, with a round curse; "I have my orders from citizen Danton himself about these six aristos. You hinder me at your peril."

He was challenged over and over again in the same way, and so were his friends who were carrying papa and maman and the children; but they were always ready with a reply, ready with an invective or a curse; with eyes that could not see, one could imagine them as hideous, as vengeful, as cruel as the rest of the crowd.

I think that soon I must have fainted from sheer excitement and terror, for I remember nothing more till I felt myself deposited on a hard floor, propped against the wall, and the stifling piece of sacking taken off my head and face.

I looked around me, dazed and bewildered; gradually the horrors of the past hour came back to me, and I had to close my eyes again, for I felt sick and giddy with the sheer memory of it all.

But presently I felt stronger and looked around me again. Jean and Andre were squatting in a corner close by, gazing wide-eyed at the group of men in filthy, ragged clothing, who sat round a deal table in the centre of a small, ill-furnished room.

Maman was lying on a horsehair sofa at the other end of the room, with Marguerite beside her, and papa sat in a low chair by her side, holding her hand.

The voice I loved was speaking in its quaint, somewhat drawly cadence:

"You are quite safe now, my dear Monsieur Lemercier," it said; "after Madame and the young people have had a rest, some of my friends will find you suitable disguises, and they will escort you out of Paris, as they have some really genuine passports in their possessions, which we obtain from time to time through the agency of a personage highly placed in this murdering government, and with the help of English banknotes. Those passports are not always unchallenged, I must confess," added my hero with a quaint laugh; "but to-night everyone is busy murdering in one part of Paris, so the other parts are comparatively safe."

Then he turned to one of his friends and spoke to him in English:

"You had better see this through, Tony," he said, "with Hastings and Mackenzie. Three of you will be enough; I shall have need of the others."

No one seemed to question his orders. He had spoken, and the others made ready to obey. Just then papa spoke up:

"How are we going to thank you, sir?" he asked, speaking broken English, but with his habitual dignity of manner.

"By leaving your welfare in our hands, Monsieur," replied our gallant rescuer quietly.

Papa tried to speak again, but the Englishman put up his hand to stop any further talk.

"There is no time now, Monsieur," he said with gentle courtesy. "I must leave you, as I have much work yet to do."

"Where are you going, Blakeney?" asked one of the others.

"Back to the Abbaye prison," he said; "there are other women and children to be rescued there!"

VIII

The Traitor

Not one of them had really trusted him for some time now. Heaven and his conscience alone knew what had changed my Lord Kulmsted from a loyal friend and keen sportsman into a surly and dissatisfied adherent—adherent only in name.

Some say that lack of money had embittered him. He was a confirmed gambler, and had been losing over-heavily of late; and the League of the Scarlet Pimpernel demanded sacrifices of money at times from its members, as well as of life if the need arose. Others averred that jealousy against the chief had outweighed Kulmsted's honesty. Certain it is that his oath of fealty to the League had long ago been broken in the spirit. Treachery hovered in the air.

But the Scarlet Pimpernel himself, with that indomitable optimism of his, and almost maddening insouciance, either did not believe in Kulmsted's disloyalty or chose not to heed it.

He even asked him to join the present expedition—one of the most dangerous undertaken by the League for some time, and which had for its object the rescue of some women of the late unfortunate Marie Antoinette's household: maids and faithful servants, ruthlessly condemned to die for their tender adherence to a martyred queen. And yet eighteen pairs of faithful lips had murmured words of warning.

It was towards the end of November, 1793. The rain was beating down in a monotonous drip, drip, drip on to the roof of a derelict house in the Rue Berthier. The wan light of a cold winter's morning peeped in through the curtainless window and touched with its weird grey brush the pallid face of a young girl—a mere child—who sat in a dejected attitude on a rickety chair, with elbows leaning on the rough deal table before her, and thin, grimy fingers wandering with pathetic futility to her tearful eyes.

In the farther angle of the room a tall figure in dark clothes was made one, by the still lingering gloom, with the dense shadows beyond.

"We have starved," said the girl, with rebellious tears. "Father and I and the boys are miserable enough, God knows; but we have always been honest."

From out the shadows in that dark corner of the room there came the sound of an oath quickly suppressed.

"Honest!" exclaimed the man, with a harsh, mocking laugh, which made the girl wince as if with physical pain. "Is it honest to harbour the enemies of your country? Is it honest—"

But quickly he checked himself, biting his lips with vexation, feeling that his present tactics were not like to gain the day.

He came out of the gloom and approached the girl with every outward sign of eagerness. He knelt on the dusty floor beside her, his arms stole round her meagre shoulders, and his harsh voice was subdued to tones of gentleness.

"I was only thinking of your happiness, Yvonne," he said tenderly; "of poor blind papa and the two boys to whom you have been such a devoted little mother. My only desire is that you should earn the gratitude of your country by denouncing her most bitter enemy—an act of patriotism which will place you and those for whom you care for ever beyond the reach of sorrow or of want."

The voice, the appeal, the look of love, was more than the poor, simple girl could resist. Milor was so handsome, so kind, so good.

It had all been so strange: these English aristocrats coming here, she knew not whence, and who seemed fugitives even though they had plenty of money to spend. Two days ago they had sought shelter like malefactors escaped from justice—in this same tumbledown, derelict house where she, Yvonne, with her blind father and two little brothers, crept in of nights, or when the weather was too rough for them all to stand and beg in the streets of Paris.

There were five of them altogether, and one seemed to be the chief. He was very tall, and had deep blue eyes, and a merry voice that went echoing along the worm-eaten old rafters. But milor—the one whose arms were encircling her even now—was the handsomest among them all. He had sought Yvonne out on the very first night when she had crawled shivering to that corner of the room where she usually slept.

The English aristocrats had frightened her at first, and she was for flying from the derelict house with her family and seeking shelter elsewhere; but he who appeared to be the chief had quickly reassured her. He seemed so kind and good, and talked so gently to blind papa, and made such merry jests with Francois and Clovis that she herself could scarce refrain from laughing through her tears.

But later on in the night, milor—her milor, as she soon got to call him—came and talked so beautifully that she, poor girl, felt as if no music could ever sound quite so sweetly in her ear.

That was two days ago, and since then milor had often talked to her in the lonely, abandoned house, and Yvonne had felt as if she dwelt in Heaven. She still took blind papa and the boys out to beg in the streets, but in the morning she prepared some hot coffee for the English aristocrats, and in the evening she cooked them some broth. Oh! they gave her money lavishly; but she quite understood that they were in hiding, though what they had to fear, being English, she could not understand.

And now milor—her milor—was telling her that these Englishmen, her friends, were spies and traitors, and that it was her duty to tell citizen Robespierre and the Committee of Public Safety all about them and their mysterious doings. And poor Yvonne was greatly puzzled and deeply distressed, because, of course, whatever milor said, that was the truth; and yet her conscience cried out within her poor little bosom, and the thought of betraying those kind Englishmen was horrible to her.

"Yvonne," whispered milor in that endearing voice of his, which was like the loveliest music in her ear, "my little Yvonne, you do trust me, do you not?"

"With all my heart, milor," she murmured fervently.

"Then, would you believe it of me that I would betray a real friend?"

"I believe, milor, that whatever you do is right and good."

A sigh of infinite relief escaped his lips.

"Come, that's better!" he said, patting her cheek kindly with his hand. "Now, listen to me, little one. He who is the chief among us here is the most unscrupulous and daring rascal whom the world has ever known. He it is who is called the 'Scarlet Pimpernel!'"

"The Scarlet Pimpernel!" murmured Yvonne, her eyes dilated with superstitious awe, for she too had heard of the mysterious Englishman and of his followers, who rescued aristocrats and traitors from the death to which the tribunal of the people had justly condemned them, and on whom the mighty hand of the Committee of Public Safety had never yet been able to fall.

"This Scarlet Pimpernel," said milor earnestly after a while, "is also mine own most relentless enemy. With lies and promises he induced me to join him in his work of spying and of treachery, forcing me to do this work against which my whole soul rebels. You can save me from this hated bondage, little one. You can make me free to live again, make me free to love and place my love at your feet."

His voice had become exquisitely tender, and his lips, as he whispered the heavenly words, were quite close to her ear. He, a great gentleman, loved the miserable little waif whose kindred consisted of a blind father and two half-starved little brothers, and whose only home was this miserable hovel, whence milor's graciousness and bounty would soon take her.

Do you think that Yvonne's sense of right and wrong, of honesty and treachery, should have been keener than that primeval instinct of a simple-hearted woman to throw herself trustingly into the arms of the man who has succeeded in winning her love?

Yvonne, subdued, enchanted, murmured still through her tears:

"What would milor have me do?"

Lord Kulmsted rose from his knees satisfied.

"Listen to me, Yvonne," he said. "You are acquainted with the Englishman's plans, are you not?"

"Of course," she replied simply. "He has had to trust me."

"Then you know that at sundown this afternoon I and the three others are to leave for Courbevoie on foot, where we are to obtain what horses we can whilst awaiting the chief."

"I did not know whither you and the other three gentlemen were going, milor," she replied; "but I did know that some of you were to make a start at four o'clock, whilst I was to wait here for your leader and prepare some supper against his coming."

"At what time did he tell you that he would come?"

"He did not say; but he did tell me that when he returns he will have friends with him—a lady and two little children. They will be hungry and cold. I believe that they are in great danger now, and that the brave English gentleman means to take them away from this awful Paris to a place of safety."

"The brave English gentleman, my dear," retorted milor, with a sneer, "is bent on some horrible work of spying. The lady and the two children are, no doubt, innocent tools in his hands, just as I am, and when he no longer needs them he will deliver them over to the Committee of Public Safety, who will, of a surety, condemn them to death. That will also be my fate, Yvonne, unless you help me now."

"Oh, no, no!" she exclaimed fervently. "Tell me what to do, milor, and I will do it."

"At sundown," he said, sinking his voice so low that even she could scarcely hear, "when I and the three others have started on our way, go straight to the house I spoke to you about in the Rue Dauphine—you know where it is?"

"Oh, yes, milor."

"You will know the house by its tumbledown portico and the tattered red flag that surmounts it. Once there, push the door open and walk in boldly. Then ask to speak with citizen Robespierre."

"Robespierre?" exclaimed the child in terror.

"You must not be afraid, Yvonne," he said earnestly; "you must think of me and of what you are doing for me. My word on it—Robespierre will listen to you most kindly."

"What shall I tell him?" she murmured.

"That a mysterious party of Englishmen are in hiding in this house—that their chief is known among them as the Scarlet Pimpernel. The rest leave to Robespierre's discretion. You see how simple it is?"

It was indeed very simple! Nor did the child recoil any longer from the ugly task which milor, with suave speech and tender voice, was so ardently seeking to impose on her.

A few more words of love, which cost him nothing, a few kisses which cost him still less, since the wench loved him, and since she was young and pretty, and Yvonne was as wax in the hands of the traitor.

II

Silence reigned in the low-raftered room on the ground floor of the house in the Rue Dauphine.

Citizen Robespierre, chairman of the Cordeliers Club, the most bloodthirsty, most Evolutionary club of France, had just re-entered the room.

He walked up to the centre table, and through the close atmosphere, thick with tobacco smoke, he looked round on his assembled friends.

"We have got him," he said at last curtly.

"Got him! Whom?" came in hoarse cries from every corner of the room.

"That Englishman," replied the demagogue, "the Scarlet Pimpernel!"

A prolonged shout rose in response—a shout not unlike that of a caged herd of hungry wild beasts to whom a succulent morsel of flesh has unexpectedly been thrown.

"Where is he?" "Where did you get him?" "Alive or dead?" And many more questions such as these were hurled at the speaker from every side.

Robespierre, calm, impassive, immaculately neat in his tightly fitting coat, his smart breeches, and his lace cravat, waited awhile until the din had somewhat subsided. Then he said calmly:

"The Scarlet Pimpernel is in hiding in one of the derelict houses in the Rue Berthier."

Snarls of derision as vigorous as the former shouts of triumph drowned the rest of his speech.

"Bah! How often has that cursed Scarlet Pimpernel been said to be alone in a lonely house? Citizen Chauvelin has had him at his mercy several times in lonely houses."

And the speaker, a short, thick-set man with sparse black hair plastered over a greasy forehead, his shirt open at the neck, revealing a powerful chest and rough, hairy skin, spat in ostentatious contempt upon the floor.

"Therefore will we not boast of his capture yet, citizen Roger," resumed Robespierre imperturbably. "I tell you where the Englishman is. Do you look to it that he does not escape."

The heat in the room had become intolerable. From the grimy ceiling an oil-lamp, flickering low, threw lurid, ruddy lights on tricolour cockades, on hands that seemed red with the blood of innocent victims of lust and hate, and on faces glowing with desire and with anticipated savage triumph.

"Who is the informer?" asked Roger at last.

"A girl," replied Robespierre curtly. "Yvonne Lebeau, by name; she and her family live by begging. There are a blind father and two boys; they herd together at night in the derelict house in the Rue Berthier. Five Englishmen have been in hiding there these past few days. One of them is their leader. The girl believes him to be the Scarlet Pimpernel."

"Why has she not spoken of this before?" muttered one of the crowd, with some scepticism.

"Frightened, I suppose. Or the Englishman paid her to hold her tongue."

"Where is the girl now?"

"I am sending her straight home, a little ahead of us. Her presence should reassure the Englishman whilst we make ready to surround the house. In the meanwhile, I have sent special messengers to every gate of Paris with strict orders to the guard not to allow anyone out of the city until further orders from the Committee of Public Safety. And now," he added, throwing back his head with a gesture of proud challenge, "citizens, which of you will go man-hunting to-night?"

This time the strident roar of savage exultation was loud and deep enough to shake the flickering lamp upon its chain.

A brief discussion of plans followed, and Roger—he with the broad, hairy chest and that gleam of hatred for ever lurking in his deep-set, shifty eyes—was chosen the leader of the party.

Thirty determined and well-armed patriots set out against one man, who mayhap had supernatural powers. There would, no doubt, be some aristocrats, too, in hiding in the derelict house—the girl Lebeau, it seems, had spoken of a woman and two children. Bah! These would not count. It would be thirty to one, so let the Scarlet Pimpernel look to himself.

From the towers of Notre Dame the big bell struck the hour of six, as thirty men in ragged shirts and torn breeches, shivering beneath a cold November drizzle, began slowly to wend their way towards the Rue Berthier.

They walked on in silence, not heeding the cold or the rain, but with eyes fixed in the direction of their goal, and nostrils quivering in the evening air with the distant scent of blood.

III

At the top of the Rue Berthier the party halted. On ahead—some two hundred metres farther—Yvonne Lebeau's little figure, with her ragged skirt pulled over her head and her bare feet pattering in the mud, was seen crossing one of those intermittent patches of light formed by occasional flickering street lamps, and then was swallowed up once more by the inky blackness beyond.

The Rue Berthier is a long, narrow, ill-paved and ill-lighted street, composed of low and irregular houses, which abut on the line of fortifications at the back, and are therefore absolutely inaccessible save from the front.

Midway down the street a derelict house rears ghostly debris of roofs and chimney-stacks upward to the sky. A tiny square of yellow light, blinking like a giant eye through a curtainless window, pierced the wall of the house. Roger pointed to that light.

"That," he said, "is the quarry where our fox has run to earth."

No one said anything; but the dank night air seemed suddenly alive with all the passions of hate let loose by thirty beating hearts.

The Scarlet Pimpernel, who had tricked them, mocked them, fooled them so often, was there, not two hundred metres away; and they were thirty to one, and all determined and desperate.

The darkness was intense.

Silently now the party approached the house, then again they halted, within sixty metres of it.

"Hist!"

The whisper could scarce be heard, so low was it, like the sighing of the wind through a misty veil.

"Who is it?" came in quick challenge from Roger.

"I—Yvonne Lebeau!"

"Is he there?" was the eager whispered query.

"Not yet. But he may come at any moment. If he saw a crowd round the house, mayhap he would not come."

"He cannot see a crowd. The night is as dark as pitch."

"He can see in the darkest night," and the girl's voice sank to an awed whisper, "and he can hear through a stone wall."

Instinctively, Roger shuddered. The superstitious fear which the mysterious personality of the Scarlet Pimpernel evoked in the heart of every Terrorist had suddenly seized this man in its grip.

Try as he would, he did not feel as valiant as he had done when first he emerged at the head of his party from under the portico of the Cordeliers Club, and it was with none too steady a voice that he ordered the girl roughly back to the house. Then he turned once more to his men.

The plan of action had been decided on in the Club, under the presidency of Robespierre; it only remained to carry the plans through with success.

From the side of the fortifications there was, of course, nothing to fear. In accordance with military regulations, the walls of the houses there rose sheer from the ground without doors or windows, whilst the broken-down parapets and dilapidated roofs towered forty feet above the ground.

The derelict itself was one of a row of houses, some inhabited, others quite abandoned. It was the front of that row of houses, therefore, that had to be kept in view. Marshalled by Roger, the men flattened their meagre bodies against the walls of the houses opposite, and after that there was nothing to do but wait.

To wait in the darkness of the night, with a thin, icy rain soaking through ragged shirts and tattered breeches, with bare feet frozen by the mud of the road—to wait in silence while turbulent hearts beat well-nigh to bursting—to wait for food whilst hunger gnaws the bowels—to wait for drink whilst the parched tongue cleaves to the roof of the mouth—to wait for revenge whilst the hours roll slowly by and the cries of the darkened city are stilled one by one!

Once—when a distant bell tolled the hour of ten—a loud prolonged laugh, almost impudent in its suggestion of merry insouciance, echoed through the weird silence of the night.

Roger felt that the man nearest to him shivered at that sound, and he heard a volley or two of muttered oaths.

"The fox seems somewhere near," he whispered. "Come within. We'll wait for him inside his hole."

He led the way across the street, some of the men following him.

The door of the derelict house had been left on the latch. Roger pushed it open.

Silence and gloom here reigned supreme; utter darkness, too, save for a narrow streak of light which edged the framework of a door on the right. Not a sound stirred the quietude of this miserable hovel, only the creaking of boards beneath the men's feet as they entered.

Roger crossed the passage and opened the door on the right. His friends pressed closely round to him and peeped over his shoulder into the room beyond.

A guttering piece of tallow candle, fixed to an old tin pot, stood in the middle of the floor, and its feeble, flickering light only served to accentuate the darkness that lay beyond its range. One or two rickety chairs and a rough deal table showed vaguely in the gloom, and in the far corner of the room there lay a bundle of what looked like heaped-up rags, but from which there now emerged the sound of heavy breathing and also a little cry of fear.

"Yvonne," came in feeble, querulous accents from that same bundle of wretchedness, "are these the English milors come back at last?"

"No, no, father," was the quick whispered reply.

Roger swore a loud oath, and two puny voices began to whimper piteously.

"It strikes me the wench has been fooling us," muttered one of the men savagely.

The girl had struggled to her feet. She crouched in the darkness, and two little boys, half-naked and shivering, were clinging to her skirts. The rest of the human bundle seemed to consist of an oldish man, with long, gaunt legs and arms blue with the cold. He turned vague, wide-open eyes in the direction whence had come the harsh voices.

"Are they friends, Yvonne?" he asked anxiously.

The girl did her best to reassure him.

"Yes, yes, father," she whispered close to his ear, her voice scarce above her breath; "they are good citizens who hoped to find the English milor here. They are disappointed that he has not yet come."

"Ah! but he will come, of a surety," said the old man in that querulous voice of his. "He left his beautiful clothes here this morning, and surely he will come to fetch them." And his long, thin hand pointed towards a distant corner of the room.

Roger and his friends, looking to where he was pointing, saw a parcel of clothes, neatly folded, lying on one of the chairs. Like so many wild cats snarling at sight of prey, they threw themselves upon those clothes, tearing them out from one another's hands, turning them over and over as if to force the cloth and satin to yield up the secret that lay within their folds.

In the skirmish a scrap of paper fluttered to the ground. Roger seized it with avidity, and, crouching on the floor, smoothed the paper out against his knee.

It contained a few hastily scrawled words, and by the feeble light of the fast-dying candle Roger spelt them out laboriously:

"If the finder of these clothes will take them to the cross-roads opposite the foot-bridge which leads straight to Courbevoie, and will do so before the clock of Courbevoie Church has struck the hour of midnight, he will be rewarded with the sum of five hundred francs."

"There is something more, citizen Roger," said a raucous voice close to his ear.

"Look! Look, citizen—in the bottom corner of the paper!"

"The signature."

"A scrawl done in red," said Roger, trying to decipher it.

"It looks like a small flower."

"That accursed Scarlet Pimpernel!"

And even as he spoke the guttering tallow candle, swaying in its socket, suddenly went out with a loud splutter and a sizzle that echoed through the desolate room like the mocking laugh of ghouls.

IV

Once more the tramp through the dark and deserted streets, with the drizzle—turned now to sleet—beating on thinly clad shoulders. Fifteen men only on this tramp. The others remained behind to watch the house. Fifteen men, led by Roger, and with a blind old man, a young girl carrying a bundle of clothes, and two half-naked children dragged as camp-followers in the rear.

Their destination now was the sign-post which stands at the cross-roads, past the footbridge that leads to Courbevoie.

The guard at the Maillot Gate would have stopped the party, but Roger, member of the Committee of Public Safety, armed with his papers and his tricolour scarf, overruled Robespierre's former orders, and the party mached out of the gate.

They pressed on in silence, instinctively walking shoulder to shoulder, vaguely longing for the touch of another human hand, the sound of a voice that would not ring weirdly in the mysterious night.

There was something terrifying in this absolute silence, in such intense darkness, in this constant wandering towards a goal that seemed for ever distant, and in all this weary, weary fruitless waiting; and these men, who lived their life through, drunken with blood, deafened by the cries of their victims, satiated with the moans of the helpless and the innocent, hardly dared to look around them, lest they should see ghoulish forms flitting through the gloom.

Soon they reached the cross-roads, and in the dense blackness of the night the gaunt arms of the sign-post pointed ghostlike towards the north.

The men hung back, wrapped in the darkness as in a pall, while Roger advanced alone.

"Hola! Is anyone there?" he called softly.

Then, as no reply came, he added more loudly:

"Hola! A friend—with some clothes found in the Rue Berthier. Is anyone here? Hola! A friend!"

But only from the gently murmuring river far away the melancholy call of a waterfowl seemed to echo mockingly:

"A friend!"

Just then the clock of Courbevoie Church struck the midnight hour.

"It is too late," whispered the men.

They did not swear, nor did they curse their leader. Somehow it seemed as if they had expected all along that the Englishman would evade their vengeance yet again, that he would lure them out into the cold and into the darkness, and then that he would mock them, fool them, and finally disappear into the night.

It seemed futile to wait any longer. They were so sure that they had failed again.

"Who goes there?"

The sound of naked feet and of wooden sabots pattering on the distant footbridge had caused Roger to utter the quick challenge.

"Hola! Hola! Are you there?" was the loud, breathless response.

The next moment the darkness became alive with men moving quickly forward, and raucous shouts of "Where are they?" "Have you got them?" "Don't let them go!" filled the air.

"Got whom?" "Who are they?" "What is it?" were the wild counter-cries.

"The man! The girl! The children! Where are they?"

"What? Which? The Lebeau family? They are here with us."

"Where?"

Where, indeed? To a call to them from Roger there came no answer, nor did a hasty search result in finding them—the old man, the two boys, and the girl carrying the bundle of clothes had vanished into the night.

"In the name of—, what does this mean?" cried hoarse voices in the crowd.

The new-comers, breathless, terrified, shaking with superstitious fear, tried to explain.

"The Lebeau family—the old man, the girl, the two boys—we discovered after your departure, locked up in the cellar of the house—prisoners."

"But, then—the others?" they gasped.

"The girl and the children whom you saw must have been some aristocrats in disguise. The old man who spoke to you was that cursed Englishman—the Scarlet Pimpernel!"

And as if in mocking confirmation of these words there suddenly rang, echoing from afar, a long and merry laugh.

"The Scarlet Pimpernel!" cried Roger. "In rags and barefooted! At him, citizens; he cannot have got far!"

"Hush! Listen!" whispered one of the men, suddenly gripping him by the arm.

And from the distance—though Heaven only knew from what direction—came the sound of horses' hoofs pawing the soft ground; the next moment they were heard galloping away at breakneck speed.

The men turned to run in every direction, blindly, aimlessly, in the dark, like bloodhounds that have lost the trail.

One man, as he ran, stumbled against a dark mass prone upon the ground. With a curse on his lips, he recovered his balance.

"Hold! What is this?" he cried.

Some of his comrades gathered round him. No one could see anything, but the dark mass appeared to have human shape, and it was bound round and round with cords. And now feeble moans escaped from obviously human lips.

"What is it? Who is it?" asked the men.

"An Englishman," came in weak accents from the ground.

"Your name?"

"I am called Kulmsted."

"Bah! An aristocrat!"

"No! An enemy of the Scarlet Pimpernel, like yourselves. I would have delivered him into your hands. But you let him escape you. As for me, he would have been wiser if he had killed me."

They picked him up and undid the cords from round his body, and later on took him with them back into Paris.

But there, in the darkness of the night, in the mud of the road, and beneath the icy rain, knees were shaking that had long ago forgotten how to bend, and hasty prayers were muttered by lips that were far more accustomed to blaspheme.

IX

The Cabaret de la Liberte

I

"Eight!"

"Twelve!"

"Four!"

A loud curse accompanied this last throw, and shouts of ribald laughter greeted it.

"No luck, Guidal!"

"Always at the tail end of the cart, eh, citizen?"

"Do not despair yet, good old Guidal! Bad beginnings oft make splendid ends!"

Then once again the dice rattled in the boxes; those who stood around pressed closer round the gamesters; hot, avid faces, covered with sweat and grime, peered eagerly down upon the table.

"Eight and eleven—nineteen!"

"Twelve and zero! By Satan! Curse him! Just my luck!"

"Four and nine—thirteen! Unlucky number!"

"Now then—once more! I'll back Merri! Ten assignats of the most worthless kind! Who'll take me that Merri gets the wench in the end?"

This from one of the lookers-on, a tall, cadaverous-looking creature, with sunken eyes and broad, hunched up shoulders, which were perpetually shaken by a dry, rasping cough that proclaimed the ravages of some mortal disease, left him trembling as with ague and brought beads of perspiration to the roots of his lank hair. A recrudescence of excitement went the round of the spectators. The gamblers sitting round a narrow deal table, on which past libations had left marks of sticky rings, had scarce room to move their elbows.

"Nineteen and four—twenty-three!"

"You are out of it, Desmonts!"

"Not yet!"

"Twelve and twelve!"

"There! What did I tell you?"

"Wait! wait! Now, Merri! Now! Remember I have backed you for ten assignats, which I propose to steal from the nearest Jew this very night."

"Thirteen and twelve! Twenty-five, by all the demons and the ghouls!" came with a triumphant shout from the last thrower.

"Merri has it! Vive Merri!" was the unanimous and clamorous response.

Merri was evidently the most popular amongst the three gamblers. Now he sprawled upon the bench, leaning his back against the table, and surveyed the assembled company with the air of an Achilles having vanquished his Hector.

"Good luck to you and to your aristo!" began his backer lustily—would, no doubt, have continued his song of praise had not a violent fit of coughing smothered the words in his throat. The hand which he had raised in order to slap his friend genially on the back now went with a convulsive clutch to his own chest.

But his obvious distress did not apparently disturb the equanimity of Merri, or arouse even passing interest in the lookers-on.

"May she have as much money as rumour avers," said one of the men sententiously.

Merri gave a careless wave of his grubby hand.

"More, citizen; more!" he said loftily.

Only the two losers appeared inclined to scepticism.

"Bah!" one of them said—it was Desmonts. "The whole matter of the woman's money may be a tissue of lies!"

"And England is a far cry!" added Guidal.

But Merri was not likely to be depressed by these dismal croakings.

"'Tis simple enough," he said philosophically, "to disparage the goods if you are not able to buy."

Then a lusty voice broke in from the far corner of the room:

"And now, citizen Merri, 'tis time you remembered that the evening is hot and your friends thirsty!"

The man who spoke was a short, broad-shouldered creature, with crimson face surrounded by a shock of white hair, like a ripe tomato wrapped in cotton wool.

"And let me tell you," he added complacently, "that I have a cask of rum down below, which came straight from that accursed country, England, and is said to be the nectar whereon feeds that confounded Scarlet Pimpernel. It gives him the strength, so 'tis said, to intrigue successfully against the representatives of the people."

“Then by all means, citizen,” concluded Merri’s backer, still hoarse and spent after his fit of coughing, “let us have some of your nectar. My friend, citizen Merri, will need strength and wits too, I’ll warrant, for, after he has married the aristo, he will have to journey to England to pluck the rich dowry which is said to lie hidden there.”

“Cast no doubt upon that dowry, citizen Rateau, curse you!” broke in Merri, with a spiteful glance directed against his former rivals, “or Guidal and Desmonts will cease to look glum, and half my joy in the aristo will have gone.”

After which, the conversation drifted to general subjects, became hilarious and ribald, while the celebrated rum from England filled the close atmosphere of the narrow room with its heady fumes.

II

Open to the street in front, the locality known under the pretentious title of “Cabaret de la Liberte” was a favoured one among the flotsam and jetsam of the population of this corner of old Paris; men and sometimes women, with nothing particular to do, no special means of livelihood save the battening on the countless miseries and sorrows which this Revolution, which was to have been so glorious, was bringing in its train; idlers and loafers, who would crawl desultorily down the few worn and grimy steps which led into the cabaret from the level of the street. There was always good brandy or eau de vie to be had there, and no questions asked, no scares from the revolutionary guards or the secret agents of the Committee of Public Safety, who knew better than to interfere with the citizen host and his dubious clientele. There was also good Rhine wine or rum to be had, smuggled across from England or Germany, and no interference from the spies of some of those countless Committees, more autocratic than any ci-devant despot. It was, in fact, an ideal place wherein to conduct those shady transactions which are unavoidable corollaries of an unfettered democracy. Projects of burglary, pillage, rapine, even murder, were hatched within this underground burrow, where, as soon as evening drew in, a solitary, smoky oil-lamp alone cast a dim light upon faces that liked to court the darkness, and whence no sound that was not meant for prying ears found its way to the street above. The walls were thick with grime and smoke, the floor mildewed and cracked; dirt vied with squalor to make the place a fitting abode for thieves and cut-throats, for some of those sinister night-birds, more vile even than those who shrieked with satisfied lust at sight of the tumbril, with its daily load of unfortunates for the guillotine.

On this occasion the project that was being hatched was one of the most abject. A young girl, known by some to be possessed of a fortune, was the stake for which these workers of iniquity gambled across one of mine host's greasy tables. The latest decree of the Convention, encouraging, nay, commanding, the union of aristocrats with so-called patriots, had fired the imagination of this nest of jail-birds with thoughts of glorious possibilities. Some of them had collected the necessary information; and the report had been encouraging.

That self-indulgent aristo, the ci-devant banker Amede Vincent, who had expiated his villainies upon the guillotine, was known to have been successful in abstracting the bulk of his ill-gotten wealth and concealing it somewhere—it was not exactly known where, but thought to be in England—out of the reach, at any rate, of deserving patriots.

Some three or four years ago, before the glorious principles of Liberty, Equality, and Fraternity had made short shrift of all such pestilential aristocrats, the ci-devant banker, then a widower with an only daughter, Esther, had journeyed to England. He soon returned to Paris, however, and went on living there with his little girl in comparative retirement, until his many crimes found him out at last and he was made to suffer the punishment which he so justly deserved. Those crimes consisted for the most part in humiliating the aforesaid deserving patriots with his benevolence, shaming them with many kindnesses, and the simplicity of his home-life, and, above all, in flouting the decrees of the Revolutionary Government, which made every connection with ci-devant churches and priests a penal offence against the security of the State.

Amede Vincent was sent to the guillotine, and the representatives of the people confiscated his house and all his property on which they could lay their hands; but they never found the millions which he was supposed to have concealed. Certainly his daughter Esther—a young girl, not yet nineteen—had not found them either, for after her father's death she went to live in one of the poorer quarters of Paris, alone with an old and faithful servant named Lucienne. And while the Committee of Public Safety was deliberating whether it would be worth while to send Esther to the guillotine, to follow in her father's footsteps, a certain number of astute jail-birds plotted to obtain possession of her wealth.

The wealth existed, over in England; of that they were ready to take their oath, and the project which they had formed was as ingenious as it was diabolic: to feign a denunciation, to enact a pretended arrest, to place before the unfortunate girl the alternative of death or marriage with one of the gang, were the chief incidents of this inquitous project, and it was in the Cabaret de la Liberte that lots were thrown as to which among the herd of miscreants should be the favoured one to play the chief role in the sinister drama.

The lot fell to Merri; but the whole gang was to have a share in the putative fortune—even Rateau, the wretched creature with the hacking cough, who looked as if he had one foot in the grave, and shivered as if he were stricken with ague, put in a word now and again to remind his good friend Merri that he, too, was looking forward to his share of the spoils. Merri, however, was inclined to repudiate him altogether.

"Why should I share with you?" he said roughly, when, a few hours later, he and Rateau parted in the street outside the Cabaret de la Liberte. "Who are you, I would like to know, to try and poke your ugly nose into my affairs? How do I know where you come from, and whether you are not some crapulent spy of one of those pestilential committees?"

From which eloquent flow of language we may infer that the friendship between these two worthies was not of very old duration. Rateau would, no doubt, have protested loudly, but the fresh outer air had evidently caught his wheezy lungs, and for a minute or two he could do nothing but cough and splutter and groan, and cling to his unresponsive comrade for support. Then at last, when he had succeeded in recovering his breath, he said dolefully and with a ludicrous attempt at dignified reproach:

"Do not force me to remind you, citizen Merri, that if it had not been for my suggestion that we should all draw lots, and then play hazard as to who shall be the chosen one to woo the ci-devant millionairess, there would soon have been a free fight inside the cabaret, a number of broken heads, and no decision whatever arrived at; whilst you, who were never much of a fighter, would probably be lying now helpless, with a broken nose, and deprived of some of your teeth, and with no chance of entering the lists for the heiress. Instead of which, here you are, the victor by a stroke of good fortune, which you should at least have the good grace to ascribe to me."

Whether the poor wretch's argument had any weight with citizen Merri, or whether that worthy patriot merely thought that procrastination would, for the nonce, prove the best policy, it were impossible to say. Certain it is that in response to his companion's tirade he contented himself with a dubious grunt, and without another word turned on his heel and went slouching down the street.

III

For the persistent and optimistic romanticist, there were still one or two idylls to be discovered flourishing under the shadow of the grim and relentless Revolution. One such was that which had Esther Vincent and Jack Kennard for hero and heroine. Esther, the orphaned daughter of one of the richest bankers of pre-Revolution days, now a daily governess and household drudge at ten francs a week in the house of a retired butcher in the Rue Richelieu, and Jack Kennard, formerly the representative of a big English firm of woollen manufacturers, who had thrown up his employment and prospects in England in order to watch over the girl whom he loved. He, himself an alien enemy, an Englishman, in deadly danger of his life every hour that he remained in France; and she, unwilling at the time to leave the horrors of revolutionary Paris while her father was lingering at the Conciergerie awaiting condemnation, as such forbidden to leave the city. So Kennard stayed on, unable to tear himself away from her, and obtained an unlucrative post as accountant in a small wine shop over by Montmartre. His life, like hers, was hanging by a thread; any day, any hour now, some malevolent denunciation might, in the sight of the Committee of Public Safety, turn the eighteen years old "suspect" into a living peril to the State, or the alien enemy into a dangerous spy.

Some of the happiest hours these two spent in one another's company were embittered by that ever-present dread of the peremptory knock at the door, the portentous: "Open, in the name of the Law!" the perquisition, the arrest, to which the only issue, these days, was the guillotine.

But the girl was only just eighteen, and he not many years older, and at that age, in spite of misery, sorrow, and dread, life always has its compensations. Youth cries out to happiness so insistently that happiness is forced to hear, and for a few moments, at the least, drives care and even the bitterest anxiety away.

For Esther Vincent and her English lover there were moments when they believed themselves to be almost happy. It was in the evenings mostly, when she came home from her work and he was free to spend an hour or two with her. Then old Lucienne, who had been Esther's nurse in the happy, olden days, and was an unpaid maid-of-all-work and a loved and trusted friend now, would bring in the lamp and pull the well-darned curtains over the windows. She would spread a clean cloth upon the table and bring in a meagre supper of coffee and black bread, perhaps a little butter or a tiny square of cheese. And the two young people would talk of the future, of the time when they would settle down in Kennard's old home, over in England, where his mother and sister even now were eating out their hearts with anxiety for him.

"Tell me all about the South Downs," Esther was very fond of saying; "and your village, and your house, and the rambler roses and the clematis arbour."

She never tired of hearing, or he of telling. The old Manor House, bought with his father's savings; the garden which was his mother's hobby; the cricket pitch on the village green. Oh, the cricket! She thought that so funny—the men in high, sugar-loaf hats, grown-up men, spending hours and hours, day after day, in banging at a ball with a wooden bat!

"Oh, Jack! The English are a funny, nice, dear, kind lot of people. I remember—"

She remembered so well that happy summer which she had spent with her father in England four years ago. It was after the Bastille had been stormed and taken, and the banker had journeyed to England with his daughter in something of a hurry. Then her father had talked of returning to France and leaving her behind with friends in England. But Esther would not be left. Oh, no! Even now she glowed with pride at the thought of her firmness in the matter. If she had remained in England she would never have seen her dear father again. Here remembrances grew bitter and sad, until Jack's hand reached soothingly, consolingly out to her, and she brushed away her tears, so as not to sadden him still more.

Then she would ask more questions about his home and his garden, about his mother and the dogs and the flowers; and once more they would forget that hatred and envy and death were already stalking their door.

IV

"Open, in the name of the Law!"

It had come at last. A bolt from out the serene blue of their happiness. A rough, dirty, angry, cursing crowd, who burst through the heavy door even before they had time to open it. Lucienne collapsed into a chair, weeping and lamenting, with her apron thrown over her head. But Esther and Kennard stood quite still and calm, holding one another by the hand, just to give one another courage.

Some half dozen men stalked into the little room. Men? They looked like ravenous beasts, and were unspeakably dirty, wore soiled tricolour scarves above their tattered breeches in token of their official status. Two of them fell on the remnants of the meagre supper and devoured everything that remained on the table—bread, cheese, a piece of home-made sausage. The others ransacked the two attic-rooms which had been home for Esther and Lucienne: the little living-room under the sloping roof, with the small hearth on which very scanty meals were wont to be cooked, and the bare, narrow room beyond, with the iron bedstead, and the palliasse on the floor for Lucienne.

The men poked about everywhere, struck great, spiked sticks through the poor bits of bedding, and ripped up the palliasse. They tore open the drawers of the rickety chest and of the broken-down wardrobe, and did not spare the unfortunate young girl a single humiliation or a single indignity.

Kennard, burning with wrath, tried to protest.

"Hold that cub!" commanded the leader of the party, almost as soon as the young Englishman's hot, indignant words had resounded above the din of overturned furniture. "And if he opens his mouth again throw him into the street!" And Kennard, terrified lest he should be parted from Esther, thought it wiser to hold his peace.

They looked at one another, like two young trapped beasts—not despairing, but trying to infuse courage one into the other by a look of confidence and of love. Esther, in fact, kept her eyes fixed on her good-looking English lover, firmly keeping down the shudder of loathing which went right through her when she saw those awful men coming nigh her. There was one especially whom she abominated worse than the others, a bandy-legged ruffian, who regarded her with a leer that caused her an almost physical nausea. He did not take part in the perquisition, but sat down in the centre of the room and sprawled over the table with the air of one who was in authority. The others addressed him as "citizen Merri," and alternately ridiculed and deferred to him. And there was another, equally hateful, a horrible, cadaverous creature, with huge bare feet thrust into sabots, and lank hair, thick with grime. He did most of the talking, even though his loquacity occasionally broke down in a racking cough, which literally seemed to tear at his chest, and left him panting, hoarse, and with beads of moisture upon his low, pallid forehead.

Of course, the men found nothing that could even remotely be termed compromising. Esther had been very prudent in deference to Kennard's advice; she also had very few possessions. Nevertheless, when the wretches had turned every article of furniture inside out, one of them asked curtly:

"What do we do next, citizen Merri?"

"Do?" broke in the cadaverous creature, even before Merri had time to reply. "Do? Why, take the wench to—to—"

He got no further, became helpless with coughing. Esther, quite instinctively, pushed the carafe of water towards him.

"Nothing of the sort!" riposted Merri sententiously. "The wench stays here!"

Both Esther and Jack had much ado to suppress an involuntary cry of relief, which at this unexpected pronouncement had risen to their lips.

The man with the cough tried to protest.

"But—" he began hoarsely.

"I said, the wench stays here!" broke in Merri peremptorily. "Ah ça!" he added, with a savage imprecation. "Do you command here, citizen Rateau, or do I?"

The other at once became humble, even cringing.

"You, of course, citizen," he rejoined in his hollow voice. "I would only remark—"

"Remark nothing," retorted the other curtly. "See to it that the cub is out of the house. And after that put a sentry outside the wench's door. No one to go in and out of here under any pretext whatever. Understand?"

Kennard this time uttered a cry of protest. The helplessness of his position exasperated him almost to madness. Two men were holding him tightly by his sinewy arms. With an Englishman's instinct for a fight, he would not only have tried, but also succeeded in knocking these two down, and taken the other four on after that, with quite a reasonable chance of success. That tuberculous creature, now! And that bandy-legged ruffian! Jack Kennard had been an amateur middle-weight champion in his day, and these brutes had no more science than an enraged bull! But even as he fought against that instinct he realised the futility of a struggle. The danger of it, too—not for himself, but for her. After all, they were not going to take her away to one of those awful places from which the only egress was the way to the guillotine; and if there was that amount of freedom there was bound to be some hope. At twenty there is always hope!

So when, in obedience to Merri's orders, the two ruffians began to drag him towards the door, he said firmly:

"Leave me alone. I'll go without this unnecessary struggling."

Then, before the wretches realised his intention, he had jerked himself free from them and run to Esther.

"Have no fear," he said to her in English, and in a rapid whisper. "I'll watch over you. The house opposite. I know the people. I'll manage it somehow. Be on the look-out."

They would not let him say more, and she only had the chance of responding firmly: "I am not afraid, and I'll be on the look-out." The next moment Merri's compeers seized him from behind—four of them this time.

Then, of course, prudence went to the winds. He hit out to the right and left. Knocked two of those recreants down, and already was prepared to seize Esther in his arms, make a wild dash for the door, and run with her, whither only God knew, when Rateau, that awful consumptive reprobate, crept slyly up behind him and dealt him a swift and heavy blow on the skull with his weighted stick. Kennard staggered, and the bandits closed upon him. Those on the floor had time to regain their feet. To make assurance doubly sure, one of them emulated Rateau's tactics, and hit the Englishman once more on the head from behind. After that, Kennard became inert; he had partly lost consciousness. His head ached furiously. Esther, numb with horror, saw him bundled out of the room. Rateau, coughing and spluttering, finally closed the door upon the unfortunate and the four brigands who had hold of him.

Only Merri and that awful Rateau had remained in the room. The latter, gasping for breath now, poured himself out a mugful of water and drank it down at one draught. Then he swore, because he wanted rum, or brandy, or even wine. Esther watched him and Merri, fascinated. Poor old Lucienne was quietly weeping behind her apron.

"Now then, my wench," Merri began abruptly, "suppose you sit down here and listen to what I have to say."

He pulled a chair close to him and, with one of those hideous leers which had already caused her to shudder, he beckoned her to sit. Esther obeyed as if in a dream. Her eyes were dilated like those of one in a waking trance. She moved mechanically, like a bird attracted by a serpent, terrified, yet unresisting. She felt utterly helpless between these two villainous brutes, and anxiety for her English lover seemed further to numb her senses. When she was sitting she turned her gaze, with an involuntary appeal for pity, upon the bandy-legged ruffian beside her. He laughed.

"No! I am not going to hurt you," he said with smooth condescension, which was far more loathsome to Esther's ears than his comrades' savage oaths had been. "You are pretty and you have pleased me. 'Tis no small matter, forsooth!" he added, with loud-voiced bombast, "to have earned the good-will of citizen Merri. You, my wench, are in luck's way. You realise what has occurred just now. You are amenable to the law which has decreed you to be suspect. I hold an order for your arrest. I can have you seized at once by my men, dragged to the Conciergerie, and from thence nothing can save you—neither your good looks nor the protection of citizen Merri. It means the guillotine. You understand that, don't you?"

She sat quite still; only her hands were clutched convulsively together. But she contrived to say quite firmly:

"I do, and I am not afraid."

Merri waved a huge and very dirty hand with a careless gesture.

"I know," he said with a harsh laugh. "They all say that, don't they, citizen Rateau?"

"Until the time comes," assented that worthy dryly.

"Until the time comes," reiterated the other. "Now, my wench," he added, once more turning to Esther, "I don't want that time to come. I don't want your pretty head to go rolling down into the basket, and to receive the slap on the face which the citizen executioner has of late taken to bestowing on those aristocratic cheeks which Mme. la Guillotine has finally blanched for ever. Like this, you see."

And the inhuman wretch took up one of the round cushions from the nearest chair, held it up at arm's length, as if it were a head which he held by the hair, and then slapped it twice with the palm of his left hand. The gesture was so horrible and withal so grotesque, that Esther closed her eyes with a shudder, and her pale cheeks took on a leaden hue. Merri laughed aloud and threw the cushion down again.

"Unpleasant, what? my pretty wench! Well, you know what to expect. . . unless," he added significantly, "you are reasonable and will listen to what I am about to tell you."

Esther was no fool, nor was she unsophisticated. These were not times when it was possible for any girl, however carefully nurtured and tenderly brought up, to remain ignorant of the realities and the brutalities of life. Even before Merri had put his abominable proposition before her, she knew what he was driving at. Marriage—marriage to him! that ignoble wretch, more vile than any dumb creature! In exchange for her life!

It was her turn now to laugh. The very thought of it was farcical in its very odiousness. Merri, who had embarked on his proposal with grandiloquent phraseology, suddenly paused, almost awed by that strange, hysterical laughter.

"By Satan and all his ghouls!" he cried, and jumped to his feet, his cheeks paling beneath the grime.

Then rage seized him at his own cowardice. His egregious vanity, wounded by that laughter, egged him on. He tried to seize Esther by the waist. But she, quick as some panther on the defence, had jumped up, too, and pounced upon a knife—the very one she had been using for that happy little supper with her lover a brief half hour ago. Unguarded, unthinking, acting just with a blind instinct, she raised it and cried hoarsely:

"If you dare touch me, I'll kill you!"

It was ludicrous, of course. A mouse threatening a tiger. The very next moment Rateau had seized her hand and quietly taken away the knife. Merri shook himself like a frowsy dog.

"Whew!" he exclaimed. "What a vixen! But," he added lightly, "I like her all the better for that—eh, Rateau? Give me a wench with a temperament, I say!"

But Esther, too, had recovered herself. She realised her helplessness, and gathered courage from the consciousness of it! Now she faced the infamous villain more calmly.

"I will never marry you," she said loudly and firmly. "Never! I am not afraid to die. I am not afraid of the guillotine. There is no shame attached to death. So now you may do as you please—denounce me, and send me to follow in the footsteps of my dear father, if you wish. But whilst I am alive you will never come nigh me. If you ever do but lay a finger upon me, it will be because I am dead and beyond the reach of your polluting touch. And now I have said all that I will ever say to you in this life. If you have a spark of humanity left in you, you will, at least, let me prepare for death in peace."

She went round to where poor old Lucienne still sat, like an insentient log, panic-stricken. She knelt down on the floor and rested her arm on the old woman's knees. The light of the lamp fell full upon her, her pale face, and mass of chestnut-brown hair. There was nothing about her at this moment to inflame a man's desire. She looked pathetic in her helplessness, and nearly lifeless through the intensity of her pallor, whilst the look in her eyes was almost maniacal.

Merri cursed and swore, tried to hearten himself by turning on his friend. But Rateau had collapsed—whether with excitement or the ravages of disease, it were impossible to say. He sat upon a low chair, his long legs, his violet-circled eyes staring out with a look of hebetude and overwhelming fatigue. Merri looked around him and shuddered. The atmosphere of the place had become strangely weird and uncanny; even the tablecloth, dragged half across the table, looked somehow like a shroud.

"What shall we do, Rateau?" he asked tremulously at last.

"Get out of this infernal place," replied the other huskily. "I feel as if I were in my grave-clothes already."

"Hold your tongue, you miserable coward! You'll make the aristo think that we are afraid."

"Well?" queried Rateau blandly. "Aren't you?"

"No!" replied Merri fiercely. "I'll go now because. . . because. . . well! because I have had enough to-day. And the wench sickens me. I wish to serve the Republic by marrying her, but just now I feel as if I should never really want her. So I'll go! But, understand!" he added, and turned once more to Esther, even though he could not bring himself to go nigh her again. "Understand that to-morrow I'll come again for my answer. In the meanwhile, you may think matters over, and, maybe, you'll arrive at a more reasonable frame of mind. You will not leave these rooms until I set you free. My men will remain as sentinels at your door."

He beckoned to Rateau, and the two men went out of the room without another word.

V

THE WHOLE OF THAT NIGHT Esther remained shut up in her apartment in the Petite Rue Taranne. All night she heard the measured tramp, the movements, the laughter and loud talking of men outside her door. Once or twice she tried to listen to what they said. But the doors and walls in these houses of old Paris were too stout to allow voices to filter through, save in the guise of a confused murmur. She would have felt horribly lonely and frightened but for the fact that in one window on the third floor in the house opposite the light of a lamp appeared like a glimmer of hope. Jack Kennard was there, on the watch. He had the window open and sat beside it until a very late hour; and after that he kept the light in, as a beacon, to bid her be of good cheer.

In the middle of the night he made an attempt to see her, hoping to catch the sentinels asleep or absent. But, having climbed the five stories of the house wherein she dwelt, he arrived on the landing outside her door and found there half a dozen ruffians squatting on the stone floor and engaged in playing hazard with a pack of greasy cards. That wretched consumptive, Rateau, was with them, and made a facetious remark as Kennard, pale and haggard, almost ghostlike, with a white bandage round his head, appeared upon the landing.

"Go back to bed, citizen," the odious creature said, with a raucous laugh. "We are taking care of your sweetheart for you."

Never in all his life had Jack Kennard felt so abjectly wretched as he did then, so miserably helpless. There was nothing that he could do, save to return to the lodging, which a kind friend had lent him for the occasion, and from whence he could, at any rate, see the windows behind which his beloved was watching and suffering.

When he went a few moments ago, he had left the porte cochere ajar. Now he pushed it open and stepped into the dark passage beyond. A tiny streak of light filtrated through a small curtained window in the concierge's lodge; it served to guide Kennard to the foot of the narrow stone staircase which led to the floors above. Just at the foot of the stairs, on the mat, a white paper glimmered in the dim shaft of light. He paused, puzzled, quite certain that the paper was not there five minutes ago when he went out. Oh! it may have fluttered in from the courtyard beyond, or from anywhere, driven by the draught. But, even so, with that mechanical action peculiar to most people under like circumstances, he stooped and picked up the paper, turned it over between his fingers, and saw that a few words were scribbled on it in pencil. The light was too dim to read by, so Kennard, still quite mechanically, kept the paper in his hand and went up to his room. There, by the light of the lamp, he read the few words scribbled in pencil:

"Wait in the street outside."

Nothing more. The message was obviously not intended for him, and yet. . . A strange excitement possessed him. If it should be! If. . . !

He had heard—everyone had—of the mysterious agencies that were at work, under cover of darkness, to aid the unfortunate, the innocent, the helpless. He had heard of that legendary English gentleman who had before now defied the closest vigilance of the Committees, and snatched their intended victims out of their murderous clutches, at times under their very eyes.

If this should be. . . ! He scarce dared put his hope into words. He could not bring himself really to believe. But he went. He ran downstairs and out into the street, took his stand under a projecting doorway nearly opposite the house which held the woman he loved, and leaning against the wall, he waited.

After many hours—it was then past three o'clock in the morning, and the sky of an inky blackness—he felt so numb that despite his will a kind of trance-like drowsiness overcame him. He could no longer stand on his feet; his knees were shaking; his head felt so heavy that he could not keep it up. It rolled round from shoulder to shoulder, as if his will no longer controlled it. And it ached furiously. Everything around him was very still. Even "Paris-by-Night," that grim and lurid giant, was for the moment at rest. A warm summer rain was falling; its gentle, pattering murmur into the gutter helped to lull Kennard's senses into somnolence. He was on the point of dropping off to sleep when something suddenly roused him. A noise of men shouting and laughing—familiar sounds enough in these squalid Paris streets.

But Kennard was wide awake now; numbness had given place to intense quivering of all his muscles, and super-keenness of his every sense. He peered into the darkness and strained his ears to hear. The sound certainly appeared to come from the house opposite, and there, too, it seemed as if something or things were moving. Men! More than one or two, surely! Kennard thought that he could distinguish at least three distinct voices; and there was that weird, racking cough which proclaimed the presence of Rateau.

Now the men were quite close to where he—Kennard—still stood cowering. A minute or two later they had passed down the street. Their hoarse voices soon died away in the distance. Kennard crept cautiously out of his hiding-place. Message or mere coincidence, he now blessed that mysterious scrap of paper. Had he remained in his room, he might really have dropped off to sleep and not heard these men going away. There were three of them at least—Kennard thought four. But, anyway, the number of watch-dogs outside the door of his beloved had considerably diminished. He felt that he had the strength to grapple with them, even if there were still three of them left. He, an athlete, English, and master of the art of self-defence; and they, a mere pack of drink-sodden brutes! Yes! He was quite sure he could do it. Quite sure that he could force his way into Esther's rooms and carry her off in his arms—whither? God alone knew. And God alone would provide.

Just for a moment he wondered if, while he was in that state of somnolence, other bandits had come to take the place of those that were going. But this thought he quickly dismissed. In any case, he felt a giant's strength in himself, and could not rest now till he had tried once more to see her. He crept very cautiously along; was satisfied that the street was deserted.

Already he had reached the house opposite, had pushed open the porte cochere, which was on the latch—when, without the slightest warning, he was suddenly attacked from behind, his arms seized and held behind his back with a vice-like grip, whilst a vigorous kick against the calves of his legs caused him to lose his footing and suddenly brought him down, sprawling and helpless, in the gutter, while in his ear there rang the hideous sound of the consumptive ruffian's racking cough.

"What shall we do with the cub now?" a raucous voice came out of the darkness.

"Let him lie there," was the quick response. "It'll teach him to interfere with the work of honest patriots."

Kennard, lying somewhat bruised and stunned, heard this decree with thankfulness. The bandits obviously thought him more hurt than he was, and if only they would leave him lying here, he would soon pick himself up and renew his attempt to go to Esther. He did not move, feigning unconsciousness, even though he felt rather than saw that hideous Rateau stooping over him, heard his stertorous breathing, the wheezing in his throat.

"Run and fetch a bit of cord, citizen Desmonts," the wretch said presently. "A trussed cub is safer than a loose one."

This dashed Kennard's hopes to a great extent. He felt that he must act quickly, before those brigands returned and rendered him completely helpless. He made a movement to rise—a movement so swift and sudden as only a trained athlete can make. But, quick as he was, that odious, wheezing creature was quicker still, and now, when Kennard had turned on his back, Rateau promptly sat on his chest, a dead weight, with long legs stretched out before him, coughing and spluttering, yet wholly at his ease.

Oh! the humiliating position for an amateur middle-weight champion to find himself in, with that drink-sodden—Kennard was sure that he was drink-sodden—consumptive sprawling on the top of him!

"Don't trouble, citizen Desmonts," the wretch cried out after his retreating companions. "I have what I want by me."

Very leisurely he pulled a coil of rope out of the capacious pocket of his tattered coat. Kennard could not see what he was doing, but felt it with supersensitive instinct all the time. He lay quite still beneath the weight of that miscreant, feigning unconsciousness, yet hardly able to breathe. That tuberculous caitiff was such a towering weight. But he tried to keep his faculties on the alert, ready for that surprise spring which would turn the tables, at the slightest false move on the part of Rateau.

But, as luck would have it, Rateau did not make a single false move. It was amazing with what dexterity he kept Kennard down, even while he contrived to pinion him with cords. An old sailor, probably, he seemed so dexterous with knots.

My God! the humiliation of it all. And Esther a helpless prisoner, inside that house not five paces away! Kennard's heavy, wearied eyes could perceive the light in her window, five stories above where he lay, in the gutter, a helpless log. Even now he gave a last desperate shriek:

"Esther!"

But in a second the abominable brigand's hand came down heavily upon his mouth, whilst a raucous voice spluttered rather than said, right through an awful fit of coughing:

"Another sound, and I'll gag as well as bind you, you young fool!"

After which, Kennard remained quite still.

VI

Esther, up in her little attic, knew nothing of what her English lover was even then suffering for her sake. She herself had passed, during the night, through every stage of horror and of fear. Soon after midnight that execrable brigand Rateau had poked his ugly, cadaverous face in at the door and peremptorily called for Lucienne. The woman, more dead than alive now with terror, had answered with mechanical obedience.

"I and my friends are thirsty," the man had commanded. "Go and fetch us a litre of eau-de-vie."

Poor Lucienne stammered a pitiable: "Where shall I go?"

"To the house at the sign of 'Le fort Samson,' in the Rue de Seine," replied Rateau curtly. "They'll serve you well if you mention my name."

Of course Lucienne protested. She was a decent woman, who had never been inside a cabaret in her life.

"Then it's time you began," was Rateau's dry comment, which was greeted with much laughter from his abominable companions.

Lucienne was forced to go. It would, of course, have been futile and madness to resist. This had occurred three hours since. The Rue de Seine was not far, but the poor woman had not returned. Esther was left with this additional horror weighing upon her soul. What had happened to her unfortunate servant? Visions of outrage and murder floated before the poor girl's tortured brain. At best, Lucienne was being kept out of the way in order to make her—Esther—feel more lonely and desperate! She remained at the window after that, watching that light in the house opposite and fingering her prayer-book, the only solace which she had. Her attic was so high up and the street so narrow, that she could not see what went on in the street below. At one time she heard a great to-do outside her door. It seemed as if some of the bloodhounds who were set to watch her had gone, or that others came. She really hardly cared which it was. Then she heard a great commotion coming from the street immediately beneath her: men shouting and laughing, and that awful creature's rasping cough.

At one moment she felt sure that Kennard had called to her by name. She heard his voice distinctly, raised as if in a despairing cry.

After that, all was still.

So still that she could hear her heart beating furiously, and then a tear falling from her eyes upon her open book. So still that the gentle patter of the rain sounded like a soothing lullaby. She was very young, and was very tired. Out, above the line of sloping roofs and chimney pots, the darkness of the sky was yielding to the first touch of dawn. The rain ceased. Everything became deathly still. Esther's head fell, wearied, upon her folded arms.

Then, suddenly, she was wide awake. Something had roused her. A noise. At first she could not tell what it was, but now she knew. It was the opening and shutting of the door behind her, and then a quick, stealthy footstep across the room. The horror of it all was unspeakable.

Esther remained as she had been, on her knees, mechanically fingering her prayer-book, unable to move, unable to utter a sound, as if paralysed. She knew that one of those abominable creatures had entered her room, was coming near her even now. She did not know who it was, only guessed it was Rateau, for she heard a raucous, stertorous wheeze. Yet she could not have then turned to look if her life had depended upon her doing so.

The whole thing had occurred in less than half a dozen heart-beats. The next moment the wretch was close to her. Mercifully she felt that her senses were leaving her. Even so, she felt that a handkerchief was being bound over her mouth to prevent her screaming. Wholly unnecessary this, for she could not have uttered a sound. Then she was lifted off the ground and carried across the room, then over the threshold. A vague, subconscious effort of will helped her to keep her head averted from that wheezing wretch who was carrying her. Thus she could see the landing, and two of those abominable watchdogs who had been set to guard her.

The ghostly grey light of dawn came peeping in through the narrow dormer window in the sloping roof, and faintly illumined their sprawling forms, stretched out at full length, with their heads buried in their folded arms and their naked legs looking pallid and weird in the dim light. Their stertorous breathing woke the echoes of the bare, stone walls. Esther shuddered and closed her eyes. She was now like an insentient log, without power, or thought, or will—almost without feeling.

Then, all at once, the coolness of the morning air caught her full in the face. She opened her eyes and tried to move, but those powerful arms held her more closely than before. Now she could have shrieked with horror. With returning consciousness the sense of her desperate position came on her with its full and ghastly significance, its awe-inspiring details. The grey dawn, the abandoned wretch who held her, and the stillness of this early morning hour, when not one pitying soul would be astir to lend her a helping hand or give her the solace of mute sympathy. So great, indeed, was this stillness that the click of the man's sabots upon the uneven pavement reverberated, ghoul-like and weird.

And it was through that awesome stillness that a sound suddenly struck her ear, which, in the instant, made her feel that she was not really alive, or, if alive, was sleeping and dreaming strange and impossible dreams. It was the sound of a voice, clear and firm, and with a wonderful ring of merriment in its tones, calling out just above a whisper, and in English, if you please:

"Look out, Ffoulkes! That young cub is as strong as a horse. He will give us all away if you are not careful."

A dream? Of course it was a dream, for the voice had sounded very close to her ear; so close, in fact, that. . . well! Esther was quite sure that her face still rested against the hideous, tattered, and grimy coat which that repulsive Rateau had been wearing all along. And there was the click of his sabots upon the pavement all the time. So, then, the voice and the merry, suppressed laughter which accompanied it, must all have been a part of her dream. How long this lasted she could not have told you. An hour and more, she thought, while the grey dawn yielded to the roseate hue of morning. Somehow, she no longer suffered either terror or foreboding. A subtle atmosphere of strength and of security seemed to encompass her. At one time she felt as if she were driven along in a car that jolted horribly, and when she moved her face and hands they came in contact with things that were fresh and green and smelt of the country. She was in darkness then, and more than three parts unconscious, but the handkerchief had been removed from her mouth. It seemed to her as if she could hear the voice of her Jack, but far away and indistinct; also the tramp of horses' hoofs and the creaking of cart-wheels, and at times that awful, rasping cough, which reminded her of the presence of a loathsome wretch, who should not have had a part in her soothing dream.

Thus many hours must have gone by.

Then, all at once, she was inside a house—a room, and she felt that she was being lowered very gently to the ground. She was on her feet, but she could not see where she was. There was furniture; a carpet; a ceiling; the man Rateau with the sabots and the dirty coat, and the merry English voice, and a pair of deep-set blue eyes, thoughtful and lazy and infinitely kind.

But before she could properly focus what she saw, everything began to whirl and to spin around her, to dance a wild and idiotic saraband, which caused her to laugh, and to laugh, until her throat felt choked and her eyes hot; after which she remembered nothing more.

VII

The first thing of which Esther Vincent was conscious, when she returned to her senses, was of her English lover kneeling beside her. She was lying on some kind of couch, and she could see his face in profile, for he had turned and was speaking to someone at the far end of the room.

"And was it you who knocked me down?" he was saying, "and sat on my chest, and trussed me like a fowl?"

"La! my dear sir," a lazy, pleasant voice riposted, "what else could I do? There was no time for explanations. You were half-crazed, and would not have understood. And you were ready to bring all the nightwatchmen about our ears."

"I am sorry!" Kennard said simply. "But how could I guess?"

"You couldn't," rejoined the other. "That is why I had to deal so summarily with you and with Mademoiselle Esther, not to speak of good old Lucienne, who had never, in her life, been inside a cabaret. You must all forgive me ere you start upon your journey. You are not out of the wood yet, remember. Though Paris is a long way behind, France itself is no longer a healthy place for any of you."

"But how did we ever get out of Paris? I was smothered under a pile of cabbages, with Lucienne on one side of me and Esther, unconscious, on the other. I could see nothing. I know we halted at the barrier. I thought we would be recognised, turned back! My God! how I trembled!"

"Bah!" broke in the other, with a careless laugh. "It is not so difficult as it seems. We have done it before—eh, Ffoulkes? A market-gardener's cart, a villainous wretch like myself to drive it, another hideous object like Sir Andrew Ffoulkes, Bart., to lead the scraggy nag, a couple of forged or stolen passports, plenty of English gold, and the deed is done!"

Esther's eyes were fixed upon the speaker. She marvelled now how she could have been so blind. The cadaverous face was nothing but a splendid use of grease paint! The rags! the dirt! the whole assumption of a hideous character was masterly! But there were the eyes, deep-set, and thoughtful and kind. How did she fail to guess?

"You are known as the Scarlet Pimpernel," she said suddenly. "Suzanne de Tournai was my friend. She told me. You saved her and her family, and now. . . oh, my God!" she exclaimed, "how shall we ever repay you?"

"By placing yourselves unreservedly in my friend Ffoulkes' hands," he replied gently. "He will lead you to safety and, if you wish it, to England."

"If we wish it!" Kennard sighed fervently.

"You are not coming with us, Blakeney?" queried Sir Andrew Ffoulkes, and it seemed to Esther's sensitive ears as if a tone of real anxiety and also of entreaty rang in the young man's voice.

"No, not this time," replied Sir Percy lightly. "I like my character of Rateau, and I don't want to give it up just yet. I have done nothing to arouse suspicion in the minds of my savoury compeers up at the Cabaret de la Liberte. I can easily keep this up for some time to come, and frankly I admire myself as citizen Rateau. I don't know when I have enjoyed a character so much!"

"You mean to return to the Cabaret de la Liberte!" exclaimed Sir Andrew.

"Why not?"

"You will be recognised!"

"Not before I have been of service to a good many unfortunates, I hope."

"But that awful cough of yours! Percy, you'll do yourself an injury with it one day."

"Not I! I like that cough. I practised it for a long time before I did it to perfection. Such a splendid wheeze! I must teach Tony to do it some day. Would you like to hear it now?"

He laughed, that perfect, delightful, lazy laugh of his, which carried every hearer with it along the path of light-hearted merriment. Then he broke into the awful cough of the consumptive Rateau. And Esther Vincent instinctively closed her eyes and shuddered.

X

“Needs Must—”

I

The children were all huddled up together in one corner of the room. Etienne and Valentine, the two eldest, had their arms round the little one. As for Lucile, she would have told you herself that she felt just like a bird between two snakes—terrified and fascinated—oh! especially by that little man with the pale face and the light grey eyes and the slender white hands unstained by toil, one of which rested lightly upon the desk, and was only clenched now and then at a word or a look from the other man or from Lucile herself.

But Commissary Lebel just tried to browbeat her. It was not difficult, for in truth she felt frightened enough already, with all this talk of “traitors” and that awful threat of the guillotine.

Lucile Clamette, however, would have remained splendidly loyal in spite of all these threats, if it had not been for the children. She was little mother to them; for father was a cripple, with speech and mind already impaired by creeping paralysis, and maman had died when little Josephine was born. And now those fiends threatened not only her, but Etienne who was not fourteen, and Valentine who was not much more than ten, with death, unless she—Lucile—broke the solemn word which she had given to M. le Marquis. At first she had tried to deny all knowledge of M. le Marquis’ whereabouts.

“I can assure M. le Commissaire that I do not know,” she had persisted quietly, even though her heart was beating so rapidly in her bosom that she felt as if she must choke.

“Call me citizen Commissary,” Lebel had riposted curtly. “I should take it as a proof that your aristocratic sentiments are not so deep-rooted as they appear to be.”

“Yes, citizen!” murmured Lucile, under her breath.

Then the other one, he with the pale eyes and the slender white hands, leaned forward over the desk, and the poor girl felt as if a mighty and unseen force was holding her tight, so tight that she could neither move, nor breathe, nor turn her gaze away from those pale, compelling eyes.

In the remote corner little Josephine was whimpering, and Etienne's big, dark eyes were fixed bravely upon his eldest sister.

"There, there! little citizeness," the awful man said, in a voice that sounded low and almost caressing, "there is nothing to be frightened of. No one is going to hurt you or your little family. We only want you to be reasonable. You have promised to your former employer that you would never tell anyone of his whereabouts. Well! we don't ask you to tell us anything.

"All that we want you to do is to write a letter to M. le Marquis—one that I myself will dictate to you. You have written to M. le Marquis before now, on business matters, have you not?"

"Yes, monsieur—yes, citizen," stammered Lucile through her tears. "Father was bailiff to M. le Marquis until he became a cripple and now I—"

"Do not write any letter, Lucile," Etienne suddenly broke in with forceful vehemence. "It is a trap set by these miscreants to entrap M. le Marquis."

There was a second's silence in the room after this sudden outburst on the part of the lad. Then the man with the pale face said quietly:

"Citizen Lebel, order the removal of that boy. Let him be kept in custody till he has learned to hold his tongue."

But before Lebel could speak to the two soldiers who were standing on guard at the door, Lucile had uttered a loud cry of agonised protest.

"No! no! monsieur!—that is citizen!" she implored. "Do not take Etienne away. He will be silent. . . I promise you that he will be silent. . . only do not take him away! Etienne, my little one!" she added, turning her tear-filled eyes to her brother, "I entreat thee to hold thy tongue!"

The others, too, clung to Etienne, and the lad, awed and subdued, relapsed into silence.

"Now then," resumed Lebel roughly, after a while, "let us get on with this business. I am sick to death of it. It has lasted far too long already."

He fixed his blood-shot eyes upon Lucile and continued gruffly:

"Now listen to me, my wench, for this is going to be my last word. Citizen Chauvelin here has already been very lenient with you by allowing this letter business. If I had my way I'd make you speak here and now. As it is, you either sit down and write the letter at citizen Chauvelin's dictation at once, or I send you with that impudent brother of yours and your imbecile father to jail, on a charge of treason against the State, for aiding and abetting the enemies of the Republic; and you know what the consequences of such a charge usually are. The other two brats will go to a House of Correction, there to be detained during the pleasure of the Committee of Public Safety. That is my last word," he reiterated fiercely. "Now, which is it to be?"

He paused, the girl's wan cheeks turned the colour of lead. She moistened her lips once or twice with her tongue; beads of perspiration appeared at the roots of her hair. She gazed helplessly at her tormentors, not daring to look on those three huddled-up little figures there in the corner. A few seconds sped away in silence. The man with the pale eyes rose and pushed his chair away. He went to the window, stood there with his back to the room, those slender white hands of his clasped behind him. Neither the commissary nor the girl appeared to interest him further. He was just gazing out of the window.

The other was still sprawling beside the desk, his large, coarse hand—how different his hands were!—was beating a devil's tatoo upon the arm of his chair.

After a few minutes, Lucile made a violent effort to compose herself, wiped the moisture from her pallid forehead and dried the tears which still hung upon her lashes. Then she rose from her chair and walked resolutely up to the desk.

"I will write the letter," she said simply.

Lebel gave a snort of satisfaction; but the other did not move from his position near the window. The boy, Etienne, had uttered a cry of passionate protest.

"Do not give M. le Marquis away, Lucile!" he said hotly. "I am not afraid to die."

But Lucile had made up her mind. How could she do otherwise, with these awful threats hanging over them all? She and Etienne and poor father gone, and the two young ones in one of those awful Houses of Correction, where children were taught to hate the Church, to shun the Sacraments, and to blaspheme God!

"What am I to write?" she asked dully, resolutely closing her ears against her brother's protest.

Lebel pushed pen, ink and paper towards her and she sat down, ready to begin.

"Write!" now came in a curt command from the man at the window. And Lucile wrote at his dictation:

Monsieur le Marquis,

We are in grave trouble. My brother Etienne and I have been arrested on a charge of treason. This means the guillotine for us and for poor father, who can no longer speak; and the two little ones are to be sent to one of those dreadful Houses of Correction, where children are taught to deny God and to blaspheme. You alone can save us, M. le Marquis; and I beg you on my knees to do it. The citizen Commissary here says that you have in your possession certain papers which are of great value to the State, and that if I can persuade you to give these up, Etienne, father and I and the little ones will be left unmolested. M. le Marquis, you once said that you could never adequately repay my poor father for all his devotion in your service. You can do it now, M. le Marquis, by saving us all. I will be at the chateau a week from to-day. I entreat you, M. le Marquis, to come to me then and to bring the papers with you; or if you can devise some other means of sending the papers to me, I will obey your behests.—I am, M. le Marquis' faithful and devoted servant,

Lucile Clamette

The pen dropped from the unfortunate girl's fingers. She buried her face in her hands and sobbed convulsively. The children were silent, awed and subdued—tired out, too. Only Etienne's dark eyes were fixed upon his sister with a look of mute reproach.

Lebel had made no attempt to interrupt the flow of his colleague's dictation. Only once or twice did a hastily smothered "What the—!" of astonishment escape his lips. Now, when the letter was finished and duly signed, he drew it to him and strewed the sand over it. Chauvelin, more impassive than ever, was once more gazing out of the window.

"How are the ci-devant aristos to get this letter?" the commissary asked.

"It must be put in the hollow tree which stands by the side of the stable gate at Montorgueil," whispered Lucile.

"And the aristos will find it there?"

"Yes. M. le Vicomte goes there once or twice a week to see if there is anything there from one of us."

"They are in hiding somewhere close by, then?"

But to this the girl gave no reply. Indeed, she felt as if any word now might choke her.

"Well, no matter where they are!" the inhuman wretch resumed, with brutal cynicism. "We've got them now—both of them. Marquis! Vicomte!" he added, and spat on the ground to express his contempt of such titles. "Citizens Montorgueil, father and son—that's all they are! And as such they'll walk up in state to make their bow to Mme. la Guillotine!"

"May we go now?" stammered Lucile through her tears.

Lebel nodded in assent, and the girl rose and turned to walk towards the door. She called to the children, and the little ones clustered round her skirts like chicks around the mother-hen. Only Etienne remained aloof, wrathful against his sister for what he deemed her treachery. "Women have no sense of honour!" he muttered to himself, with all the pride of conscious manhood. But Lucile felt more than ever like a bird who is vainly trying to evade the clutches of a fowler. She gathered the two little ones around her. Then, with a cry like a wounded doe she ran quickly out of the room.

II

As soon as the sound of the children's footsteps had died away down the corridor, Lebel turned with a grunt to his still silent companion.

"And now, citizen Chauvelin," he said roughly, "perhaps you will be good enough to explain what is the meaning of all this tomfoolery."

"Tomfoolery, citizen?" queried the other blandly. "What tomfoolery, pray?"

"Why, about those papers!" growled Lebel savagely. "Curse you for an interfering busybody! It was I who got information that those pestilential aristos, the Montorgueils, far from having fled the country are in hiding somewhere in my district. I could have made the girl give up their hiding-place pretty soon, without any help from you. What right had you to interfere, I should like to know?"

"You know quite well what right I had, citizen Lebel," replied Chauvelin with perfect composure. "The right conferred upon me by the Committee of Public Safety, of whom I am still an unworthy member. They sent me down here to lend you a hand in an investigation which is of grave importance to them."

"I know that!" retorted Lebel sulkily. "But why have invented the story of the papers?"

"It is no invention, citizen," rejoined Chauvelin with slow emphasis. "The papers do exist. They are actually in the possession of the Montorgueils, father and son. To capture the two aristos would be not only a blunder, but criminal folly, unless we can lay hands on the papers at the same time."

"But what in Satan's name are those papers?" exclaimed Lebel with a fierce oath.

"Think, citizen Lebel! Think!" was Chauvelin's cool rejoinder. "Methinks you might arrive at a pretty shrewd guess." Then, as the other's bluster and bounce suddenly collapsed upon his colleague's calm, accusing gaze, the latter continued with impressive deliberation:

"The papers which the two aristos have in their possession, citizen, are receipts for money, for bribes paid to various members of the Committee of Public Safety by Royalist agents for the overthrow of our glorious Republic. You know all about them, do you not?"

While Chauvelin spoke, a look of furtive terror had crept into Lebel's eyes; his cheeks became the colour of lead. But even so, he tried to keep up an air of incredulity and of amazement.

"I?" he exclaimed. "What do you mean, citizen Chauvelin? What should I know about it?"

"Some of those receipts are signed with your name, citizen Lebel," retorted Chauvelin forcefully. "Bah!" he added, and a tone of savage contempt crept into his even, calm voice now. "Heriot, Foucquier, Ducros and the whole gang of you are in it up to the neck: trafficking with our enemies, trading with England, taking bribes from every quarter for working against the safety of the Republic. Ah! if I had my way, I would let the hatred of those aristos take its course. I would let the Montorgueils and the whole pack of Royalist agents publish those infamous proofs of your treachery and of your baseness to the entire world, and send the whole lot of you to the guillotine!"

He had spoken with so much concentrated fury, and the hatred and contempt expressed in his pale eyes were so fierce that an involuntary ice-cold shiver ran down the length of Lebel's spine. But, even so, he would not give in; he tried to sneer and to keep up something of his former surly defiance.

"Bah!" he exclaimed, and with a lowering glance gave hatred for hatred, and contempt for contempt. "What can you do? An I am not mistaken, there is no more discredited man in France to-day than the unsuccessful tracker of the Scarlet Pimpernel."

The taunt went home. It was Chauvelin's turn now to lose countenance, to pale to the lips. The glow of virtuous indignation died out of his eyes, his look became furtive and shamed.

"You are right, citizen Lebel," he said calmly after a while. "Recriminations between us are out of place. I am a discredited man, as you say. Perhaps it would have been better if the Committee had sent me long ago to expiate my failures on the guillotine. I should at least not have suffered, as I am suffering now, daily, hourly humiliation at thought of the triumph of an enemy, whom I hate with a passion which consumes my very soul. But do not let us speak of me," he went on quietly. "There are graver affairs at stake just now than mine own."

Lebel said nothing more for the moment. Perhaps he was satisfied at the success of his taunt, even though the terror within his craven soul still caused the cold shiver to course up and down his spine. Chauvelin had once more turned to the window; his gaze was fixed upon the distance far away. The window gave on the North. That way, in a straight line, lay Calais, Boulogne, England—where he had been made to suffer such bitter humiliation at the hands of his elusive enemy. And immediately before him was Paris, where the very walls seemed to echo that mocking laugh of the daring Englishman which would haunt him even to his grave.

Lebel, unnerved by his colleague's silence, broke in gruffly at last:

"Well then, citizen," he said, with a feeble attempt at another sneer, "if you are not thinking of sending us all to the guillotine just yet, perhaps you will be good enough to explain just how the matter stands?"

"Fairly simply, alas!" replied Chauvelin dryly. "The two Montorgueils, father and son, under assumed names, were the Royalist agents who succeeded in suborning men such as you, citizen—the whole gang of you. We have tracked them down, to this district, have confiscated their lands and ransacked the old chateau for valuables and so on. Two days later, the first of a series of pestilential anonymous letters reached the Committee of Public Safety, threatening the publication of a whole series of compromising documents if the Marquis and the Vicomte de Montorgueil were in any way molested, and if all the Montorgueil property is not immediately restored."

"I suppose it is quite certain that those receipts and documents do exist?" suggested Lebel.

"Perfectly certain. One of the receipts, signed by Heriot, was sent as a specimen."

"My God!" exclaimed Lebel, and wiped the cold sweat from his brow.

"Yes, you'll all want help from somewhere," retorted Chauvelin coolly. "From above or from below, what? if the people get to know what miscreants you are. I do believe," he added, with a vicious snap of his thin lips, "that they would cheat the guillotine of you and, in the end, drag you out of the tumbrils and tear you to pieces limb from limb!"

Once more that look of furtive terror crept into the commissary's bloodshot eyes.

"Thank the Lord," he muttered, "that we were able to get hold of the wench Clamette!"

"At my suggestion," retorted Chauvelin curtly. "I always believe in threatening the weak if you want to coerce the strong. The Montorgueils cannot resist the wench's appeal. Even if they do at first, we can apply the screw by clapping one of the young ones in gaol. Within a week we shall have those papers, citizen Lebel; and if, in the meanwhile, no one commits a further blunder, we can close the trap on the Montorgueils without further trouble."

Lebel said nothing more, and after a while Chauvelin went back to the desk, picked up the letter which poor Lucile had written and watered with her tears, folded it deliberately and slipped it into the inner pocket of his coat.

"What are you going to do?" queried Lebel anxiously.

"Drop this letter into the hollow tree by the side of the stable gate at Montorgueil," replied Chauvelin simply.

"What?" exclaimed the other. "Yourself?"

"Why, of course! Think you I would entrust such an errand to another living soul?"

III

A couple of hours later, when the two children had had their dinner and had settled down to play in the garden, and father been cosily tucked up for his afternoon sleep, Lucile called her brother Etienne to her. The boy had not spoken to her since that terrible time spent in the presence of those two awful men. He had eaten no dinner, only sat glowering, staring straight out before him, from time to time throwing a look of burning reproach upon his sister. Now, when she called to him, he tried to run away, was halfway up the stairs before she could seize hold of him.

"Etienne, mon petit!" she implored, as her arms closed around his shrinking figure.

"Let me go, Lucile!" the boy pleaded obstinately.

"Mon petit, listen to me!" she pleaded. "All is not lost, if you will stand by me."

"All is lost, Lucile!" Etienne cried, striving to keep back a flood of passionate tears. "Honour is lost. Your treachery has disgraced us all. If M. le Marquis and M. le Vicomte are brought to the guillotine, their blood will be upon our heads."

"Upon mine alone, my little Etienne," she said sadly. "But God alone can judge me. It was a terrible alternative: M. le Marquis, or you and Valentine and little Josephine and poor father, who is so helpless! But don't let us talk of it. All is not lost, I am sure. The last time that I spoke with M. le Marquis—it was in February, do you remember?—he was full of hope, and oh! so kind. Well, he told me then that if ever I or any of us here were in such grave trouble that we did not know where to turn, one of us was to put on our very oldest clothes, look as like a bare-footed beggar as we could, and then go to Paris to a place called the Cabaret de la Liberte in the Rue Christine. There we were to ask for the citizen Rateau, and we were to tell him all our troubles, whatever they might be. Well! we are in such trouble now, mon petit, that we don't know where to turn. Put on thy very oldest clothes, little one, and run bare-footed into Paris, find the citizen Rateau and tell him just what has happened: the letter which they have forced me to write, the threats which they held over me if I did not write it—everything. Dost hear?"

Already the boy's eyes were glowing. The thought that he individually could do something to retrieve the awful shame of his sister's treachery spurred him to activity. It needed no persuasion on Lucile's part to induce him to go. She made him put on some old clothes and stuffed a piece of bread and cheese into his breeches pocket.

It was close upon a couple of leagues to Paris, but that run was one of the happiest which Etienne had ever made. And he did it bare-footed, too, feeling neither fatigue nor soreness, despite the hardness of the road after a two weeks' drought, which had turned mud into hard cakes and ruts into fissures which tore the lad's feet till they bled.

He did not reach the Cabaret de la Liberte till nightfall, and when he got there he hardly dared to enter. The filth, the squalor, the hoarse voices which rose from that cellar-like place below the level of the street, repelled the country-bred lad. Were it not for the desperate urgency of his errand he never would have dared to enter. As it was, the fumes of alcohol and steaming, dirty clothes nearly choked him, and he could scarce stammer the name of "citizen Rateau" when a gruff voice presently demanded his purpose.

He realised now how tired he was and how hungry. He had not thought to pause in order to consume the small provision of bread and cheese wherewith thoughtful Lucile had provided him. Now he was ready to faint when a loud guffaw, which echoed from one end of the horrible place to the other, greeted his timid request.

"Citizen Rateau!" the same gruff voice called out hilariously. "Why, there he is! Here, citizen! there's a blooming aristo to see you."

Etienne turned his weary eyes to the corner which was being indicated to him. There he saw a huge creature sprawling across a bench, with long, powerful limbs stretched out before him. Citizen Rateau was clothed, rather than dressed, in a soiled shirt, ragged breeches and tattered stockings, with shoes down at heel and faded crimson cap. His face looked congested and sunken about the eyes; he appeared to be asleep, for stertorous breathing came at intervals from between his parted lips, whilst every now and then a racking cough seemed to tear at his broad chest.

Etienne gave him one look, shuddering with horror, despite himself, at the aspect of this bloated wretch from whom salvation was to come. The whole place seemed to him hideous and loathsome in the extreme. What it all meant he could not understand; all that he knew was that this seemed like another hideous trap into which he and Lucile had fallen, and that he must fly from it—fly at all costs, before he betrayed M. le Marquis still further to these drink-sodden brutes. Another moment, and he feared that he might faint. The din of a bibulous song rang in his ears, the reek of alcohol turned him giddy and sick. He had only just enough strength to turn and totter back into the open. There his senses reeled, the lights in the houses opposite began to dance wildly before his eyes, after which he remembered nothing more.

IV

THERE IS NOTHING NOW IN the whole countryside quite so desolate and forlorn as the chateau of Montorgueil, with its once magnificent park, now overgrown with weeds, its encircling walls broken down, its terraces devastated, and its stately gates rusty and torn.

Just by the side of what was known in happier times as the stable gate there stands a hollow tree. It is not inside the park, but just outside, and shelters the narrow lane, which skirts the park walls, against the blaze of the afternoon sun.

Its beneficent shade is a favourite spot for an afternoon siesta, for there is a bit of green sward under the tree, and all along the side of the road. But as the shades of evening gather in, the lane is usually deserted, shunned by the neighbouring peasantry on account of its eerie loneliness, so different to the former bustle which used to reign around the park gates when M. le Marquis and his family were still in residence. Nor does the lane lead anywhere, for it is a mere loop which gives on the main road at either end.

Henri de Montorgueil chose a peculiarly dark night in mid-September for one of his periodical visits to the hollow-tree. It was close on nine o'clock when he passed stealthily down the lane, keeping close to the park wall. A soft rain was falling, the first since the prolonged drought, and though it made the road heavy and slippery in places, it helped to deaden the sound of the young man's furtive footsteps. The air, except for the patter of the rain, was absolutely still. Henri de Montorgueil paused from time to time, with neck craned forward, every sense on the alert, listening, like any poor, hunted beast, for the slightest sound which might betray the approach of danger.

As many a time before, he reached the hollow tree in safety, felt for and found in the usual place the letter which the unfortunate girl Lucile had written to him. Then, with it in his hand, he turned to the stable gate. It had long since ceased to be kept locked and barred. Pillaged and ransacked by order of the Committee of Public Safety, there was nothing left inside the park walls worth keeping under lock and key.

Henri slipped stealthily through the gates and made his way along the drive. Every stone, every nook and cranny of his former home was familiar to him, and anon he turned into a shed where in former times wheelbarrows and garden tools were wont to be kept. Now it was full of debris, lumber of every sort. A more safe or secluded spot could not be imagined. Henri crouched in the furthermost corner of the shed. Then from his belt he detached a small dark lanthorn, opened its shutter, and with the aid of the tiny, dim light read the contents of the letter. For a long while after that he remained quite still, as still as a man who has received a stunning blow on the head and has partly lost consciousness. The blow was indeed a staggering one. Lucile Clamette, with the invincible power of her own helplessness, was demanding the surrender of a weapon which had been a safeguard for the Montorgueils all this while. The papers which compromised a number of influential members of the Committee of Public Safety had been the most perfect arms of defence against persecution and spoliation.

And now these were to be given up: Oh! there could be no question of that. Even before consulting with his father, Henri knew that the papers would have to be given up. They were clever, those revolutionaries. The thought of holding innocent children as hostages could only have originated in minds attuned to the villainies of devils. But it was unthinkable that the children should suffer.

After a while the young man roused himself from the torpor into which the suddenness of this awful blow had plunged him. By the light of the lanthorn he began to write upon a sheet of paper which he had torn from his pocket-book.

"My Dear Lucile," he wrote, "As you say, our debt to your father and to you all never could be adequately repaid. You and the children shall never suffer whilst we have the power to save you. You will find the papers in the receptacle you know of inside the chimney of what used to be my mother's boudoir. You will find the receptacle unlocked. One day before the term you name I myself will place the papers there for you. With them, my father and I do give up our lives to save you and the little ones from the persecution of those fiends. May the good God guard you all."

He signed the letter with his initials, H. de M. Then he crept back to the gate and dropped the message into the hollow of the tree.

A quarter of an hour later Henri de Montorgueil was wending his way back to the hiding place which had sheltered him and his father for so long. Silence and darkness then held undisputed sway once more around the hollow tree. Even the rain had ceased its gentle pattering. Anon from far away came the sound of a church bell striking the hour of ten. Then nothing more.

A few more minutes of absolute silence, then something dark and furtive began to move out of the long grass which bordered the roadside—something that in movement was almost like a snake. It dragged itself along close to the ground, making no sound as it moved. Soon it reached the hollow tree, rose to the height of a man and flattened itself against the tree-trunk. Then it put out a hand, felt for the hollow receptacle and groped for the missive which Henri de Montorgueil had dropped in there a while ago.

The next moment a tiny ray of light gleamed through the darkness like a star. A small, almost fragile, figure of a man, dressed in the mud-stained clothes of a country yokel, had turned up the shutter of a small lanthorn. By its flickering light he deciphered the letter which Henri de Montorgueil had written to Lucile Clamette.

"One day before the term you name I myself will place the papers there for you."

A sigh of satisfaction, quickly suppressed, came through his thin, colourless lips, and the light of the lanthorn caught the flash of triumph in his pale, inscrutable eyes.

Then the light was extinguished. Impenetrable darkness swallowed up that slender, mysterious figure again.

V

Six days had gone by since Chauvelin had delivered his cruel "either—or" to poor little Lucile Clamette; three since he had found Henri de Montorgueil's reply to the girl's appeal in the hollow of the tree. Since then he had made a careful investigation of the chateau, and soon was able to settle it in his own mind as to which room had been Madame la Marquise's boudoir in the past. It was a small apartment, having direct access on the first landing of the staircase, and the one window gave on the rose garden at the back of the house. Inside the monumental hearth, at an arm's length up the wide chimney, a receptacle had been contrived in the brickwork, with a small iron door which opened and closed with a secret spring. Chauvelin, whom his nefarious calling had rendered proficient in such matters, had soon mastered the workings of that spring. He could now open and close the iron door at will.

Up to a late hour on the sixth night of this weary waiting, the receptacle inside the chimney was still empty. That night Chauvelin had determined to spend at the chateau. He could not have rested elsewhere.

Even his colleague Lebel could not know what the possession of those papers would mean to the discredited agent of the Committee of Public Safety. With them in his hands, he could demand rehabilitation, and could purchase immunity from those sneers which had been so galling to his arrogant soul—sneers which had become more and more marked, more and more unendurable, and more and more menacing, as he piled up failure on failure with every encounter with the Scarlet Pimpernel.

Immunity and rehabilitation! This would mean that he could once more measure his wits and his power with that audacious enemy who had brought about his downfall.

"In the name of Satan, bring us those papers!" Robespierre himself had cried with unwonted passion, ere he sent him out on this important mission. "We none of us could stand the scandal of such disclosures. It would mean absolute ruin for us all."

And Chauvelin that night, as soon as the shades of evening had drawn in, took up his stand in the chateau, in the small inner room which was contiguous to the boudoir.

Here he sat, beside the open window, for hour upon hour, his every sense on the alert, listening for the first footfall upon the gravel path below. Though the hours went by leaden-footed, he was neither excited nor anxious. The Clamette family was such a precious hostage that the Montorgueils were bound to comply with Lucile's demand for the papers by every dictate of honour and of humanity.

"While we have those people in our power," Chauvelin had reiterated to himself more than once during the course of his long vigil, "even that meddlesome Scarlet Pimpernel can do nothing to save those cursed Montorgueils."

The night was dark and still. Not a breath of air stirred the branches of the trees or the shrubberies in the park; any footsteps, however wary, must echo through that perfect and absolute silence. Chauvelin's keen, pale eyes tried to pierce the gloom in the direction whence in all probability the aristo would come. Vaguely he wondered if it would be Henri de Montorgueil or the old Marquis himself who would bring the papers.

"Bah! whichever one it is," he muttered, "we can easily get the other, once those abominable papers are in our hands. And even if both the aristos escape," he added mentally, "'tis no matter, once we have the papers."

Anon, far away a distant church bell struck the midnight hour. The stillness of the air had become oppressive. A kind of torpor born of intense fatigue lulled the Terrorist's senses to somnolence. His head fell forward on his breast. . .

VI

Then suddenly a shiver of excitement went right through him. He was fully awake now, with glowing eyes wide open and the icy calm of perfect confidence ruling every nerve. The sound of stealthy footsteps had reached his ear.

He could see nothing, either outside or in; but his fingers felt for the pistol which he carried in his belt. The aristo was evidently alone; only one solitary footstep was approaching the chateau.

Chauvelin had left the door ajar which gave on the boudoir. The staircase was on the other side of that fateful room, and the door leading to that was closed. A few minutes of tense expectancy went by. Then through the silence there came the sound of furtive foot-steps on the stairs, the creaking of a loose board and finally the stealthy opening of the door.

In all his adventurous career Chauvelin had never felt so calm. His heart beat quite evenly, his senses were undisturbed by the slightest tingling of his nerves. The stealthy sounds in the next room brought the movements of the aristo perfectly clear before his mental vision. The latter was carrying a small dark lanthorn. As soon as he entered he flashed its light about the room. Then he deposited the lanthorn on the floor, close beside the hearth, and started to feel up the chimney for the hidden receptacle.

Chauvelin watched him now like a cat watches a mouse, savouring these few moments of anticipated triumph. He pushed open the door noiselessly which gave on the boudoir. By the feeble light of the lanthorn on the ground he could only see the vague outline of the aristo's back, bending forward to his task; but a thrill went through him as he saw a bundle of papers lying on the ground close by.

Everything was ready; the trap was set. Here was a complete victory at last. It was obviously the young Vicomte de Montorgueil who had come to do the deed. His head was up the chimney even now. The old Marquis's back would have looked narrower and more fragile. Chauvelin held his breath; then he gave a sharp little cough, and took the pistol from his belt.

The sound caused the aristo to turn, and the next moment a loud and merry laugh roused the dormant echoes of the old chateau, whilst a pleasant, drawly voice said in English:

"I am demmed if this is not my dear old friend M. Chambertin! Zounds, sir! who'd have thought of meeting you here?"

Had a cannon suddenly exploded at Chauvelin's feet he would, I think, have felt less unnerved. For the space of two heart-beats he stood there, rooted to the spot, his eyes glued on his arch-enemy, that execrated Scarlet Pimpernel, whose mocking glance, even through the intervening gloom, seemed to have deprived him of consciousness. But that phase of helplessness only lasted for a moment; the next, all the marvellous possibilities of this encounter flashed through the Terrorist's keen mind.

Everything was ready; the trap was set! The unfortunate Clamettes were still the bait which now would bring a far more noble quarry into the mesh than even he—Chauvelin—had dared to hope.

He raised his pistol, ready to fire. But already Sir Percy Blakeney was on him, and with a swift movement, which the other was too weak to resist, he wrenched the weapon from his enemy's grasp.

"Why, how hasty you are, my dear M. Chambertin," he said lightly. "Surely you are not in such a hurry to put a demmed bullet into me!"

The position now was one which would have made even a braver man than Chauvelin quake. He stood alone and unarmed in face of an enemy from whom he could expect no mercy. But, even so, his first thought was not of escape. He had not only apprised his own danger, but also the immense power which he held whilst the Clamettes remained as hostages in the hands of his colleague Lebel.

"You have me at a disadvantage, Sir Percy," he said, speaking every whit as coolly as his foe. "But only momentarily. You can kill me, of course; but if I do not return from this expedition not only safe and sound, but with a certain packet of papers in my hands, my colleague Lebel has instructions to proceed at once against the girl Clamette and the whole family."

"I know that well enough," rejoined Sir Percy with a quaint laugh. "I know what venomous reptiles you and those of your kidney are. You certainly do owe your life at the present moment to the unfortunate girl whom you are persecuting with such infamous callousness."

Chauvelin drew a sigh of relief. The situation was shaping itself more to his satisfaction already. Through the gloom he could vaguely discern the Englishman's massive form standing a few paces away, one hand buried in his breeches pockets, the other still holding the pistol. On the ground close by the hearth was the small lanthorn, and in its dim light the packet of papers gleamed white and tempting in the darkness. Chauvelin's keen eyes had fastened on it, saw the form of receipt for money with Heriot's signature, which he recognised, on the top.

He himself had never felt so calm. The only thing he could regret was that he was alone. Half a dozen men now, and this impudent foe could indeed be brought to his knees. And this time there would be no risks taken, no chances for escape. Somehow it seemed to Chauvelin as if something of the Scarlet Pimpernel's audacity and foresight had gone from him. As he stood there, looking broad and physically powerful, there was something wavering and undecided in his attitude, as if the edge had been taken off his former recklessness and enthusiasm. He had brought the compromising papers here, had no doubt helped the Montorgueils to escape; but while Lucile Clamette and her family were under the eye of Lebel no amount of impudence could force a successful bargaining.

It was Chauvelin now who appeared the more keen and the more alert; the Englishman seemed undecided what to do next, remained silent, toying with the pistol. He even smothered a yawn. Chauvelin saw his opportunity. With the quick movement of a cat pouncing upon a mouse he stooped and seized that packet of papers, would then and there have made a dash for the door with them, only that, as he seized the packet, the string which held it together gave way and the papers were scattered all over the floor.

Receipts for money? Compromising letters? No! Blank sheets of paper, all of them—all except the one which had lain tantalisingly on the top: the one receipt signed by citizen Heriot. Sir Percy laughed lightly:

"Did you really think, my good friend," he said, "that I would be such a demmed fool as to place my best weapon so readily to your hand?"

"Your best weapon, Sir Percy!" retorted Chauvelin, with a sneer. "What use is it to you while we hold Lucile Clamette?"

"While I hold Lucile Clamette, you mean, my dear Monsieur Chambertin," riposted Blakeney with elaborate blandness.

"You hold Lucile Clamette? Bah! I defy you to drag a whole family like that out of our clutches. The man a cripple, the children helpless! And you think they can escape our vigilance when all our men are warned! How do you think they are going to get across the river, Sir Percy, when every bridge is closely watched? How will they get across Paris, when at every gate our men are on the look-out for them?"

"They can't do it, my dear Monsieur Chambertin," rejoined Sir Percy blandly, "else I were not here."

Then, as Chauvelin, fuming, irritated despite himself, as he always was when he encountered that impudent Englishman, shrugged his shoulders in token of contempt, Blakeney's powerful grasp suddenly clutched his arm.

"Let us understand one another, my good M. Chambertin," he said coolly. "Those unfortunate Clamettes, as you say, are too helpless and too numerous to smuggle across Paris with any chance of success. Therefore I look to you to take them under your protection. They are all stowed away comfortably at this moment in a conveyance which I have provided for them. That conveyance is waiting at the bridgehead now. We could not cross without your help; we could not get across Paris without your august presence and your tricolour scarf of office. So you are coming with us, my dear M. Chambertin," he continued, and, with force which was quite irresistible, he began to drag his enemy after him towards the door. "You are going to sit in that conveyance with the Clamettes, and I myself will have the honour to drive you. And at every bridgehead you will show your pleasing countenance and your scarf of office to the guard and demand free passage for yourself and your family, as a representative member of the Committee of Public Safety. And then we'll enter Paris by the Porte d'Ivry and leave it by the Batignolles; and everywhere your charming presence will lull the guards' suspicions to rest. I pray you, come! There is no time to consider! At noon to-morrow, without a moment's grace, my friend Sir Andrew Ffoulkes, who has the papers in his possession, will dispose of them as he thinks best unless I myself do claim them from him."

While he spoke he continued to drag his enemy along with him, with an assurance and an impudence which were past belief. Chauvelin was trying to collect his thoughts; a whirl of conflicting plans were running riot in his mind. The Scarlet Pimpernel in his power! At any point on the road he could deliver him up to the nearest guard. . . then still hold the Clamettes and demand the papers. . .

"Too late, my dear Monsieur Chambertin!" Sir Percy's mocking voice broke in, as if divining his thoughts. "You do not know where to find my friend Ffoulkes, and at noon to-morrow, if I do not arrive to claim those papers, there will not be a single ragamuffin in Paris who will not be crying your shame and that of your precious colleagues upon the housetops."

Chauvelin's whole nervous system was writhing with the feeling of impotence. Mechanically, unresisting now, he followed his enemy down the main staircase of the chateau and out through the wide open gates. He could not bring himself to believe that he had been so completely foiled, that this impudent adventurer had him once more in the hollow of his hand.

"In the name of Satan, bring us back those papers!" Robespierre had commanded. And now he—Chauvelin—was left in a maze of doubt;

and the vital alternative was hammering in his brain: "The Scarlet Pimpernel—or those papers—" Which, in Satan's name, was the more important? Passion whispered "The Scarlet Pimpernel!" but common sense and the future of his party, the whole future of the Revolution mayhap, demanded those compromising papers. And all the while he followed that relentless enemy through the avenues of the park and down the lonely lane. Overhead the trees of the forest of Sucy, nodding in a gentle breeze, seemed to mock his perplexity.

He had not arrived at a definite decision when the river came in sight, and when anon a carriage lanthorn threw a shaft of dim light through the mist-laden air. Now he felt as if he were in a dream. He was thrust unresisting into a closed chaise, wherein he felt the presence of several other people—children, an old man who was muttering ceaselessly. As in a dream he answered questions at the bridge to a guard whom he knew well.

"You know me—Armand Chauvelin, of the Committee of Public Safety!"

As in a dream, he heard the curt words of command:

"Pass on, in the name of the Republic!"

And all the while the thought hammered in his brain: "Something must be done! This is impossible! This cannot be! It is not I—Chauvelin—who am sitting here, helpless, unresisting. It is not that impudent Scarlet Pimpernel who is sitting there before me on the box, driving me to utter humiliation!"

And yet it was all true. All real. The Clamette children were sitting in front of him, clinging to Lucile, terrified of him even now. The old man was beside him—imbecile and not understanding. The boy Etienne was up on the box next to that audacious adventurer, whose broad back appeared to Chauvelin like a rock on which all his hopes and dreams must for ever be shattered.

The chaise rattled triumphantly through the Batignolles. It was then broad daylight. A brilliant early autumn day after the rains. The sun, the keen air, all mocked Chauvelin's helplessness, his humiliation. Long before noon they passed St. Denis. Here the barouche turned off the main road, halted at a small wayside house—nothing more than a cottage. After which everything seemed more dreamlike than ever. All that Chauvelin remembered of it afterwards was that he was once more alone in a room with his enemy, who had demanded his signature to a number of safe-conducts, ere he finally handed over the packet of papers to him.

"How do I know that they are all here?" he heard himself vaguely muttering, while his trembling fingers handled that precious packet.

"That's just it!" his tormentor retorted airily. "You don't know. I don't know myself," he added, with a light laugh. "And, personally, I don't see how either of us can possibly ascertain. In the meanwhile, I must bid you au revoir, my dear M. Chambertin. I am sorry that I cannot provide you with a conveyance, and you will have to walk a league or more ere you meet one, I fear me. We, in the meanwhile, will be well on our way to Dieppe, where my yacht, the Day Dream, lies at anchor, and I do not think that it will be worth your while to try and overtake us. I thank you for the safe-conducts. They will make our journey exceedingly pleasant. Shall I give your regards to M. le Marquis de Montorgueil or to M. le Vicomte? They are on board the Day Dream, you know. Oh! and I was forgetting! Lady Blakeney desired to be remembered to you."

The next moment he was gone. Chauvelin, standing at the window of the wayside house, saw Sir Percy Blakeney once more mount the box of the chaise. This time he had Sir Andrew Ffoulkes beside him. The Clamette family were huddled together—happy and free—inside the vehicle. After which there was the usual clatter of horses' hoofs, the creaking of wheels, the rattle of chains. Chauvelin saw and heard nothing of that. All that he saw at the last was Sir Percy's slender hand, waving him a last adieu.

After which he was left alone with his thoughts. The packet of papers was in his hand. He fingered it, felt its crispness, clutched it with a fierce gesture, which was followed by a long-drawn-out sigh of intense bitterness.

No one would ever know what it had cost him to obtain these papers. No one would ever know how much he had sacrificed of pride, revenge and hate in order to save a few shreds of his own party's honour.

XI

A Battle of Wits

What had happened was this:

Tournefort, one of the ablest of the many sleuth-hounds employed by the Committee of Public Safety, was out during that awful storm on the night of the twenty-fifth. The rain came down as if it had been poured out of buckets, and Tournefort took shelter under the portico of a tall, dilapidated-looking house somewhere at the back of St. Lazare. The night was, of course, pitch dark, and the howling of the wind and beating of the rain effectually drowned every other sound.

Tournefort, chilled to the marrow, had at first cowered in the angle of the door, as far away from the draught as he could. But presently he spied the glimmer of a tiny light some little way up on his left, and taking this to come from the concierge's lodge, he went cautiously along the passage intending to ask for better shelter against the fury of the elements than the rickety front door afforded.

Tournefort, you must remember, was always on the best terms with every concierge in Paris. They were, as it were, his subordinates; without their help he never could have carried on his unavowable profession quite so successfully. And they, in their turn, found it to their advantage to earn the good-will of that army of spies, which the Revolutionary Government kept in its service, for the tracking down of all those unfortunates who had not given complete adhesion to their tyrannical and murderous policy.

Therefore, in this instance, Tournefort felt no hesitation in claiming the hospitality of the concierge of the squalid house wherein he found himself. He went boldly up to the lodge. His hand was already on the latch, when certain sounds which proceeded from the interior of the lodge caused him to pause and to bend his ear in order to listen. It was Tournefort's metier to listen. What had arrested his attention was the sound of a man's voice, saying in a tone of deep respect:

"Bien, Madame la Comtesse, we'll do our best."

No wonder that the servant of the Committee of Public Safety remained at attention, no longer thought of the storm or felt the cold blast chilling him to the marrow. Here was a wholly unexpected piece of good luck. "Madame la Comtesse!" Peste! There were not many such left in Paris these days. Unfortunately, the tempest of the wind and the rain made such a din that it was difficult to catch every sound which came from the interior of the lodge. All that Tournefort caught definitely were a few fragments of conversation.

"My good M. Bertin. . ." came at one time from a woman's voice. "Truly I do not know why you should do all this for me."

And then again: "All I possess in the world now are my diamonds. They alone stand between my children and utter destitution."

The man's voice seemed all the time to be saying something that sounded cheerful and encouraging. But his voice came only as a vague murmur to the listener's ears. Presently, however, there came a word which set his pulses tingling. Madame said something about "Gentilly," and directly afterwards: "You will have to be very careful, my dear M. Bertin. The chateau, I feel sure, is being watched."

Tournefort could scarce repress a cry of joy. "Gentilly? Madame la Comtesse? The chateau?" Why, of course, he held all the necessary threads already. The ci-devant Comte de Sucy—a pestilential aristo if ever there was one!—had been sent to the guillotine less than a fortnight ago. His chateau, situated just outside Gentilly, stood empty, it having been given out that the widow Sucy and her two children had escaped to England. Well! she had not gone apparently, for here she was, in the lodge of the concierge of a mean house in one of the desolate quarters of Paris, begging some traitor to find her diamonds for her, which she had obviously left concealed inside the chateau. What a haul for Tournefort! What commendation from his superiors! The chances of a speedy promotion were indeed glorious now! He blessed the storm and the rain which had driven him for shelter to this house, where a poisonous plot was being hatched to rob the people of valuable property, and to aid a few more of those abominable aristos in cheating the guillotine of their traitorous heads.

He listened for a while longer, in order to get all the information that he could on the subject of the diamonds, because he knew by experience that those perfidious aristos, once they were under arrest, would sooner bite out their tongues than reveal anything that might be of service to the Government of the people. But he learned little else. Nothing was revealed of where Madame la Comtesse was in hiding, or how the diamonds were to be disposed of once they were found. Tournefort would have given much to have at least one of his colleagues with him. As it was, he would be forced to act single-handed and on his own initiative. In his own mind he had already decided that he would wait until Madame la Comtesse came out of the concierge's lodge, and that he would follow her and apprehend her somewhere out in the open streets, rather than here where her friend Bertin might prove to be a stalwart as well as a desperate man, ready with a pistol, whilst he—Tournefort—was unarmed. Bertin, who had, it seemed, been entrusted with the task of finding the diamonds, could then be shadowed and arrested in the very act of filching property which by decree of the State belonged to the people.

So he waited patiently for a while. No doubt the aristo would remain here under shelter until the storm had abated. Soon the sound of voices died down, and an extraordinary silence descended on this miserable, abandoned corner of old Paris. The silence became all the more marked after a while, because the rain ceased its monotonous pattering and the soughing of the wind was stilled. It was, in fact, this amazing stillness which set citizen Tournefort thinking. Evidently the aristo did not intend to come out of the lodge to-night. Well! Tournefort had not meant to make himself unpleasant inside the house, or to have a quarrel just yet with the traitor Bertin, whoever he was; but his hand was forced and he had no option.

The door of the lodge was locked. He tugged vigorously at the bell again and again, for at first he got no answer. A few minutes later he heard the sound of shuffling footsteps upon creaking boards. The door was opened, and a man in night attire, with bare, thin legs and tattered carpet slippers on his feet, confronted an exceedingly astonished servant of the Committee of Public Safety. Indeed, Tournefort thought that he must have been dreaming, or that he was dreaming now. For the man who opened the door to him was well known to every agent of the Committee. He was an ex-soldier who had been crippled years ago by the loss of one arm, and had held the post of concierge in a house in the Ruelle du Paradis ever since. His name was Grosjean. He was very old, and nearly doubled up with rheumatism, had scarcely any hair on his head or flesh on his bones. At this moment he appeared to be suffering from a cold in the head, for his eyes were streaming and his narrow, hooked nose was adorned by a drop of moisture at its tip. In fact, poor old Grosjean looked more like a dilapidated scarecrow than a dangerous conspirator. Tournefort literally gasped at sight of him, and Grosjean uttered a kind of croak, intended, no doubt, for complete surprise.

"Citizen Tournefort!" he exclaimed. "Name of a dog! What are you doing here at this hour and in this abominable weather? Come in! Come in!" he added, and, turning on his heel, he shuffled back into the inner room, and then returned carrying a lighted lamp, which he set upon the table. "Amelie left a sup of hot coffee on the hob in the kitchen before she went to bed. You must have a drop of that."

He was about to shuffle off again when Tournefort broke in roughly:

"None of that nonsense, Grosjean! Where are the aristos?"

"The aristos, citizen?" queried Grosjean, and nothing could have looked more utterly, more ludicrously bewildered than did the old concierge at this moment. "What aristos?"

"Bertin and Madame la Comtesse," retorted Tournefort gruffly. "I heard them talking."

"You have been dreaming, citizen Tournefort," the old man said, with a husky little laugh. "Sit down, and let me get you some coffee—"

"Don't try and hoodwink me, Grosjean!" Tournefort cried now in a sudden access of rage. "I tell you that I saw the light. I heard the aristos talking. There was a man named Bertin, and a woman he called 'Madame la Comtesse,' and I say that some devilish royalist plot is being hatched here, and that you, Grosjean, will suffer for it if you try and shield those aristos."

"But, citizen Tournefort," replied the concierge meekly, "I assure you that I have seen no aristos. The door of my bedroom was open, and the lamp was by my bedside. Amelie, too, has only been in bed a few minutes. You ask her! There has been no one, I tell you—no one! I should have seen and heard them—the door was open," he reiterated pathetically.

"We'll soon see about that!" was Tournefort's curt comment.

But it was his turn indeed to be utterly bewildered. He searched—none too gently—the squalid little lodge through and through, turned the paltry sticks of furniture over, hauled little Amelie, Grosjean's granddaughter, out of bed, searched under the mattresses, and even poked his head up the chimney.

Grosjean watched him wholly unperturbed. These were strange times, and friend Tournefort had obviously gone a little off his head. The worthy old concierge calmly went on getting the coffee ready. Only when presently Tournefort, worn out with anger and futile exertion, threw himself, with many an oath, into the one armchair, Grosjean remarked coolly:

"I tell you what I think it is, citizen. If you were standing just by the door of the lodge you had the back staircase of the house immediately behind you. The partition wall is very thin, and there is a disused door just there also. No doubt the voices came from there. You see, if there had been any aristos here," he added naively, "they could not have flown up the chimney, could they?"

That argument was certainly unanswerable. But Tournefort was out of temper. He roughly ordered Grosjean to bring the lamp and show him the back staircase and the disused door. The concierge obeyed without a murmur. He was not in the least disturbed or frightened by all this blustering. He was only afraid that getting out of bed had made his cold worse. But he knew Tournefort of old. A good fellow, but inclined to be noisy and arrogant since he was in the employ of the Government. Grosjean took the precaution of putting on his trousers and wrapping an old shawl round his shoulders. Then he had a final sip of hot coffee; after which he picked up the lamp and guided Tournefort out of the lodge.

The wind had quite gone down by now. The lamp scarcely flickered as Grosjean held it above his head.

"Just here, citizen Tournefort," he said, and turned sharply to his left. But the next sound which he uttered was a loud croak of astonishment.

"That door has been out of use ever since I've been here," he muttered.

"And it certainly was closed when I stood up against it," rejoined Tournefort, with a savage oath, "or, of course, I should have noticed it."

Close to the lodge, at right angles to it, a door stood partially open. Tournefort went through it, closely followed by Grosjean. He found himself in a passage which ended in a cul de sac on his right; on the left was the foot of the stairs. The whole place was pitch dark save for the feeble light of the lamp. The cul de sac itself reeked of dirt and fustiness, as if it had not been cleaned or ventilated for years.

"When did you last notice that this door was closed?" queried Tournefort, furious with the sense of discomfiture, which he would have liked to vent on the unfortunate concierge.

"I have not noticed it for some days, citizen," replied Grosjean meekly. "I have had a severe cold, and have not been outside my lodge since Monday last. But we'll ask Amelie!" he added more hopefully.

Amelie, however, could throw no light upon the subject. She certainly kept the back stairs cleaned and swept, but it was not part of her duties to extend her sweeping operations as far as the cul de sac. She had quite enough to do as it was, with grandfather now practically helpless. This morning, when she went out to do her shopping, she had not noticed whether the disused door did or did not look the same as usual.

Grosjean was very sorry for his friend Tournefort, who appeared vastly upset, but still more sorry for himself, for he knew what endless trouble this would entail upon him.

Nor was the trouble slow in coming, not only on Grosjean, but on every lodger inside the house; for before half an hour had gone by Tournefort had gone and come back, this time with the local commissary of police and a couple of agents, who had every man, woman and child in that house out of bed and examined at great length, their identity books searchingly overhauled, their rooms turned topsy-turvy and their furniture knocked about.

It was past midnight before all these perquisitions were completed. No one dared to complain at these indignities put upon peaceable citizens on the mere denunciation of an obscure police agent. These were times when every regulation, every command, had to be accepted without a murmur. At one o'clock in the morning, Grosjean himself was thankful to get back to bed, having satisfied the commissary that he was not a dangerous conspirator.

But of anyone even remotely approaching the description of the ci-devant Comtesse de Sucy, or of any man called Bertin, there was not the faintest trace.

II

But no feeling of discomfort ever lasted very long with citizen Tournefort. He was a person of vast resource and great buoyancy of temperament.

True, he had not apprehended two exceedingly noxious aristos, as he had hoped to do; but he held the threads of an abominable conspiracy in his hands, and the question of catching both Bertin and Madame la Comtesse red-handed was only a question of time. But little time had been lost. There was always someone to be found at the offices of the Committee of Public Safety, which were open all night. It was possible that citizen Chauvelin would be still there, for he often took on the night shift, or else citizen Gourdon.

It was Gourdon who greeted his subordinate, somewhat ill-humouredly, for he was indulging in a little sleep, with his toes turned to the fire, as the night was so damp and cold. But when he heard Tournefort's story, he was all eagerness and zeal.

"It is, of course, too late to do anything now," he said finally, after he had mastered every detail of the man's adventures in the Ruelle du Paradis; "but get together half a dozen men upon whom you can rely, and by six o'clock in the morning, or even five, we'll be on our way to Gentilly. Citizen Chauvelin was only saying to-day that he strongly suspected the ci-devant Comtesse de Sucy of having left the bulk of her valuable jewellery at the chateau, and that she would make some effort to get possession of it. It would be rather fine, citizen Tournefort," he added with a chuckle, "if you and I could steal a march on citizen Chauvelin over this affair, what? He has been extraordinarily arrogant of late and marvellously in favour, not only with the Committee, but with citizen Robespierre himself."

"They say," commented Tournefort, "that he succeeded in getting hold of some papers which were of great value to the members of the Committee."

"He never succeeded in getting hold of that meddlesome Englishman whom they call the Scarlet Pimpernel," was Gourdon's final dry comment.

Thus was the matter decided on. And the following morning at daybreak, Gourdon, who was only a subordinate officer on the Committee of Public Safety, took it upon himself to institute a perquisition in the chateau of Gentilly, which is situated close to the commune of that name. He was accompanied by his friend Tournefort and a gang of half a dozen ruffians recruited from the most disreputable cabarets of Paris.

The intention had been to steal a march on citizen Chauvelin, who had been over arrogant of late; but the result did not come up to expectations. By midday the chateau had been ransacked from attic to cellar; every kind of valuable property had been destroyed, priceless works of art irretrievably damaged. But priceless works of art had no market in Paris these days; and the property of real value—the Sucy diamonds namely—which had excited the cupidity or the patriotic wrath of citizens Gourdon and Tournefort could nowhere be found.

To make the situation more deplorable still, the Committee of Public Safety had in some unexplainable way got wind of the affair, and the two worthies had the mortification of seeing citizen Chauvelin presently appear upon the scene.

It was then two o'clock in the afternoon. Gourdon, after he had snatched a hasty dinner at a neighbouring cabaret, had returned to the task of pulling the chateau of Gentilly about his own ears if need be, with a view to finding the concealed treasure.

For the nonce he was standing in the centre of the finely proportioned hall. The rich ormolu and crystal chandelier lay in a tangled, broken heap of scraps at his feet, and all around there was a confused medley of pictures, statuettes, silver ornaments, tapestry and brocade hangings, all piled up in disorder, smashed, tattered, kicked at now and again by Gourdon, to the accompaniment of a savage oath.

The house itself was full of noises; heavy footsteps tramping up and down the stairs, furniture turned over, curtains torn from their poles, doors and windows battered in. And through it all the ceaseless hammering of pick and axe, attacking these stately walls which had withstood the wars and sieges of centuries.

Every now and then Tournefort, his face perspiring and crimson with exertion, would present himself at the door of the hall. Gourdon would query gruffly: "Well?"

And the answer was invariably the same: "Nothing!"

Then Gourdon would swear again and send curt orders to continue the search, relentlessly, ceaselessly.

"Leave no stone upon stone," he commanded. "Those diamonds must be found. We know they are here, and, name of a dog! I mean to have them."

When Chauvelin arrived at the chateau he made no attempt at first to interfere with Gourdon's commands. Only on one occasion he remarked curtly:

"I suppose, citizen Gourdon, that you can trust your search party?"

"Absolutely," retorted Gourdon. "A finer patriot than Tournefort does not exist."

"Probably," rejoined the other dryly. "But what about the men?"

"Oh! they are only a set of barefooted, ignorant louts. They do as they are told, and Tournefort has his eye on them. I dare say they'll contrive to steal a few things, but they would never dare lay hands on valuable jewellery. To begin with, they could never dispose of it. Imagine a va-nu-pieds peddling a diamond tiara!"

"There are always receivers prepared to take risks."

"Very few," Gourdon assured him, "since we decreed that trafficking with aristo property was a crime punishable by death."

Chauvelin said nothing for the moment. He appeared wrapped in his own thoughts, listened for a while to the confused hubbub about the house, then he resumed abruptly:

"Who are these men whom you are employing, citizen Gourdon?"

"A well-known gang," replied the other. "I can give you their names."

"If you please."

Gourdon searched his pockets for a paper which he found presently and handed to his colleague. The latter perused it thoughtfully.

"Where did Tournefort find these men?" he asked.

"For the most part at the Cabaret de la Liberte—a place of very evil repute down in the Rue Christine."

"I know it," rejoined the other. He was still studying the list of names which Gourdon had given him. "And," he added, "I know most of these men. As thorough a set of ruffians as we need for some of our work. Merri, Guidal, Rateau, Desmonds. TIENS!" he exclaimed. "Rateau! Is Rateau here now?"

"Why, of course! He was recruited, like the rest of them, for the day. He won't leave till he has been paid, you may be sure of that. Why do you ask?"

"I will tell you presently. But I would wish to speak with citizen Rateau first."

Just at this moment Tournefort paid his periodical visit to the hall. The usual words, "Still nothing," were on his lips, when Gourdon curtly ordered him to go and fetch the citizen Rateau.

A minute or two later Tournefort returned with the news that Rateau could nowhere be found. Chauvelin received the news without any comment; he only ordered Tournefort, somewhat roughly, back to his work. Then, as soon as the latter had gone, Gourdon turned upon his colleague.

"Will you explain—" he began with a show of bluster.

"With pleasure," replied Chauvelin blandly. "On my way hither, less than an hour ago, I met your man Rateau, a league or so from here."

"You met Rateau!" exclaimed Gourdon impatiently. "Impossible! He was here then, I feel sure. You must have been mistaken."

"I think not. I have only seen the man once, when I, too, went to recruit a band of ruffians at the Cabaret de la Liberte, in connection with some work I wanted doing. I did not employ him then, for he appeared to me both drink-sodden and nothing but a miserable, consumptive creature, with a churchyard cough you can hear half a league away. But I would know him anywhere. Besides which, he stopped and wished me good morning. Now I come to think of it," added Chauvelin thoughtfully, "he was carrying what looked like a heavy bundle under his arm."

"A heavy bundle!" cried Gourdon, with a forceful oath. "And you did not stop him!"

"I had no reason for suspecting him. I did not know until I arrived here what the whole affair was about, or whom you were employing. All that the Committee knew for certain was that you and Tournefort and a number of men had arrived at Gentilly before daybreak, and I was then instructed to follow you hither to see what mischief you were up to. You acted in complete secrecy, remember, citizen Gourdon, and without first ascertaining the wishes of the Committee of Public Safety, whose servant you are. If the Sucy diamonds are not found, you alone will be held responsible for their loss to the Government of the People."

Chauvelin's voice had now assumed a threatening tone, and Gourdon felt all his audacity and self-assurance fall away from him, leaving him a prey to nameless terror.

"We must round up Rateau," he murmured hastily. "He cannot have gone far."

"No, he cannot," rejoined Chauvelin dryly. "Though I was not specially thinking of Rateau or of diamonds when I started to come hither. I did send a general order forbidding any person on foot or horseback to enter or leave Paris by any of the southern gates. That order will serve us well now. Are you riding?"

"Yes. I left my horse at the tavern just outside Gentilly. I can get to horse within ten minutes."

"To horse, then, as quickly as you can. Pay off your men and dismiss them—all but Tournefort, who had best accompany us. Do not lose a single moment. I'll be ahead of you and may come up with Rateau before you overtake me. And if I were you, citizen Gourdon," he concluded, with ominous emphasis, "I would burn one or two candles to your compeer the devil. You'll have need of his help if Rateau gives us the slip."

III

The first part of the road from Gentilly to Paris runs through the valley of the Biere, and is densely wooded on either side. It winds in and out for the most part, ribbon-like, through thick coppice of chestnut and birch. Thus it was impossible for Chauvelin to spy his quarry from afar; nor did he expect to do so this side of the Hopital de la Sante. Once past that point, he would find the road quite open and running almost straight, in the midst of arid and only partially cultivated land.

He rode at a sharp trot, with his caped coat wrapped tightly round his shoulders, for it was raining fast. At intervals, when he met an occasional wayfarer, he would ask questions about a tall man who had a consumptive cough, and who was carrying a cumbersome burden under his arm.

Almost everyone whom he thus asked remembered seeing a personage who vaguely answered to the description: tall and with a decided stoop—yes, and carrying a cumbersome-looking bundle under his arm. Chauvelin was undoubtedly on the track of the thief.

Just beyond Meuves he was overtaken by Gourdon and Tournefort. Here, too, the man Rateau's track became more and more certain. At one place he had stopped and had a glass of wine and a rest, at another he had asked how close he was to the gates of Paris.

The road was now quite open and level; the irregular buildings of the hospital appeared vague in the rain-sodden distance. Twenty minutes later Tournefort, who was riding ahead of his companions, spied a tall, stooping figure at the spot where the Chemin de Gentilly forks, and where stands a group of isolated houses and bits of garden, which belong to la Sante. Here, before the days when the glorious Revolution swept aside all such outward signs of superstition, there had stood a Calvary. It was now used as a signpost. The man stood before it, scanning the half-obliterated indications.

At the moment that Tournefort first caught sight of him he appeared uncertain of his way. Then for a while he watched Tournefort, who was coming at a sharp trot towards him. Finally, he seemed to make up his mind very suddenly and, giving a last, quick look round, he walked rapidly along the upper road. Tournefort drew rein, waited for his colleagues to come up with him. Then he told them what he had seen.

"It is Rateau, sure enough," he said. "I saw his face quite distinctly and heard his abominable cough. He is trying to get into Paris. That road leads nowhere but to the barrier. There, of course, he will be stopped, and—"

The other two had also brought their horses to a halt. The situation had become tense, and a plan for future action had at once to be decided on. Already Chauvelin, masterful and sure of himself, had assumed command of the little party. Now he broke in abruptly on Tournefort's vapid reflections.

"We don't want him stopped at the barrier," he said in his usual curt, authoritative manner. "You, citizen Tournefort," he continued, "will ride as fast as you can to the gate, making a detour by the lower road. You will immediately demand to speak with the sergeant who is in command, and you will give him a detailed description of the man Rateau. Then you will tell him in my name that, should such a man present himself at the gate, he must be allowed to enter the city unmolested."

Gourdon gave a quick cry of protest.

"Let the man go unmolested? Citizen Chauvelin, think what you are doing!"

"I always think of what I am doing," retorted Chauvelin curtly, "and have no need of outside guidance in the process." Then he turned once more to Tournefort. "You yourself, citizen," he continued, in sharp, decisive tones which admitted of no argument, "will dismount as soon as you are inside the city. You will keep the gate under observation. The moment you see the man Rateau, you will shadow him, and on no account lose sight of him. Understand?"

"You may trust me, citizen Chauvelin," Tournefort replied, elated at the prospect of work which was so entirely congenial to him. "But will you tell me—"

"I will tell you this much, citizen Tournefort," broke in Chauvelin with some acerbity, "that though we have traced the diamonds and the thief so far, we have, through your folly last night, lost complete track of the ci-devant Comtesse de Sucy and of the man Bertin. We want Rateau to show us where they are."

"I understand," murmured the other meekly.

"That's a mercy!" riposted Chauvelin dryly. "Then quickly man. Lose no time! Try to get a few minutes' advance on Rateau; then slip in to the guard-room to change into less conspicuous clothes. Citizen Gourdon and I will continue on the upper road and keep the man in sight in case he should think of altering his course. In any event, we'll meet you just inside the barrier. But if, in the meanwhile, you have to get on Rateau's track before we have arrived on the scene, leave the usual indications as to the direction which you have taken."

Having given his orders and satisfied himself that they were fully understood, he gave a curt command, "En avant," and once more the three of them rode at a sharp trot down the road towards the city.

IV

Citizen Rateau, if he thought about the matter at all, must indeed have been vastly surprised at the unwonted amiability or indifference of sergeant Ribot, who was in command at the gate of Gentilly. Ribot only threw a very perfunctory glance at the greasy permit which Rateau presented to him, and when he put the usual query, "What's in that parcel?" and Rateau gave the reply: "Two heads of cabbage and a bunch of carrots," Ribot merely poked one of his fingers into the bundle, felt that a cabbage leaf did effectually lie on the top, and thereupon gave the formal order: "Pass on, citizen, in the name of the Republic!" without any hesitation.

Tournefort, who had watched the brief little incident from behind the window of a neighbouring cabaret, could not help but chuckle to himself. Never had he seen game walk more readily into a trap. Rateau, after he had passed the barrier, appeared undecided which way he would go. He looked with obvious longing towards the cabaret, behind which the keenest agent on the staff of the Committee of Public Safety was even now ensconced. But seemingly a halt within those hospitable doors did not form part of his programme, and a moment or two later he turned sharply on his heel and strode rapidly down the Rue de l'Oursine.

Tournefort allowed him a fair start, and then made ready to follow.

Just as he was stepping out of the cabaret he spied Chauvelin and Gourdon coming through the gates. They, too, had apparently made a brief halt inside the guard-room, where—as at most of the gates—a store of various disguises was always kept ready for the use of the numerous sleuth-hounds employed by the Committee of Public Safety. Here the two men had exchanged their official garments for suits of sombre cloth, which gave them the appearance of a couple of humble bourgeois going quietly about their business. Tournefort had donned an old blouse, tattered stockings, and shoes down at heel. With his hands buried in his breeches' pockets, he, too, turned into the long narrow Rue de l'Oursine, which, after a sharp curve, abuts on the Rue Mouffetard.

Rateau was walking rapidly, taking big strides with his long legs. Tournefort, now sauntering in the gutter in the middle of the road, now darting in and out of open doorways, kept his quarry well in sight. Chauvelin and Gourdon lagged some little way behind. It was still raining, but not heavily—a thin drizzle, which penetrated almost to the marrow. Not many passers-by haunted this forlorn quarter of old Paris.

To right and left tall houses almost obscured the last, quickly-fading light of the grey September day.

At the bottom of the Rue Mouffetard, Rateau came once more to a halt. A network of narrow streets radiated from this centre. He looked all round him and also behind. It was difficult to know whether he had a sudden suspicion that he was being followed; certain it is that, after a very brief moment of hesitation, he plunged suddenly into the narrow Rue Contrescarpe and disappeared from view.

Tournefort was after him in a trice. When he reached the corner of the street he saw Rateau, at the further end of it, take a sudden sharp turn to the right. But not before he had very obviously spied his pursuer, for at that moment his entire demeanour changed. An air of furtive anxiety was expressed in his whole attitude. Even at that distance Tournefort could see him clutching his bulky parcel close to his chest.

After that the pursuit became closer and hotter. Rateau was in and out of that tight network of streets which cluster around the Place de Fourci, intent, apparently, on throwing his pursuers off the scent, for after a while he was running round and round in a circle. Now up the Rue des Poules, then to the right and to the right again; back in the Place de Fourci. Then straight across it once more to the Rue Contrescarpe, where he presently disappeared so completely from view that Tournefort thought that the earth must have swallowed him up.

Tournefort was a man capable of great physical exertion. His calling often made heavy demands upon his powers of endurance; but never before had he grappled with so strenuous a task. Puffing and panting, now running at top speed, anon brought to a halt by the doubling-up tactics of his quarry, his great difficulty was the fact that citizen Chauvelin did not wish the man Rateau to be apprehended; did not wish him to know that he was being pursued. And Tournefort had need of all his wits to keep well under the shadow of any projecting wall or under cover of open doorways which were conveniently in the way, and all the while not to lose sight of that consumptive giant, who seemed to be playing some intricate game which well-nigh exhausted the strength of citizen Tournefort.

What he could not make out was what had happened to Chauvelin and to Gourdon. They had been less than three hundred metres behind him when first this wild chase in and out of the Rue Contrescarpe had begun. Now, when their presence was most needed, they seemed to have lost track both of him—Tournefort—and of the very elusive quarry. To make matters more complicated, the shades of evening were drawing in very fast, and these narrow streets of the Faubourg were very sparsely lighted.

Just at this moment Tournefort had once more caught sight of Rateau, striding leisurely this time up the street. The worthy agent quickly took refuge under a doorway and was mopping his streaming forehead, glad of this brief respite in the mad chase, when that awful churchyard cough suddenly sounded so close to him that he gave a great jump and well-nigh betrayed his presence then and there. He had only just time to withdraw further still into the angle of the doorway, when Rateau passed by.

Tournefort peeped out of his hiding-place, and for the space of a dozen heart beats or so, remained there quite still, watching that broad back and those long limbs slowly moving through the gathering gloom. The next instant he perceived Chauvelin standing at the end of the street.

Rateau saw him too—came face to face with him, in fact, and must have known who he was for, without an instant's hesitation and just like a hunted creature at bay, he turned sharply on his heel and then ran back down the street as hard as he could tear. He passed close to within half a metre of Tournefort, and as he flew past he hit out with his left fist so vigorously that the worthy agent of the Committee of Public Safety, caught on the nose by the blow, staggered and measured his length upon the flagged floor below.

The next moment Chauvelin had come by. Tournefort, struggling to his feet, called to him, panting:

"Did you see him? Which way did he go?"

"Up the Rue Bordet. After him, citizen!" replied Chauvelin grimly, between his teeth.

Together the two men continued the chase, guided through the intricate mazes of the streets by their fleeing quarry. They had Rateau well in sight, and the latter could no longer continue his former tactics with success now that two experienced sleuth-hounds were on his track.

At a given moment he was caught between the two of them. Tournefort was advancing cautiously up the Rue Bordet; Chauvelin, equally stealthily, was coming down the same street, and Rateau, once more walking quite leisurely, was at equal distance between the two.

V

THERE ARE NO SIDE TURNINGS out of the Rue Bordet, the total length of which is less than fifty metres; so Tournefort, feeling more at his ease, ensconced himself at one end of the street, behind a doorway, whilst Chauvelin did the same at the other. Rateau, standing in the gutter, appeared once more in a state of hesitation. Immediately in front of him the door of a small cabaret stood invitingly open; its signboard, "Le Bon Copain," promised rest and refreshment. He peered up and down the road, satisfied himself presumably that, for the moment, his pursuers were out of sight, hugged his parcel to his chest, and then suddenly made a dart for the cabaret and disappeared within its doors.

Nothing could have been better. The quarry, for the moment, was safe, and if the sleuth-hounds could not get refreshment, they could at least get a rest. Tournefort and Chauvelin crept out of their hiding-places. They met in the middle of the road, at the spot where Rateau had stood a while ago. It was then growing dark and the street was innocent of lanterns, but the lights inside the cabaret gave a full view of the interior. The lower half of the wide shop-window was curtained off, but above the curtain the heads of the customers of "Le Bon Copain," and the general comings and goings, could very clearly be seen.

Tournefort, never at a loss, had already climbed upon a low projection in the wall of one of the houses opposite. From this point of vantage he could more easily observe what went on inside the cabaret, and in short, jerky sentences he gave a description of what he saw to his chief.

"Rateau is sitting down. . . he has his back to the window. . . he has put his bundle down close beside him on the bench. . . he can't speak for a minute, for he is coughing and spluttering like an old walrus. . . A wench is bringing him a bottle of wine and a hunk of bread and cheese. . . He has started talking. . . is talking volubly. . . the people are laughing. . . some are applauding. . . And here comes Jean Victor, the landlord. . . you know him, citizen. . . a big, hulking fellow, and as good a patriot as I ever wish to see. . . He, too, is laughing and talking to Rateau, who is doubled up with another fit of coughing—"

Chauvelin uttered an exclamation of impatience:

"Enough of this, citizen Tournefort. Keep your eye on the man and hold your tongue. I am spent with fatigue."

"No wonder," murmured Tournefort. Then he added insinuatingly: "Why not let me go in there and apprehend Rateau now? We should have the diamonds and—"

"And lose the ci-devant Comtesse de Sucy and the man Bertin," retorted Chauvelin with sudden fierceness. "Bertin, who can be none other than that cursed Englishman, the—"

He checked himself, seeing Tournefort was gazing down on him, with awe and bewilderment expressed in his lean, hatchet face.

"You are losing sight of Rateau, citizen," Chauvelin continued calmly. "What is he doing now?"

But Tournefort felt that this calmness was only on the surface; something strange had stirred the depths of his chief's keen, masterful mind. He would have liked to ask a question or two, but knew from experience that it was neither wise nor profitable to try and probe citizen Chauvelin's thoughts. So after a moment or two he turned back obediently to his task.

"I can't see Rateau for the moment," he said, "but there is much talking and merriment in there. Ah! there he is, I think. Yes, I see him! . . . He is behind the counter, talking to Jean Victor. . . and he has just thrown some money down upon the counter. . . gold too! name of a dog. . ."

Then suddenly, without any warning, Tournefort jumped down from his post of observation. Chauvelin uttered a brief:

"What the——are you doing, citizen?"

"Rateau is going," replied Tournefort excitedly. "He drank a mug of wine at a draught and has picked up his bundle, ready to go."

Once more cowering in the dark angle of a doorway, the two men waited, their nerves on edge, for the reappearance of their quarry.

"I wish citizen Gourdon were here," whispered Tournefort. "In the darkness it is better to be three than two."

"I sent him back to the Station in the Rue Mouffetard," was Chauvelin's curt retort; "there to give notice that I might require a few armed men presently. But he should be somewhere about here by now, looking for us. Anyway, I have my whistle, and if—"

He said no more, for at that moment the door of the cabaret was opened from within and Rateau stepped out into the street, to the accompaniment of loud laughter and clapping of hands which came from the customers of the "Bon Copain."

This time he appeared neither in a hurry nor yet anxious. He did not pause in order to glance to right or left, but started to walk quite leisurely up the street. The two sleuth-hounds quietly followed him. Through the darkness they could only vaguely see his silhouette, with the great bundle under his arm. Whatever may have been Rateau's fears of being shadowed awhile ago, he certainly seemed free of them now. He sauntered along, whistling a tune, down the Montagne Ste. Genevieve to the Place Maubert, and thence straight towards the river.

Having reached the bank, he turned off to his left, sauntered past the Ecole de Medecine and went across the Petit Pont, then through the New Market, along the Quai des Orfevres. Here he made a halt, and for awhile looked over the embankment at the river and then round about him, as if in search of something. But presently he appeared to make up his mind, and continued his leisurely walk as far as the Pont Neuf, where he turned sharply off to his right, still whistling, Tournefort and Chauvelin hard upon his heels.

"That whistling is getting on my nerves," muttered Tournefort irritably; "and I haven't heard the ruffian's churchyard cough since he walked out of the 'Bon Copain.'"

Strangely enough, it was this remark of Tournefort's which gave Chauvelin the first inkling of something strange and, to him, positively awesome. Tournefort, who walked close beside him, heard him suddenly mutter a fierce exclamation.

"Name of a dog!"

"What is it, citizen?" queried Tournefort, awed by this sudden outburst on the part of a man whose icy calmness had become proverbial throughout the Committee.

"Sound the alarm, citizen!" cried Chauvelin in response. "Or, by Satan, he'll escape us again!"

"But—" stammered Tournefort in utter bewilderment, while, with fingers that trembled somewhat, he fumbled for his whistle.

"We shall want all the help we can," retorted Chauvelin roughly. "For, unless I am much mistaken, there's more noble quarry here than even I could dare to hope!"

Rateau in the meanwhile had quietly lolled up to the parapet on the right-hand side of the bridge, and Tournefort, who was watching him with intense keenness, still marvelled why citizen Chauvelin had suddenly become so strangely excited. Rateau was merely lolling against the parapet, like a man who has not a care in the world. He had placed his bundle on the stone ledge beside him. Here he waited a moment or two, until one of the small craft upon the river loomed out of the darkness immediately below the bridge. Then he picked up the bundle and threw it straight into the boat. At that same moment Tournefort had the whistle to his lips. A shrill, sharp sound rang out through the gloom.

"The boat, citizen Tournefort, the boat!" cried Chauvelin. "There are plenty of us here to deal with the man."

Immediately, from the quays, the streets, the bridges, dark figures emerged out of the darkness and hurried to the spot. Some reached the bridgehead even as Rateau made a dart forward, and two men were upon him before he succeeded in running very far. Others had scrambled down the embankment and were shouting to some unseen boatman to "halt, in the name of the people!"

But Rateau gave in without a struggle. He appeared more dazed than frightened, and quietly allowed the agents of the Committee to lead him back to the bridge, where Chauvelin had paused, waiting for him.

VI

A MINUTE OR TWO LATER Tournefort was once more beside his chief. He was carrying the precious bundle, which, he explained, the boatman had given up without question.

"The man knew nothing about it," the agent said. "No one, he says, could have been more surprised than he was when this bundle was suddenly flung at him over the parapet of the bridge."

Just then the small group, composed of two or three agents of the Committee, holding their prisoner by the arms, came into view. One man was walking ahead and was the first to approach Chauvelin. He had a small screw of paper in his hand, which he gave to his chief.

"Found inside the lining of the prisoner's hat, citizen," he reported curtly, and opened the shutter of a small, dark lantern which he wore at his belt.

Chauvelin took the paper from his subordinate. A weird, unexplainable foreknowledge of what was to come caused his hand to shake and beads of perspiration to moisten his forehead. He looked up and saw the prisoner standing before him. Crushing the paper in his hand he snatched the lantern from the agent's belt and flashed it in the face of the quarry who, at the last, had been so easily captured.

Immediately a hoarse cry of disappointment and of rage escaped his throat.

"Who is this man?" he cried.

One of the agents gave reply:

"It is old Victor, the landlord of the 'Bon Copain.' He is just a fool, who has been playing a practical joke."

Tournefort, too, at sight of the prisoner had uttered a cry of dismay and of astonishment.

"Victor!" he exclaimed. "Name of a dog, citizen, what are you doing here?"

But Chauvelin had gripped the man by the arm so fiercely that the latter swore with the pain.

"What is the meaning of this?" he queried roughly.

"Only a bet, citizen," retorted Victor reproachfully. "No reason to fall on an honest patriot for a bet, just as if he were a mad dog."

"A joke? A bet?" murmured Chauvelin hoarsely, for his throat now felt hot and parched. "What do you mean? Who are you, man? Speak, or I'll—"

"My name is Jean Victor," replied the other. "I am the landlord of the 'Bon Copain.' An hour ago a man came into my cabaret. He was a queer, consumptive creature, with a churchyard cough that made you shiver. Some of my customers knew him by sight, told me that the man's name was Rateau, and that he was an habitue of the 'Liberte,' in the Rue Christine. Well; he soon fell into conversation, first with me, then with some of my customers—talked all sorts of silly nonsense, made absurd bets with everybody. Some of these he won, and others he lost; but I must say that when he lost he always paid up most liberally. Then we all got excited, and soon bets flew all over the place. I don't rightly know how it happened at the last, but all at once he bet me that I would not dare to walk out then and there in the dark, as far as the Pont Neuf, wearing his blouse and hat and carrying a bundle the same as his under my arm. I not dare? . . . I, Jean Victor, who was a fine fighter in my day! I bet him a gold piece that I would and he said that he would make it five if I came back without my bundle, having thrown it over the parapet into any passing boat. Well, citizen!" continued Jean Victor with a laugh, "I ask you, what would you have done? Five gold pieces means a fortune these hard times, and I tell you the man was quite honest and always paid liberally when he lost. He slipped behind the counter and took off his blouse and hat, which I put on. Then we made up a bundle with some cabbage heads and a few carrots, and out I came. I didn't think there could be anything wrong in the whole affair—just the tomfoolery of a man who has got the betting mania and in whose pocket money is just burning a hole. And I have won my bet," concluded Jean Victor, still unabashed, "and I want to go back and get my money. If you don't believe me, come with me to my CABARET. You will find the citizen Rateau there, for sure; and I know that I shall find my five gold pieces."

Chauvelin had listened to the man as he would to some weird dream-story, wherein ghouls and devils had played a part. Tournefort, who was watching him, was awed by the look of fierce rage and grim hopelessness which shone from his chief's pale eyes. The other agents laughed. They were highly amused at the tale, but they would not let the prisoner go.

"If Jean Victor's story is true, citizen," their sergeant said, speaking to Chauvelin, "there will be witnesses to it over at 'Le Bon Copain.' Shall we take the prisoner straightway there and await further orders?"

Chauvelin gave a curt acquiescence, nodding his head like some insentient wooden automaton. The screw of paper was still in his hand; it seemed to sear his palm. Tournefort even now broke into a grim laugh. He had just undone the bundle which Jean Victor had thrown over the parapet of the bridge. It contained two heads of cabbage and a bunch of carrots. Then he ordered the agents to march on with their prisoner, and they, laughing and joking with Jean Victor, gave a quick turn, and soon their heavy footsteps were echoing down the flagstones of the bridge.

Chauvelin waited, motionless and silent, the dark lantern still held in his shaking hand, until he was quite sure that he was alone. Then only did he unfold the screw of paper.

It contained a few lines scribbled in pencil—just that foolish rhyme which to his fevered nerves was like a strong irritant, a poison which gave him an unendurable sensation of humiliation and impotence:

"We seek him here, we seek him there!
Chauvelin seeks him everywhere!
Is he in heaven? Is he in hell?
That demmed, elusive Pimpernel!"

He crushed the paper in his hand and, with a loud groan, of misery, fled over the bridge like one possessed.

VII

Madame la Comtesse de Sucy never went to England. She was one of those French women who would sooner endure misery in their own beloved country than comfort anywhere else. She outlived the horrors of the Revolution and speaks in her memoirs of the man Bertin.

She never knew who he was nor whence he came. All that she knew was that he came to her like some mysterious agent of God, bringing help, counsel, a semblance of happiness, at the moment when she was at the end of all her resources and saw grim starvation staring her and her children in the face. He appointed all sorts of strange places in out-of-the-way Paris where she was wont to meet him, and one night she confided to him the history of her diamonds, and hardly dared to trust his promise that he would get them for her.

Less than twenty-four hours later he brought them to her, at the poor lodgings in the Rue Blanche which she occupied with her children under an assumed name. That same night she begged him to dispose of them. This also he did, bringing her the money the next day.

She never saw him again after that.

But citizen Tournefort never quite got over his disappointment of that night. Had he dared, he would have blamed citizen Chauvelin for the discomfiture. It would have been better to have apprehended the man Rateau while there was a chance of doing so with success.

As it was, the impudent ruffian slipped clean away, and was never heard of again either at the "Bon Copain" or at the "Liberte." The customers at the cabaret certainly corroborated the story of Jean Victor. The man Rateau, they said, had been honest to the last. When time went on and Jean Victor did not return, he said that he could no longer wait, had work to do for the Government over the other side of the water and was afraid he would get punished if he dallied. But, before leaving, he laid the five gold pieces on the table. Every one wondered that so humble a workman had so much money in his pocket, and was withal so lavish with it. But these were not the times when one inquired too closely into the presence of money in the pocket of a good patriot.

And citizen Rateau was a good patriot, for sure.

And a good fellow to boot!

They all drank his health in Jean Victor's sour wine; then each went his way.

A Note About the Author

Baroness Emmuska Orczy (1865–1947) was initially born in Hungary but raised throughout Europe. She was educated in Brussels, London, Paris and Budapest where she studied creative arts. In 1899, Orczy would publish her first novel entitled, *The Emperor's Candlesticks*. It wasn't a massive success but led to more writing opportunities including a series of detective stories. A few years later, she wrote and produced a stage play called *The Scarlet Pimpernel*, which she'd later adapt into a novel. It went on to become her most famous work and is considered a literary masterpiece of the twentieth century.

A Note from the Publisher

CPSIA information can be obtained
at www.ICGtesting.com
Printed in the USA
JSHW060927180723
44896JS00011B/114

9 781513 272184